STRONG WOMEN IN CHICAGO

FERN KUPFER

Culicidae Press, LLC
PO Box 5069
Middleton, WI 53705-5069
USA
culicidaepress.com
editor@culicidaepress.com

STRONG WOMEN IN CHICAGO

ISBN: 978-1-68315-115-9

Library of Congress Cataloging Number: 2025933600

Our books may be purchased in bulk for promotional, educational or business use. Please contact your local bookseller or the Culicidae Press Sales Department at +1-352-215-7558
or by email at sales@culicidaepress.com

culicidaepress.bsky.social – facebook.com/culicidaepress
threads.net/@culicidaepress – instagram.com/culicidaepress
x.com/culicidaepress

Cover design and interior layout © 2025 by polytekton

Dedication

For the strong women I love most of all:
Gabi, Megan, Katie, and Ruthie

Table of Contents

Prologue

itzi Solomon got up from the desk chair, her left hip hurting. So much hurt these days. But the papers on the desk were signed and ready to go back to the lawyers. Everything was finally settled. What a relief!

The sound of women's laughter came from the smaller studio. Not giggles, but hearty, full-throated laughter. Then it was quiet and Lily's voice, loud and clear, called a command: "If the attacker comes toward you in a straight line, you have the advantage. So hold your breath, grab the pendant firmly, and turn to face him as if you were holding a gun. Flick, then press."

If Mitzi had had a daughter, she would be Lily Lerner: happy and kind but also brave. If Mitzi had a daughter, she would certainly inherit what had been built over so many years: this courage, this gift.

In the studio, someone asked a question, but Mitzi couldn't hear what it was. Lily's voice was softer now in response, assuring. Lily was strong. Stronger than she even knew. Mitzi was a good judge of character. She sensed these things, and understood them more clearly. Especially now in the short time she had left. Whatever was going to happen, what she had created in Chicago, the city of her birth, would continue. The legacy of Mitzi Solomon, who was now over seventy years old and one of the richest women in Chicago—this legacy would endure.

Chapter 1

Lily: This Can't Be Happening, But It Is

December. The attack happened in the women's bathroom of Union Station at a time when most people were traveling for the holiday. The afternoon was dull and gray, the wind whipping mercilessly as Lily maneuvered her way through the crowds with her luggage. She was wearing the puffy down coat her mother had bought for her last year. Although the coat was not what Lily would have chosen, it was protection against the Chicago winter. Lily went inside to go to the bathroom before she boarded the Megabus for Des Moines. The cold always made her want to pee.

There were a few creepy characters hanging around the station including a wild-eyed man clicking his teeth like castanets. There were college students waiting for the Megabus, tired young mothers trying to keep track of toddlers and old women who looked too frail to travel anywhere alone. No one was in the bathroom except a woman holding up a little boy against the sink so he could wash his hands.

Lily had a backpack and an old suitcase whose wheels kept getting stuck when she turned corners. Because of the suitcase, she thought it would be acceptable to use the handicapped stall, although ordinarily she would not.

"Devon, that's enough soap," the woman said to the boy. "Finish up." Lily smiled as she passed, but the pair did not acknowledge her presence. She walked to the last stall, placed the suitcase on the floor away from the toilet, and carefully laid paper across the seat.

"You press now, Devon," Lily heard the woman say. "Press hard." The blower was noisy. Then the door opened. Whooshed closed.

Out of habit, Lily looked down under the stalls; no feet were visible, though perhaps he had been there already, hiding in wait. Her backpack was on top of the suitcase in front of her, both with luggage tags attached. The name was written in black marker, all caps: LILY LERNER. The name suited her. Sometimes when she told people her full name, they smiled. She noticed this in school when teachers took attendance and her hand shot up eagerly, happily present. Her father, a careful man, had written her name and address in his neat printing. He was recovering from the accident he'd had the month before. No longer even using the cane, her mom had texted the other day.

The presents Lily packed were modest: gourmet caramel popcorn for her father, and hand-woven scarves for her mother and her sister. The suitcase was half-empty because her mother offered to take the girls shopping after Christmas. Most of the clothes she was bringing home needed to be washed, a chore for which her mother would volunteer, Lily would demur, and her mother would eventually accomplish it, folding everything into tidy packages smelling of fabric softener. Lily was looking forward to being home in her parents' clean house for a whole week, sleeping late, and hanging out with her sister, Megan.

Lily looked like her mother, everyone said, which was good because Betsy Lerner was pretty, a petite natural blonde with a flawless complexion. Megan was dark-haired like her dad. "But thank god," Grandma Roberta assured everyone, "Both of the girls have Betsy's nose."

Lily did well in school but not in the way of the genius kids in gifted classes. Her work was neat, handed in on time and she was adept at guessing the correct answers on multiple-choice tests. In interpersonal relations, she excelled and even as a little girl, always shared toys and had many friends. Works and plays well with others. A pleasure to have in class, the teachers wrote. "She comes into the room, like a ray of sunshine," her grandmother Roberta said.

She was two years out of college with a journalism degree and a job editing grants; she was two months out of a relationship she ended with Todd, a nice man—a boy, really—who lived in the same doorman building where she shared a small two-bedroom apartment with three friends.

Todd was attractive in a thick-necked, jocky way, but he turned out to be not a very interesting person. They had met in the elevator going down to the scary basement to do laundry. "Propinquity is all," she once told him. Later, Todd confessed that he looked up the word propinquity. He was always trying to improve his vocabulary.

They remained friends. Albeit ones without benefits.

***

Flushing the toilet, Lily rose to put on her coat, opened the door to the stall and there he was, standing there holding a knife. "Get back," he growled, reaching out, and pushing her against the stool. Then he locked the door. It was crowded with the two of them, her backpack and suitcase. She gasped, not fully believing that he was real. "I won't hurt you," he said, pressing the knife against the side of her neck, right under her ear.

And then he did.

Perhaps he didn't mean to cut her. He seemed young, about her age, and had a narrow, sharky face; dirty, brown hair stuck out in odd places, the rest matted to his head. He pushed her down so that she was sitting on the toilet. Lily looked up at him, thinking this can't be happening, though indeed it was; she had a sudden stillness, looking at him, willing herself to keep calm and remember what he looked like. Details. Remember the details. The collar on his brown jacket was frayed. His thin lips were dry and cracked. He sniffed a few times in rapid succession.

"Give me money," he said. "The money," he repeated, as if it were something she owed him. She reached down and slowly unzipped one side of her backpack. "I only have about ten dollars, " she told him.

He grabbed the wallet from her hands and looked at it before stuffing it into his jacket pocket. "There's fifteen here." Still, he sounded disappointed. She told him she was sorry. In the wallet was a debit card, a college ID with a picture of her smiling, her Iowa driver's license where she was not, an unflattering picture where she looked almost grim.

He discarded the wallet behind her on the bathroom floor. "Take off your clothes," he said, a request that seemed impossible. She was wearing a down coat. A scarf, identical to the one she had bought for her mother and sister. She had on a hooded sweater and under the sweater was a tee shirt tucked into her jeans. The bus was often cold.

Lily looked at him, pleading. "Please," she said. His eyes were cold, the color of stone.

"Don't look at me." The knife scraped against her throat in a shallow line. It did not hurt much, more like a stinging scratch, but drops of bright blood fell along the front of the down coat, standing out on the waterproof fabric like tiny jewels. She put her hand up to her neck and her fingers became wet. She smelled the blood. And him. Like stale cigarettes. His breath was close to her face, dank and putrid. He took a fistful of her pony-tail, yanking it so hard, that her head snapped back. "Don't look at me, I told you!"

"Please," she started to say again, looking up at the ceiling of the stall. Please, she prayed for someone to come into the bathroom and save her.

"Take your pants off," he said. He breathed raggedly, his arms and shoulders making jerky, twitchy movements. With one hand, Lily began to unzip her jeans. The other lifted the collar of the tee shirt against her neck to absorb the blood.

Then she heard the door to the bathroom opening. Whoosh. Involuntarily, Lily made little mewing sounds, but she couldn't call out. The whole time he held his hands over her mouth, practically covering her nose so that she couldn't breathe. His fingers pressed into the sides of her face so tightly that she thought her jaw would break. His palms were calloused and dry. Lily heard someone go to the first stall, farthest away from hers. The sound immediately followed an urgent stream hitting the bowl. Flush. The woman left just as quickly, not stopping to wash her hands.

"Shit," he said, seeing the blood on his fingers. Lily sat mute in front of him on the stool, her face at his crotch. He plucked some toilet paper out of the dispenser and began wiping, but everything was sticky. Dry bits of paper clung to his hands. "Why don't you just suck me off then," he said.

Lily felt apart from her body as if she were floating atop the bathroom stall, watching this like a scene played out in a movie. His words were also floating like little bubbles above their heads. He opened his fly, took out his penis, and started jabbing the side of her cheek, though he was barely erect. "Take it," he said. "Take it in your fucking mouth." He smelled awful down there. Like urine and dirty laundry. She opened her mouth, but before he pushed himself in, she began to gag.

When Lily was in college, a speaker came to lecture in her women's studies class about self-defense. There was some acronym about knowing escape routes, general preparedness, keeping calm, or choosing to scream. There was advice about how to gain sympathy with the attacker or how to make oneself a less desirable victim, feigning illness, even throwing up. "Whatever you have to do to stay alive, do it," the woman said. "Don't give up. Do not give up."

Lily felt herself spinning, starting to pass out. But giving up all the same.

***

There was blood. The ambulance came. She didn't know how much time had passed, sitting among the chaos in the hospital emergency room. There were children crying and a sleeping old man who looked as if he was going to fall over. Someone was brought in on a stretcher emitting deep-belly groans. She couldn't find her phone. There was no one she could have called in Chicago anyway since all her friends had left for the holiday. She felt unmoored from the world without her phone. Had he stolen it? Then he would know who she was and how to find her. But she was told at the hospital that her parents had already been contacted from the phone numbers on the luggage tags. They were on their way.

Under a triage system of people brought in with gunshot wounds and heart attacks, Lily sat along the wall in a plastic chair with a towel held up to her neck, waiting, it seemed, for a long time before a doctor saw her and declared that, despite all the blood, the knife cut was superficial.

Lily winced as he peeled off the towel. "Sorry, luv," the doctor said. The towel was red with blood, but the part pressed against her neck had already dried. "I know it looks quite messy," the doctor told her. He had a clipped British accent that made him seem like someone who should be in charge. "That is because twenty percent of the body's blood flows to the head. Your wound is not as bad as it looks, though." He rolled over a cart. Pausing before he began to disinfect the wound, he asked: "You all right now, luv?"

"Yes," Lily said.

"I was told he didn't hurt you, then?" She opened her mouth to say something, but nothing came out and the doctor added hurriedly: "I mean any more than this cut." He squinted at the wound over his glasses and furrowed his brow, looking pained.

"No."

"The bastard," he said, under his breath. With his accent, the word sounded almost elegant: The bahstard. Before he left, he told her that she was lucky, the assailant had missed an artery. "It's a matter of depth, not location," he assured her.

Apart from feeling terrorized, that was what she felt. Lucky that woman came into the bathroom when she did and called 911. "Yes, lucky for that woman," the doctor said.

Lily's savior, the woman he referred to, was a middle-school music teacher, the leader of a Girl Scout troop on Chicago's South Side. Her girls, successful the year before at selling cookies and fund-raising, were going to a recital by the Chicago Youth Symphony orchestra.

Lily had been surprised at the insistent pounding on the stall door as the assailant was tightly holding her jaw steady. The woman didn't stop. "Sweet Jesus. Oh, my lord. Oh my lord," the woman yelled. Her voice was almost operatic. "What are you doin' in there? What are you two doin' in there?"

After she was stitched up, Lily recalled the entire event to the police. She was on the toilet. He was standing, astride her. Everything stopped. Lily had heard twittering in the background. Nervous laughter. More pounding. Tilting her head, she could see around him under the stall two feet encased in unfashionable winter boots. "You get your sorry asses out of there right now. I know what you're doin' in there. I know what you're doin'. This is a public restroom. I got young girls with me here. I'm gonna call the po-lice. I am calling the cops right now, " a woman's voice said, clear and strong. "You hear me in there?" All the while she continued pounding on the door of the cubicle.

Lily's assailant opened the door and pushed the woman aside, knocking her against the wall; a bevy of young Black girls behind her stopped their tittering and began screaming in unison. Their voices, echoing against the tile, were very loud. "Help me," Lily managed to call out, still straddling the toilet, her blood- splayed hand held tight against her neck.

"Oh, my dear sweet Jesus," the woman said when she turned and looked inside the stall. Everything happened quickly. There was screaming and crying. A large girl in a red hat, buoyed by her leader's anger, got a punch at the assailant's back before he reached the exit door. "Motherfucker," she yelled after him, shaking a balled fist. In the lobby of the train station, there were dozens of people who turned to look as a scruffy young man with matted brown hair ran out of the front entrance into the street.

Except for Lily, no one in the bathroom or anyone left in the train station lobby could seem to give a coherent description to the police. The information varied. The attacker was young. He was middle-aged. He was tall and thin. He was short and scrawny. He wore denim. His jacket was brown. He wore a baseball cap. His hair was wild. He was white. He was Hispanic. He might have been an Arab.

***

The police were polite and matter-of-fact. After the kind doctor in the emergency room attended to the wound on her neck, Lily met with a police officer, a woman, thankfully. Lily was exhausted. She wished her parents were there. Hours had passed. The police officer told her that her parents had been regularly calling the hospital and were already in Illinois. And they had her phone. The Girl Scout leader had found it on the bathroom floor and turned it in.

"I'm sorry, I know this is hard. Just a few more questions, the officer said. What exactly could Lily remember? The cliché of a bad dream was what she kept thinking. But the smell of him—the smell "down there" lingered.

At one point, the officer offered Lily a glossy, color brochure: SWIC- Strong Women in Chicago! On the cover were five women of different ages and ethnicities in athletic gear, posed together with arms on each other's shoulders. Inside was information about self-defense classes and counseling. "There's also a sexual assault support group, " the officer said. "And all the initial classes for survivors are free."

Lily said, "I wasn't raped, you know. And he actually didn't..." What he didn't do, Lily wasn't sure, which indicated that perhaps there was some denial concerning the horrific nature of what had happened.

"I know. I know," The officer said. She reminded Lily of the pregnant policewoman in the movie Fargo. She wasn't pregnant but wholesome in a way that suggested stability and confidence. She told Lily her name: Lois Lane.

"Is that really your name? Lois Lane?" Lily asked. Then added: "I'm sorry. I guess you hear that a lot."

Officer Lois Lane was in her forties, blond, short and thick, built like a fire plug. "I married into it," she said. "I wasn't going to change my name, but then thought it was kind of cool. My maiden name was Suvelouski. It was a pain in the ass spelling it all the time." Officer Lane had a nice, smile.

Lily looked down at the brochure. "Strong Women in Chicago. I heard about this before." The teacher in her women's studies class had mentioned SWIC.

"You'll like the woman who runs it. Actually, she owns it as well, That and a number of women's self-defense and athletic clubs. Her name is Mitzi Solomon. I send assault victims to her. She'll want to meet you. Hear your story. She's great. Just like a grandma. Especially if your grandma is a kick-ass black belt who owns half of Chicago."

"Thank you." Lily smiled at the image of Grandma Roberta kicking anyone's ass. At least physically. Settled in a Florida condominium, Roberta did nothing more strenuous than get up from her chair at the card table to change partners in a canasta game.

Officer Lane gave Lily a card. "I'll be in touch," she said. "And call me if you remember anything else." She paused in the doorway: "And maybe you don't believe this now. But you're a very lucky girl."

"Oh, I believe that," Lily told her.

***

It was evening by the time her parents arrived and by then Lily was in a cubicle in the emergency room, curled up on a bed, sleeping uneasily in the din. A white bandage covered the right side of her neck

"We're here. We're here, sweetheart." Her father's voice sounded croaky as if he hadn't used it for a while.

The British doctor was gone. Officer Lois Lane was gone. Lily looked like herself. Her face was flushed a bit, but her blond ponytail was still in place. "What time is it? You made it quickly, " Lily said, sitting up. "Daddy, did you drive?" Under the best of circumstances, Howard Lerner was a distracted driver, overly polite or simply not paying attention at four-way stop signs until his wife reminded him it was his turn to go.

Betsy, her usually composed mother, started to cry. "You're all right, Lily. You're all right." Sitting at the edge of the bed, her mother held both of Lily's cheeks in her hands, looking at her as if she were the most beautiful angel. "We spoke to the nurses. They said you were so brave." Betsy forced a smile. "You're going to be all right," she said.

There was something in her mother's fragility, something that Lily had not sensed before. "I'm all right, Mom," Lily assured her mother. "Really, I am." She meant it, too.

"I know you are, lovey," Betsy said, wiping her nose with a handkerchief that Howard offered. He was a man who always had a clean, white hankie in his pocket. Unusual. When Lily and Megan were little and had runny noses or dirty fingers, they depended on that. And if ever there was a father who was dependable, it was Howard Lerner.

Chapter 2

Howard: The Two Terrible Things That Happened That Winter

Not that the two terrible things were anywhere near awfulness in comparison. Howard Lerner felt guilty thinking of the events together, but he did, identifying the winter when their lives changed. How painful and bleak everything appeared. And then how strange when everything began to snowball. Snow. Winter had hardly begun, and there was snow, that slippery slope, gathering momentum in a way that could not be stopped.

The first terrible thing occurred on a real slippery, icy slope outside the building where Dr. Howard Lerner worked. In late middle age, he was a respected scientist, the country's leading expert in porcine diseases (It occurred to Howard sometimes, the oddity of his career choice given his background. "Pigs, Howie?" his mother said. "Trafe?").

That November, a surprising snowstorm had roared through the Midwest before most people had even gotten out their shovels. Coming out of the Veterinary Pathology building, Howard had fallen on a patch of ice, fracturing his hip in a way that made the orthopedist shake his head in dismay and prepare for emergency surgery.

After the operation, navigating on his crutches, and getting in and out of the car, Howard felt for the first time disappointment with the dependable body of his adult life. To aid in the rehabilitation, the orthopedist suggested swimming. Howard Lerner had reached his fifties without ever quite learning how to swim. He hated the water. Always he had been a creature of habit. Sunday mornings at the lab; running the same route every day when he could get away; a quick nap on the fold-out chair before he left the office at six.

The few weeks following the accident, he began to feel creaky and old, with a sense of his physical frailty looming large. The orthopod, who looked as young as one of Howard's graduate students, warned against running, even after the healing. "All those years were hell on your knees. The joints can't take it. Gotta give it up," he said in what Howard considered a tone too casual for this life-altering news.

He had been running almost daily for decades, having made the decision to lose weight when he was a senior in college and still living with his mother and sister in an apartment in Queens where he studied hours every night in a corner of the tiny kitchen. While he studied, his mother would bring up surprises from the bakery on the corner: seven-layer cake, rugelach, black-and-white cookies the size of his open hand.

Always a chubby, unathletic boy, Howard left Queens to go to graduate school in Wisconsin, a shy biochemistry major with thick glasses. There, with the same dogged reliability that organized his life of study, he began running, lost fifty pounds, and bulked up at the gym with muscle. He got contact lenses. When he came home for the first time after his year away, no one recognized him. "Can I help you, son?" Old Mr. Fein from 4F asked when Howard, who had forgotten the keys, was trying to ring into the apartment house his family had lived in for many years.

He was not used to it that the college girls at the University of Wisconsin found him attractive. He was swarthy, with thick, dark curls—possibly seen as exotic to them. He was unaggressive and polite, smart, and destined to make a good living. Howard Lerner was solid husband material.

The last year of graduate school in Wisconsin, he met Betsy Randall, a pretty blond, so low maintenance that she never even once asked what was he thinking because she presumed, unlike his mother, that he was permitted to keep his thoughts to himself.

Betsy had been in a chemistry class, a lecture for undergraduates and he was the teaching assistant for the smaller group. When he proctored the final exam for the entire class, he couldn't help looking at her as he went up and down the aisles. She was wearing a fuzzy, blue sweater that puffed around her like a cloud. He knew she already had an A in the class because he graded her other tests. He also knew she was an English major, a senior, who had probably put off her dreaded science requirement until the last semester.

Betsy was sitting by the door and was one of the last to leave. When she handed in her final, Howard told her the grades would be posted at the end of the week.

Betsy smiled: "Yes, you told us that already." She pointed to the blackboard, where Howard had scrawled the information.

After the exams were graded and handed in, he ran into her on campus. Inanely, he asked if she had liked the class. She was kind, saying the subject was difficult, then adding that he had explained things very well.

Summoning up his courage he cleared his throat and asked if she would like to go out sometime. "I mean, now that you're not in the class." She looked at him directly, her bright, blue eyes almost mocking. "Sure."

***

The second terrible thing played over and over again in his mind: Winter break. Lily, in Union Station, waiting for her ride. Howard worried about Lily driving home as much as he worried about her living in Chicago, alone in her apartment after her roommates had already left for the holiday. She had a whistle on her keychain. Howard had bought her a can of pepper spray. He worried. Oh, he worried all the time. He was a worrier, his family knew that. Sometimes they even kept things from him.

Lily rented that apartment with her friends. Not in the best neighborhood. Howard didn't approve. As a teenager, he had to take two subways and a bus to his high school in lower Manhattan, but he never thought of his own children as having the watchful street-smarts he had acquired growing up as a city boy in New York.

Don't worry, Daddy, Lily had said. She was going to meet a friend at Union Station, then get a ride to Des Moines where they could pick her up. She was supposed to text them when they got on the road. They didn't know the last name of Lily's ride—just Brian Somebody. Howard was plagued with guilt. What kind of parents don't know the last name of their daughter's friend?

Brian Somebody had waited on Jackson in front of the Megabus stop and idled for almost half an hour, texting Lily and not getting any response. He even parked—though it was fairly impossible to find a space—and went up and down the street to look for her. Then finally, thinking maybe she got another ride, he left.

Howard replayed in his mind the information the police told him. The man waiting in the woman's bathroom at the Union Station, leering at Lily, the knife at her throat. Lily helpless in the stall. His daughter riding in the ambulance through Chicago streets, alone and bleeding, admitted to the chaos of the city's emergency room.

Howard felt a rage building inside him. For some time, even before his daughter's assault, Howard Lerner believed that what was wrong with the world was men. Almost every night on the news there were scenes of rock-throwing males somewhere, their faces lit up with angry energy. Young men, over-turning vehicles, their fists pumping. Or breaking glass, taking down light poles, storming a barricade. In celebration or in protest, men in crowds were frightening.

One would think that living in a peaceful, midwestern college town would not reinforce this belief, but in fact, it did. Every home football game. There they were. The guys with their hats on backward, hooting and hollering, especially if the team won. They held up hastily made signs on the front lawns in front of their run-down student rentals. 'You Honk, We Drink.' College boys were ugly drunks. "Show us your tits," they'd yell at girls who walked by.

Perhaps it was not a stretch to go from young men celebrating a winning football team to the violence of uprisings, kidnappings, and rapes. Even wars! Something was wrong with the male species. After Howard became a father of daughters, he felt more than ever that the world, however it was rife with accident and disease, was made ever more dangerous by men.

Howard preferred the company of women and for at least the last decade his life revolved around them: his wife and daughters; his dependable secretary, Joyce Corning; and of course his brilliant post-doc, the bold Anaya Pran.

Chapter 3

A Complaint to Dr. Lerner:
My Pigs Are Vomiting

The summer before Howard's surgery and before his daughter's attack, a farmer from Vinton came into the lab. Howard recalled that innocent time with longing. Before and after. That August (before) the heat made everything shimmer. Howard dripped in sweat and the building felt good when he came back from a jog.

Howard often thought about a problem in the lab while he ran. The fields along the road changed with the season. Seedlings. Corn inching its way up. Knee-high at the Fourth of July. Then later, as the song goes—as high as an elephant's eye. Fall harvest would leave hollow husks. Cultivated, the rich earth was dark as coffee. After it rained, black mud. Later in winter, snowy barren fields, crystal white, reflecting the light.

One afternoon, a man appeared at the door of Howard's office unannounced. "My pigs are vomiting," he said.

Joyce stood in the doorway, looking apologetic. "He said he needed to meet you," she explained. "I'm sorry, Dr. Lerner. Are you busy?"

"It's all right, Joyce." Howard nodded that she could leave and return to her desk. Howard had been with Joyce Corning in the vet school almost as long as he was married to Betsy and, understanding each other, both conveyed a kind of shorthand. Joyce was protective. She was going to retire soon, but neither of them wanted to talk about that yet.

"Leroy Stang," said the man, taking a seat without being asked. "I heard you on the radio…"

Howard nodded.

"…talking about your research."

"Uh huh."

Leroy Stang described his own small operation outside of Vinton, Iowa. "Less than five hundred hogs, farrow to finish." He had run the farm for over forty years, his father for fifty years before him. He had not experienced anything like this before. There were years when feed was expensive, when drought seared the land, followed by flood the next. But nothing, nothing like this. "Something is wrong," he said. "Sounds like you're the guy who might know what it is."

Howard's research had recently been the subject of a segment on Science Friday. Just as surprising as Leroy Stang's unannounced intrusion into the lab on a Monday afternoon was the knowledge that the man in front of him was a fan of NPR.

Leroy Stang looked like something out of central casting. Overalls covered his considerable belly. The seed-corn cap pulled down over his forehead. Howard knew that if the farmer took off his tee shirt, his shoulders and chest would be the palest vanilla. Like the man himself, his kind of farm was an endangered species. Many of the small family farms were gone. Huge hog lot operations now splattered the land; established farmers had children who went to Iowa State to study agriculture or engineering but no longer planned to take over the family farm.

Howard's current research involved the diagnosis and treatment of diseases caused by mycotoxins, perhaps as a result of contaminated feed. Establishing cause-and-effect relationships between the consumption of mycotoxin-contaminated feed was not exactly clear; detection was difficult. Howard's most recent grants came not from the National Science Foundation, but from large agribusiness companies.

Also, the veterinary school had changed over the decades. When Howard was a young vet student there were only a few young women who loved animals enough to have the tenacity—indeed the audacity—to apply to vet school. It was difficult to gain admission. There was a joke: "What do you call someone who couldn't get into vet school?" Answer: "A medical student!"

The gender bias continued to shift. Now females outnumbered males in the vet school by a large margin. And many of the young women grew up not on farms, but with the domesticated dogs and cats they loved, and they wanted to be small-animal veterinarians. They would not choose to spend their careers with their hands up inside a cow's ass. Or trying to figure out why pigs were vomiting.

***

Anaya Pran happened to be in Howard's office when Leroy Stang arrived. Anaya remained quiet when the farmer came in. She stood over by the window and began to take notes although neither Howard nor Leroy took notice.

Anaya was the best colleague that Howard had ever had, her name appearing directly under his with almost every article he had recently published. She was like no one Howard had ever worked with. The science graduate students in general were respectful and diffident. The female graduate students perhaps more so. The female international students, of whom Howard had almost a dozen in the past twenty-five years— it didn't matter how smart they were, how many awards and accolades they came with—these young women simply did not call attention to themselves.

But Anaya was different in every possible way: gregarious, outspoken, confident. Some might say brash. Often, she treated Howard as an equal partner rather than a mentor. Howard didn't mind. He was proud when he and Anaya presented together at a conference and afterward, some stuffy, old scientist would ask: "Who IS that girl?" looking at Anya's spiked black hair, her strong jaw, her jangly silver jewelry.

Recently Anaya had the opportunity for a position at a major research center at another university. Then she, too, would leave Howard's lab. But Howard didn't want to think about that either. He couldn't imagine his professional life without Joyce and Anaya any more than he could imagine his domestic life without Betsy. He was a man who didn't like change.

There had already been too much change that summer with both daughters away from home, though Betsy seemed agreeable about this phase. At night, they locked up the house at ten and his wife was relieved not having to listen for a teenager's car pulling in. Lily once observed that her mother seemed awfully happy when she and her sister left for college after summer vacation. "That's the point of being a parent," Betsy assured her. She and Howard had helped to create capable, confident young women going out into the world.

But no one was more confident than Anaya Pran. Although, truth be told, she sometimes scared Howard with her bold intensity. "Interesting," she said, when Leroy Stang left.

"I forgot you were there," Howard said.

"I was quiet."

"Yes, unusual."

"I was listening. What do you make of it?" Anaya asked.

"It could be something. It could be more than…"

Just then Joyce Corning knocked on the open door. "Dr. Lerner, there's a grants committee meeting in the conference room. They're waiting for you."

"Oh, yes, thank you Joyce. I was just heading out," Howard said. He had read so many proposals in the past week that they all blended together, every scientist an apparent candidate for a Nobel prize.

Anaya headed back to her own office. "It could be something," she said. I mean. Something really…something."

***

Sometimes, despite the professional success Howard Lerner had for so many years, with all the articles and the keynote addresses at conferences all over the world, he felt like a fraud. A different Howard Lerner appeared from time to time. Not the esteemed Dr. Lerner whose work was validated by the most respected scientists; but clumsy Howie from Queens, the kid who was never picked for the team in gym; the boy who began to cry so hard in third grade when the class was assigned to make Father's Day cards that he had to be sent to the nurse.

As a city boy, the closest he had ever got to livestock was one summer when his parents rented a cabin for a vacation week in upstate New York, and they drove past cows on the side of the road. "Look! Moo-Moos!" Roberta Lerner excitedly pointed out the exotic landscape to Howard and his little sister.

It was their last family vacation. One of the only happy times Howard could remember from his childhood. The following winter—Howard was six years old, his sister, three—their father, a muscular soda delivery driver, was killed in a hold-up in the Bronx. The truck was still running when Jake Lerner surprised a man who was in the process of running out of the deli he had just robbed. "Hey," said Jake when he saw the gunman and the man tripped and fell. But not before he shot Jake Lerner in the chest, killing him instantly.

A witness to the robbery said that Jake was a hero, the way he blocked the entrance like that, trying to stop a dangerous criminal. That was the statement reported the next day in the paper.

Howard can still only murkily recall what followed. For days after, so many people came to the house. His mother wailing, incapacitated by mourning, took the children to sleep in her bed. Then followed a run of bad relationships including a short marriage to a gambler who ran through all the insurance money.

They were poor. His mother was lonely. By the time Howard and his sister were teenagers, they were living in a small apartment in Queens; he worked every day after school while Roberta had a job selling ladies' lingerie in Bloomingdales.

As an adult, Howard realized that he had never known what his parents' marriage had actually been like. His father was idealized by Roberta and every time their wedding picture was taken out of the living room when she was dating someone, it was put back up when the relationship faltered. "There was never a man good like your father," Roberta said, again displaying their wedding photograph prominently on the living room credenza. "Your father. He was a man. He protected us."

Now years older than his father had been when he was killed, Howard could not recall the man with any clarity. He remembered his father's strong arms. He recalled that his father had a mustache that tickled. Though perhaps that memory was created from the photo in the living room of a dark man with a suave mustache. The cows along the side of the road from that vacation in upstate New York remained more vivid in Howard's mind.

After Lily's attack, he began to think of his father, a man he had barely known, killed while working at a job to support his family. The loss became fresh, painful. Because a father should be there, should be a protector, after all.

Chapter 4

Lily: Strong Women in Chicago

Walking to the studio, Lily mused that perhaps she was repressing her emotions. Would the stress kick up later as some post-trauma drama? When she talked to her sister about the attack, Megan's reaction was fury. "I could kill that little fucker, that sicko jerk," she raged. Megan knew that Lily's attacker was slight in build and so referred to him as "that little fucker," as if to diminish the horror of what he had done.

Also, what he attempted to do, Lily might say. She was a victim of a sexual assault. She had bled from a knife wound. She had seen his limp, smelly penis. But he had not actually put it in her mouth, had he?

On Van Buren Street, Lily stood on the curb in front of the SWIC building for a few moments before going in. SWIC. Strong Women in Chicago. The strongest woman was the owner, Mitzi Solomon. Even recalling what Lois Lane, the police officer, told her that night in the emergency room, Lily was still surprised when she met Mitzi. Of course, it was unusual to be instructed in the art of self-defense by a gray-haired woman well into her sixties. Or maybe seventies. It was hard to tell with gray-haired women. And then there was her voice, issuing directions with intensity.

As an instructor, Mitzi Solomon was amazing. Clear, powerful in execution, but eventually a comforting maternal presence to the women in the class. Although Mitzi was the owner of SWIC, she still taught one of the self-defense classes, especially when the newbies were signed up. Lily loved that first class.

That was when Mitzi shared her personal story. Forty-five years ago, her younger sister was raped, beaten and left for dead in the vestibule of her apartment reaching inside her purse for her keys. But Mitzi's sister Grace was not dead; she went on to become an interior decorator, to marry, have children and move to Highland Park. It was Mitzi who became trained as a black belt in karate, a certified martial arts instructor and who began Strong Women in Chicago. Currently, there was a chain of popular and financially thriving SWIC studios in the city. Mitzi Solomon had made the protection of women her life's work.

Lily was not, by nature, an aggressive or even a particularly physical person. But, like her father, she was a rule follower, an attentive and determined student, and so did very well in the class. Soon Lily came to be one of Mitzi's favorites and was frequently called on to demonstrate newly learned techniques. Before doing this, Lily sometimes thought about her attacker, touching the wound on her neck. The scar, first an angry red, was now a silver line following from her right ear to her collarbone.

She and Todd had split up amicably. She needed space, she told him, and the cliché was true. He seemed relieved. Lily would have preferred to be comforted by a boyfriend who had the right words, a boyfriend who knew who she was in the deepest way, even without the words. But that boyfriend wasn't Todd. There was no acrimony. Todd meant well and she didn't hold his limitations against him. He was sweet, texting sometimes to ask how she was.

After they broke up, Todd's mother sent a basket of chocolate and fruit to the apartment Lily shared with her college friends, and they finished the contents greedily. Then she put the basket in the bathroom and filled it with fancy soaps.

***

SWIC: The afternoon of the third meeting, the women in the class sat on mats arranged in a circle, Mitzi with a box on her lap. She passed around devices that she encouraged women to carry for self-defense. "Be prepared. Which means you are always in a state of readiness in mind and body. Be prepared for everything. Isn't that what the girl scouts say?"

It was a Boy Scout motto, Lily knew, but never mind. The Girl Scout motto had something to do with helping people.

The third meeting was the time when the women shared their own stories, describing why they were taking a class specifically designed for survivors of assault. "Would you please go first?" Mitzi said, starting with the young woman who was sitting next to her.

Maryanne, a chubby-cheeked girl with blond ringlets, looked the very picture of mid-western milkmaid. Coming home from a nightshift job at the post office, Maryanne had been raped by a man impersonating a police officer who pulled her over. Cars drove by as the man assaulted her in a ditch beside the road. "Stay here until my car is gone," he said afterward. Adding, "Good night," before driving off. Maryanne was soft-spoken and tremulous describing the attack; Mitzi placed a hand on her shoulder and gave a gently squeeze. Then led everyone in applause. "Thank you for sharing that, Maryanne," Mitzi said.

Next to Lily sat Alida, a young Hispanic nanny who had been attacked in a playground after she had put a toddler on a swing. When a man came close to her, pulled her arm and tried to drag her away behind some bushes, Alida screamed at the top of her lungs, fighting so hard, punching against the man's chest that she broke all the bones in her hand. The attacker ran off. "It was because of the baby," she explained. "I had to fight because of the baby." The class clapped again, acknowledging Alida's bravery.

Laura Murphy was older than the others in the Lily's circle. Lily knew Laura was a teacher because she had mentioned her 'kids' during one of the other classes. Hearing this for the first time, Lily thought Laura meant her own children. Laura was being stalked by a man who was calling her, texting her, following her after school. Laura had met him on a dating ap, gone out with him only once, but he became fixated on her, alternating between threatening her life and proposing marriage.

When it was Lily's turn, she shared what happened to her in the bathroom at Union Station, how she had been saved by presence of a furious Girl Scout leader. "I was lucky," she said, showing them the scar on her neck. "But I want to think that surviving this will make me stronger. What we went through has the capacity to make all of us stronger." She added: "Together!" She was surprised when everyone, including Mitzi, clapped more loudly than before.

Lily liked the women in the class. Maybe it was a sense of camaraderie that drew her to all of them; never had she been in a place that was so authentically you-go-girl. Despite sharing horrific experiences, there was also a lot of laughter.

"There are many ways to defend yourselves." Mitzi handed out a sheet that listed all the devices, including prices and availability. A tiny alarm that could be placed in the palm of one's hand sold at Walmart for $11.81. Kuba-Kickz, brass knuckles designed to be laced into shoes could be ordered on Amazon for only $15.98, with free shipping.

Alida passed Lily the 'world's smallest flashlight' which also served as a powerful alarm. AAA batteries included. There were simple objects that were made into weapons: a tactical penlight, made by Smith and Wesson which had a sharpened end that could be used as a knife; there was a stun-gun flashlight; a lipstick stun-gun; a cute cat key chain, with the cute cat's ears sharpened into deadly points; a hairbrush whose handle concealed a stiletto. Many of the objects, including the cute cat keychain, were pink.

"Understand, for all of these devices, time is of the essence. You must be always ready," Mitzi said. Holding up a can of pepper spray, she added: "Be smart. Something like this, an inhalant, that you can use to fend off an attacker, can also be taken away from you and used against you. So be smart. Be very smart."

Chapter 5

Dr. Lerner: Eureka, He Might Have Thought Among That Stinking Mess

On a Sunday at the end of February, Dr. Howard Lerner made an amazing, if accidental, discovery. Even scientists can recognize this as serendipity. Someone leaves an unattended culture in the petri dish by the windowsill. Or incubated too long and then forgotten. Two solutions are mixed together for the first time by a lab assistant and an improperly labeled chemical gets added. And one in a million, two in a million, what are the odds?

But sometimes unusual discoveries do occur: penicillin from bread mold; a bladder cancer drug from a live germ that causes tuberculosis. Scientist can make unexpected but wildly fortuitous connections.

Sunday morning was Howard's favorite time to be in the lab—when everyone else was home reading the paper, eating pancakes and bacon, or getting ready for church. Howard had a wife who did not object to his working on Sunday morning. Years before, Betsy took the girls to church but that didn't last. She came from a pale Protestant denomination with little flair; Howard was a secular Jew and a scientist to boot; when Megan and Lily became adolescents, they complained bitterly about going to church, wanting only to sleep in.

February. Howard was both distraught and distracted ever since Lily's attack. The police had found nothing. No leads. He watched the news, sometimes choking up when other parents lost children to opioids or gunfire and had to remind himself that Lily was alive and actually doing quite well.

But for the past two months, he had difficulty finishing a grant or writing a recommendation for a graduate student. Colleagues were understanding. His secretary, Joyce, maternal under ordinary circumstances, treated him with sympathy. It was horrible. Horrible. Joyce had known Lily since she was a little girl. A sweet, happy little girl.

Howard continued to work. It was the life he knew, despite his own malaise. Go to the lab every day. Direct the graduate students. Read the journals. Every day, the research was painstaking and grindingly slow.

In February, the winter in Iowa seems endless. Below zero and lots of snow. Usually, Howard didn't mind winter very much. The snow never got gray and dirty as it did in New York. He liked the Midwest. The cheery, airy cleanness of it. The big sky. A place where you could breathe. He had loved his job as a toxicologist at the best land grant institution in the country. A foxitologist, Lily used to say when she was little. She understood that there were animals in her father's lab. In first grade, she had announced proudly to the class that her father worked mostly with foxes and wolves. Years later she learned that her father worked only with pigs. Many of them already dead from unknown diseases. He was a scientist whose life's work was maintaining animal safety and figuring out the reasons for early or mysterious porcine demise.

That Sunday morning, Howard was looking at the slides from areas near the confinements in Vinton. Again, checking the molds. What was it that caused the whole herd of pigs on the farm to lose weight? Howard had tested the soil, taking samples of the earth, the feed, and especially random carcasses. All received scrupulous analysis in the pathology lab.

He surmised that the farmer's grain had been contaminated by mycotoxins. In fact, the lab had just isolated a particular mold spore when he dropped a particular slide, breaking it against the counter. He had broken or misplaced a lot of things during the past two months. Now Howard fastidiously wrapped the slide to throw it out in the bin that contained the dangerous trash, radioactive waste, and contaminants. He was careful to use gloves. Careful not to touch anything. There were two other prepared slides with samples of the same grain and neither of them was cracked.

He began to wipe down the counter with a paper towel after spraying an antiseptic, a generic all-purpose cleaner. He thought he had been careful, but realized later that he must have missed a few tiny strands of the spore. Because suddenly a strange smell hit. The odor was pungent, sweet and burnt. Not the smell of the cleaning solvent, but an acrid-sweet smell, like caramel left too long on the stove.

And then—almost immediately—Howard became sick. Struck by something that seemed to turn his body almost inside out. The first wave hit and he threw up everything he had eaten for breakfast that day. Then he vomited again. And again. The retching lasted for almost five minutes. It began that Sunday morning at exactly ten o'clock. He knew because he checked the clock on the wall just as the first wave hit. He did not even have time to make it to the lab sink over in the corner of the room. The first spasm began that quickly.

Never had he thrown up that violently and with such sustained intensity. Not with the flu. Not with the food poisoning he had once had after eating a bowl of mussels. The contractions began in earnest immediately after the first whiff reached his nostrils and didn't ebb until almost five minutes past the hour. Afterward, he leaned on the counter, shaken and weak, barely able to stand. The lab counter was disgusting. There was vomit on the windowsill, on his shoes, on the computer. The smell permeated the room.

He had made a discovery. Something was created there that morning in the lab. But what exactly?

Chapter 6

As Dr. Jerry Ketcham Knows: There Used to Be Some Anthrax Around Here Somewhere

Following the attack on the World Trade Center, letters containing a toxic substance were sent to media outlets and United States senators' offices. Seven letters altogether. The first person to die of anthrax in what was considered to be a terrorist attack, was a photographer for a newspaper in Florida. The FBI believed then that the bacteria came from a laboratory at the veterinary school in Ames, Iowa.

A story in the New Yorker just a few months following 9/11 led with the headline: How a sick cow in Iowa may have helped to create a lethal bioweapon. The article described how in the late seventies, a farmer found his apparently healthy cow dead in the field. The farmer suspected anthrax poisoning. The veterinarian who examined the carcass agreed. The cow would have looked perfectly healthy in death "except for the blood streaming from its nostrils, ears, and rectum," the article said. Anthrax kills quickly.

The cow had probably contracted anthrax from eating spores that were in the dirt; perhaps contaminated bone meal had been given to the herd. Spores could remain dormant for a long time—years, in fact—until they were possibly reconstituted when eaten along with a clump of wet grass by an animal who then got sick and died.

Although the reports were mistaken and the anthrax did not originate in Ames, the College of Veterinary Medicine had been nervous. "We want the public to know our commitment is to animal health and public safety," Dr. Jerry Ketcham, the Vice Provost for academic research, assured the public. His was a job demanding rigor and scrupulous surveillance. Suspicion of an unaccounted toxin could have dire consequences, and it was Ketcham's responsibility to make sure that the university did not violate good practice.

Science had a creative side, but Jerry Ketcham was a man who did not tolerate rule-breakers. Quickly he established himself as the administrator official who would safeguard the public trust. A scientist who used nefarious practices in applying for a grant could jeopardize everyone. Carelessness, malfeasance, violation of any of the National Institute of Health standards was never to be tolerated. Certainly not if Jerry Ketcham did his job properly.

***

The contaminated feed at the farm in Vinton was found in the soil around the containment areas. Like anthrax, the spores were dormant in the lab. But then they were no longer dormant in the pig's stomach after being mixed with digestive juices. No longer dormant when the smear on Dr. Howard Lerner's broken slide inadvertently mixed with a cleaning solution.

When combined, two single chemical agents can become lethal. That's what the underwear bomber was attempting to do with a plunger that was supposed to be mixed with chemicals to ignite explosives. That's what was involved in the airport killing of the North Korean leader's half-brother: VX nerve gas in two elements, mixed before delivery, resulted in muscle contractions that locked the ability to breathe.

There has been a long history of secret—and not so secret—poisonings, especially from Russia. The attempts on the lives of dissidents, lawyers, journalists. The stuff of spy novels occurred many times in real life: poison tipped umbrellas; rare toxic plants; tainted dinners. In other countries, scientists removed themselves from bioweapons research and began to concentrate on discovering vaccines against the poisons. The vaccine for anthrax was an example.

If something was identified as a possibility to be used as a bioweapon, there were immediate restrictions on research. Politicians weren't scientists. Call something a bioweapon and there were sanctions. Call something a weapon and rules hardly applied. Congress understood guns, but they didn't understand pathogens. Bombs and guns don't grow or reproduce themselves. But pathogens could be frozen in a lab, even for years. Something that is discovered and planned to be used for a good purpose can get in the hands of bad people. Perhaps if protocol on research wasn't so very restrictive, something useful that could thwart bad behavior could be used by good people.

Contamination with anthrax resulted in a few dead cows. On the farm in Vinton, there were vomiting pigs. But even though the animals were violently ill, they didn't die.

Nor did Howard Lerner when he inadvertently inhaled the mixed agents. The result was similar to inhalation anthrax and VX nerve gas. But without lethal consequences. Muscle contractions that locked the ability to breathe—the result of VX nerve gas—somehow did the opposite in Howard's lab. Muscle contractions, rather than being stopped, were put on speed dial, causing the most violent anti-peristalsis imaginable.

***

The month of March offered some respite. Tricky in Iowa. It always is. No one who lived in Iowa put away shovels and boots even on the most spring-like day in March. Howard and Betsy were finishing dinner, one of his favorites—roast chicken and garlic mashed potatoes —when Howard said he had to go back to the lab. "I'll clean up before I go back if you'd like," he offered.

"Thanks," she said, kissing him on the cheek. "Are you going to be late? Maybe I'll watch one of my shows." There were so many choices. HBO. Netflix. Amazon Prime. Often it took so long to decide on something they both agreed to, that they ended up watching nothing at all.

Howard was methodical in kitchen maintenance and took pride in the proper way to stack the dishwasher, mixing silverware upside, downside. Betsy sorted by type, which Howard believed did not produce maximum results. Now, wiping down the counter with the same generic cleaner that he had in the lab, he looked at the familiar plastic spray bottle. Lemon-scented, all-purpose cleaner, kills 99.9% of bacteria. Cleans and disinfects tough grime.

> *Octyl decyl dimethyl ammonium chloride*
> *Diocytl dimethyl ammonium chloride*
> *Alkyl dimethyl benzyl ammonium chloride*
> *Keep Out of Reach of Children*

"Are you ok?" Betsy said, coming back into the kitchen, and taking out a mug for tea. "I've been calling you."

"Just thinking," Howard said.

They stood in front of the microwave and hugged each other tight. A pattern of random embrace emerged with some frequency since Lily's attack. They pulled away when the microwave stopped; Betsy took out the mug, put in a bag of Orange Spice and noticed that Howard had tears in his eyes.

The sadness ambushed him at random times: riding his bike and passing a jogging college girl, her ponytail swinging behind her; or Anaya, her neck bent over a microscope, seeming inexplicably vulnerable; or waiting for the ding of the microwave.

"Oh, honey," Betsy said, taking him back into her arms. They remained this way for a while. "Why don't you stay home tonight? You've been working such long hours lately."

"I just have a few things to check up on. We'll watch something when I get home." Then he added: "But don't wait up, just in case."

"Just in case," Betsy said, smiling.

***

Around seven o'clock that evening, Howard drove back to the lab where the animals were kept, found a parking space on the quiet south side of the building, walked out of the car, and breathed in the fecund odor of pig shit.

The research animals were kept under lock-up, the security greater since animal rights activists had staged protests years ago. But the truth was that there was not all that much support at the university for PETA and their sympathizers. Many of the students at Iowa State came from rural areas where there was not a sentimental view regarding either animal research or food.

For months, he had been working tirelessly with tissue samples of sick pigs and trying to reproduce the clinical results after feeding. But these trials were going slowly. They were also expensive, and grant money was tight.

When he had first come to Iowa State, there was not so much paperwork, not so much accountability, not nearly so many restrictions. Now there was IACUC, the Institute for Animal Care and Use Committee, which had to approve every single animal experiment. And Jerry Ketcham was more scrupulous than he ever needed to be, micromanaging every facet of research. While Howard tolerated Jerry Ketcham, Joyce was compliant but nervous in any interaction with him, and Anaya despised him. Ketcham was one of the reasons she had given Howard for leaving his lab. "How can anyone do science with all those drudges watching over your every move?"

By the time Howard pulled into the parking lot, it was already quite dark. Soon it would be daylight savings. Fall back. Spring ahead. No one in the family except him could remember which way to turn the clocks. He walked gingerly to the front entrance and unlocked the door, down the corridor to the lab where the animals were kept and looked around before punching in the security code. The hall was empty.

The warm room, smelling of flesh and straw, was already lit, and the friendly piglets came to greet him, pushing their snouts against the mesh of their cages, their tails wagging, happy to see him. Often these same pigs were anesthetized for research procedures, some many times. Pigs were smart. They remembered. But perhaps they just didn't carry a grudge.

Pigs were also an excellent model in use for human study. Like humans, they were monogastric, having only one stomach. Other internal organs matched in all sorts of interesting ways, making pigs compatible donors for transplants and grafts. Pigs were used in research for diabetes and even alcoholism. Like humans, pigs loved beer and often a good Chianti.

Choosing a sturdy first specimen, he stood in front of a cage, checking to see that the area was clean. "Hey there, sport," he said. The piglet was perfectly pink except for a black coloration over one eye that made it seem jaunty.

To prepare, Howard had covered himself with protective clothing, gloves, and a mask. On the table beside the cages, he added a small amount of cleaning fluid and a tiny spore onto a tray. Then, using, a bulb syringe, he sucked in both the liquid and particle, inserting the tip of the syringe in between the wire of the cage. The piglet, one of the largest and soon to be euthanized, came over to investigate. "Sorry," Howard said gently, before spraying the pig directly in the snout. He held his breath, anticipating that the activated mycotoxin would produce immediate results.

Which it did. The antiperistalsis was quick and violent. Recording the reaction and the recovery time, Howard repeated the preparation, moving on to the next cage and the next, recording the start and stop of each event.

He felt bad, watching the pigs become so terribly sick. But they recovered quickly, as he had anticipated, seemingly not disturbed. The pigs even cleaned up after themselves and then went back to happily rooting in the straw.

***

Betsy was asleep by the time he came home. He showered and crawled into bed alongside her. "How'd it go, hon?" she mumbled, turning toward him. "Good, really good," he said. "Sorry, Bets. Go back to sleep." "Mmm." She turned and was soon breathing evenly.

It was past midnight, but sleep seemed a far way off. In the quiet of night, he had flashes of Lily being attacked by a monster in a bathroom stall. Sometimes, even after he had fallen asleep, that image startled him awake, and he sat up in bed in a sweat, his heart racing.

Now, not wanting to risk waking Betsy by getting out of bed to read, he did his sleep tricks: deep breathing—four breathes in, hold for seven, out for eight. Another: remembering all the rooms he had ever lived in: the family apartment in Queens, his graduate dorm room in Madison, a ramshackle house the last two years there; first apartments with Betsy in the early years of marriage.

Sleepless still, he began to recall the names of famous scientists he admired and their life's work. He knew of dedicated, brave, and perhaps foolish scientists who, against protocol and reason, had experimented upon themselves, their assistants, even their own families.

There was a scientist named Bier who discovered spinal anesthesia through a method involving injecting cocaine into cerebrospinal fluid. This left Bier with a hole in his spine but did not dissuade him from experimenting further on his agreeable assistant.

Then there was a man with the strange name of Stubbins Ffirth (1784-1820) who—during the Yellow Fever epidemic—tested the disease's characteristic 'black vomit' by drinking it.

Perhaps the most famous and least wacky researcher was Jonas Salk who volunteered himself and his entire family for a vaccine trial. He was successful: all the hosts tested positive for anti-polio antibodies. Salk was not only an inspiration as a scientist, but he was also an inspiration as a man. Salk refused to patent the vaccine, and never received financial compensation for his discovery. When he was interviewed and asked who owned the patent on the vaccine,

Salk responded: "Well, the people, I would say. There is no patent. Could you patent the sun?"

***

This next week was spring break at the university. Anaya would be with her wife Vera Perez in Las Vegas, a belated honeymoon. Joyce and her husband would be vacationing with the grandchildren at Disney World. Over spring break the janitorial staff was going to clean and wax all the floors in the building, but Howard had given notice not to enter his lab. Alone, without interruption, without Anaya or Joyce to witness, he would be able to continue the inhalation experiment. The knowledge of what he was about to begin was a cause for comfort rather than alarm. It was unlike him, this rash, randomless move. And why? A little after three in the morning, he finally fell asleep.

Chapter 7

The Town Empties Out Over Spring Break

It was the middle of March, and many students on spring break were heading for even warmer climes: San Padre Island, Cancun. Maybe being already thousands of dollars in debt, college students figured, what the hell: we're only young once.

Howard wasn't feeling quite as fragile, riding his bike on new trails. The orthopedist had recommended swimming and biking; Howard was enjoying the latter. His hip felt good. There was even one sleepy moment, when he rose to go to the bathroom in the middle of the night and thought: which hip was it?

On Sunday morning Betsy packed the car, rushing the season by adding spring clothes for the girls. She had decided to drive to Chicago to see Lily and was picking up Megan on the way: just her girls, shopping, and eating out.

Although he would have liked to see Lily, Howard had been encouraging. In truth, he was relieved. They had both been quietly mourning since the attack. Not every day was painful; they were back to their usual routines, but something had been lost. Betsy was teaching Zumba classes at the senior citizen center and tutoring special-needs children. She kept busy. But sometimes he saw her face in repose and wondered what she was thinking.

Their intimate life had changed, and he was determined to be patient, knowing that men were different from women, more able to compartmentalize. He remembered there were times in their marriage, just when he and Betsy were having sex and a baby cried in the night; he could keep going, while Betsy, suddenly drawn to the call, had lost all passion.

The police had not caught Lily's attacker. Officer Lois Lane, she was certainly nice enough when Howard spoke to her, but she was not optimistic. It seemed likely that the man would not be found. Howard thought about that often. Too often. Howard was looking forward to staying as long as he wanted in the lab, recording the data, seeing if any of his weird suppositions were perhaps not weird after all. There was excitement building in this.

After breakfast Howard walked Betsy to the car, checking the tires out of habit, asking if she had her phone. Then he stood in the driveway and waved before walking back into the house through the garage.

It was strange being alone in the home they shared; a cozy, welcoming place, made more so by Betsy's touch with colorful pillows on cream-colored couches; on the shelves in the living room was a mix of books and tasteful tchotchkes: glass-blown vases, ceramic bowls, a few family photos in antique frames. He stared at the hard-back books, many he didn't know they owned. Did Betsy read all of them?

This was the peaceful, familiar home that she made, but alone he felt lost. At night, cleaning up the kitchen, he stood holding a spatula aloft at the counter. Where did it go? The following week he didn't make the bed, although he disliked getting into an unmade bed at the end of the day; breakfast dishes were left in the sink; he forgot to take in the mail or close the curtains at night. But he wasn't home very much that week anyway.

***

He reviewed the data again in his office, carefully detailing the work he had done with the lab animals. He recorded the amount of activated mycotoxin: the times, start, and stop of each anti-peristaltic event. The pigs seemed to have recovered well from his controlled and limited intervention; they had become sicker on the Vinton farm because the feed times were varied and unlimited.

Most of the offices in his building were closed, the halls empty, though occasionally a graduate student or a custodian passed by. Joyce, in her meticulous way, had cleaned out the department refrigerator, left notes for him, calls that he needed return; she left her cell number in case he needed something while she was in Florida.

He wouldn't disturb her. Joyce was looking tired lately. He knew she was concerned about her youngest daughter. Caroline had been a difficult teenager, and she was into a bad crowd of drugs and petty crimes. Now a young mother with a real job, Caroline seemed to lead an even more precarious life. Joyce didn't say much about it, but the worry crease behind her glasses became prominent whenever Caroline's name was brought up. The framed photo on Joyce's desk was of Caroline and her little girl, although Joyce's other two sons-in-law figured prominently in other family pictures. Joyce did not like the man Caroline was married to.

Howard's lab was around the corner from his office, set back in an alcove beyond the women's bathroom. Since the newer wing had been built, hardly anyone came back here. It was just Joyce at the front; Anaya had her own office across from his. The laboratory was secluded in the back. He opened the door to the lab with a key that only he and Joyce and Anaya had. There was a warning note on the door, not to disturb, an experiment was in progress.

Indeed, it was. Careful to protect himself before the assigned time of inhalation, he had everything lined up, ready to go. The counters were cleaned off; he positioned himself by the slop sink and moved the computer and his notepad out of the way from anticipated projection. He began by placing a very small piece of contaminated feed in a glass cup, scraping the dried spore across with a toothpick until the spore broke off into individual threads. It looked like a tiny serving of shredded wheat for a very small person. There was a children's book that he remembered reading to the girls about a family of little people who slept in matchbooks and ate out of teeny-tiny bowls.

Strange to know what was to come. He licked his lips, his heart thumping in his chest. Pausing, he took a breath. Deep breath. He remembered watching Betsy in labor with the girls. One moment she was fine, resting, talking, asking for ice; and then, when the next contraction came, she was huffing and blowing, moaning and screaming, the veins in her neck standing out. Then it was over, and she was Betsy again before everything started up once more. This went on for hours. Watching her, Howard was exhausted, but he didn't dare say so. She was doing all the work. For hours! How did women do it?

Trying to keep a steady hand, he added just enough all-purpose cleaner (cleans and disinfects, cleans tough grime) about 0.2 milliliters, mixing it with the spores until they dampened and became limp. Then he leaned over the cup and took a breath. There was the same smell: that acrid sweetness. And so it began.

Over spring break, he did this half a dozen times. Mix. Breathe. Purge. He couldn't say that he looked forward to getting sick every time, but with the last few, he didn't dread the experience all that much. There was a cleansing that made him actually feel clean, something spiritual about giving up control so very completely. Whatever he had accidently discovered became an instant purgative. Crazy, how this very simple solution worked so very effectively. He wasn't clear about what he could to do with this discovery, what it would become. Initially he wasn't even clear about why he was doing this at all.

When Betsy came home at the end of the week, he heard the garage door go up and went to meet her as she came out of the car with packages, smiling, happy. He got her suitcase from the trunk. "I missed you," he said, realizing how much only when he first saw her as the car pulled into the garage.

Standing back after they hugged, she stepped back and looked at him. He had not shaved for a few days and was wearing old jeans and a worn, blue work-shirt. "Howie," she said, her eyes narrowing. "Have you lost weight?"

Chapter 8

What Betsy Can Hardly Remember

She had breathed a sigh of relief leaving Howard, needing this trip alone. It was the first time going to see Lily since the attack, and she was looking forward to some time with both the girls. There had been nothing from the police. No one had been picked up as a suspect. Howard was still kind of a mess. A quiet mess who was working harder than ever before but then melting down in random moments.

It was warm for mid-March, all the snow gone from the fields along the highway. Betsy was a good driver, better than Howard, although he frequently took the wheel out of gender obligation. She was a Midwestern girl, driving with her parents as soon as she got her learner's permit at fourteen. Now going down Interstate 80 toward Iowa City to pick up Megan, she was driving fast, passing every truck, enjoying both the speed and the solitude. There was an emotional burden, the aftershock of Lily's attack. When the girls were little, it was Howard who fretted about fevers and street-crossings and abductions; later about slick roads, and friends with questionable habits. With Howie, it was always about keeping safe.

Somehow, Betsy felt responsible to make him happy again. Not that he was a weak man. It was just that Howard seemed to feel things deeply, to perseverate, and to share with her all the frightening dangers available to them as parents. Since her husband was kind and considerate, she felt guilty about being annoyed.

West of the Amana Colonies, she passed a yellow school bus rollicking with teenagers, a team of boys going somewhere. They looked young. Maybe baseball had started. Betsy had grown up loving sports. But no one else in her family now did, and she eventually lost interest in being a fan. It was not so much fun to watch alone.

She smiled up at the bus as she passed, and one of the boys smiled back at her, giving a little nod of his head. Sweet. So she was shocked when a clean-cut boy sitting by the window in the front of the bus, just a few rows behind the driver, made a lewd gesture with his tongue, and the boys around him began laughing and banging on the windows. Betsy stepped hard on the gas and sped on ahead, but her throat tightened and she remained unsettled all the way to the second Iowa City exit where she got off to pick up Megan.

***

Betsy Randall was in the popular crowd at her high school, in the usual clichéd ways of popular girls. She was on the honor roll. She was a star on the girls' volleyball team. Betsy was also nice. Everyone agreed. Even the tough girls who were smoking in the bathroom and the awkward girl in gym class who had a locker in the same aisle, who thought of Betsy as a friend. It was easy for some high school girls to be nice, even if they were also popular. Betsy had good parents, two younger brothers who were sometimes pests, and an uncomplicated home life. Her mother worked part-time in the public library. Her father was an engineer with a company that made valves and regulators.

Of course, she drank in high school (something she never told her parents) but everyone did. Mostly beer and not even that much. Her family lived in a small city in Ohio, and it was not difficult to get someone older to buy beer. And then there were always the more mature-looking boys with fake IDs, those who were never questioned in the convenience stores.

The high school kids of every clique would meet at an abandoned barn in the country. Or in the parking lot behind a grocery store. Or sometimes in a house, if parents were out of town and unwise enough to leave a teenager home alone. Betsy never had a party at her house, but then her parents never went anywhere, except to a movie or out to dinner with friends. Even without cell phones, the kids found out where to meet. There was beer. Cheap wine. Grass. Betsy and her friends didn't do anything really crazy.

In June, after high school graduation, there was a party every night, sometimes two a night, until they all started summer jobs. Goodbye. Goodbye. There were yearbooks to be signed, hugs and reminisces and tears, as if everyone was going off to war, never to see each other again.

One of the last parties was in June at a public park near the quarry, a favorite place to swim. Betsy drove with a group of girls from her volleyball team. Parents brought hot dogs and watermelon, marshmallows and graham crackers to make s'mores over a campfire. There was beer in the bushes, and kids waiting for the parents to leave.

Boys and girls both played volleyball under the lights, and although Betsy was shorter than most of the girls on the team, she was strong and could really spike the ball. After the first game, she volunteered to have someone take her place.

Matt Teller had been playing on the other team. He stopped as well. Matt had a crush on Betsy, but he was shy, given to boring conversation about sports teams. "You want a beer?" he asked quietly. Adding: "You're a really good athlete."

"Sure," she said, following him behind the bathrooms, into the bushes. "Thanks." There was a cooler there, filled with cans of Red White & Blue, a cheap beer popular in their town. The colored cans made drinking this brand of beer—albeit illegally—seem patriotic. All the kids drank it. They used to call it, Red, White & Barf. "Who bought this?" Betsy was hot and sweaty; the beer tasted so good, she chugged it down.

"My brother's home from college," Matt said. "Marc? You remember him. He's wrestling now at Ohio State. Matt went into detail about his brother's wrestling career. Betsy interrupted: "Where are you going to school?"

"Ohio State. You?"

Betsy told him that she was going to Madison.

"Aren't you totally psyched? Getting out of this place?" Matt asked.

"Oh, it's not been so bad." Betsy knew she was in the minority of teenagers who actually liked high school. Senior year went way too fast; yearbook, prom, graduation parties; she didn't want it to end. But she didn't need to share this with Matt Teller.

"Yeah, it's been fun," Matt said, agreeably.

"Hey!" The big brother, Marc, appeared and helped himself to a beer. He looked a little glassy-eyed, as if he already had a few. "Help yourselves?" he said, though obviously, they already had. "Un otra vez?" He held out a beer to Betsy.

Betsy finished off the last of hers and took a second can.

"You remember my brother, Marc?" Matt said, proudly.

Betsy nodded. Marc Teller was a big deal on the wrestling team when she was still a sophomore. She had never gone to a match. The idea of sweaty guys entwined in a grunting match seemed unappealing. Not like the excitement and glamor of football. But she remembered how Marc was all over the yearbook that year.

She looked at Marc and gave him her best popular girl smile. She had straight teeth, perfect and white, with never a visit to the orthodontist. "So, are you staying in town this summer?" she asked.

Marc was handsome with high cheekbones and a set, serious jaw. He was mature, filled out, not like most of the high school boys.

Marc didn't answer. Instead, he said, "Hey, little brother. Why don't you get yourself back in the game and I'll take the lady to show her the quarry.

"Are you taking the car?" Matt asked.

"Just for a little while."

"Well, come back. Don't leave without me. "Matt didn't seem pleased but did as he was told and started walking back to the volleyball game.

It occurred to Betsy that she didn't have a say. Obediently, she followed Marc Teller to the parking lot where he took out a small bottle of Jim Beam in his glove box, took a swig, and passed it to her. "No thanks," she said, holding up the can of beer.

The quarry was a swimming hole, only about a mile around the edge of the park from where the party was. Betsy had been there many times. She felt nervous but also flattered that she was chosen. Maybe she would have a college boyfriend for the summer.

When they parked, Marc passed her the bottle of whiskey again, and this time she took a few sips. It burned going down. But in a good way. She was not usually this adventurous.

Marc leaned over to kiss her. He stopped and looked her full on in the face. "You're so pretty," he said, holding her cheek tenderly with his hand. Then he kissed her again. It was a good kiss. He smelled like liquor and soap. When they stopped, he put his hand under her jaw, tenderly rubbing the side of her neck. "I mean, really pretty. I could like you."

He got a blanket out of the back seat and spread it in front of the car where they were both hidden from view and where they could see the moonlight reflecting off the water. He passed her the bottle. She did not refuse. She laid down on her back and looked up at the stars. She felt the world spinning. This time, when he reached over her, his kiss was little more insistent, his tongue probing, but she kissed him back, feeling herself being 'taken', if that was the word, by this college man.

The stars above. A perfect, romantic night. She was thinking of the next day, of telling her girlfriends when they asked where she was, telling them that she was at the quarry, drinking whiskey, and on a blanket with Marc Teller under the moon. But when he began to touch her breast, she pulled back. "Don't," she said, taking his hand away. She was lying under him, the weight of one of his legs covering hers. A recent boyfriend had done this before, even taking her bra off one afternoon when they were at his house alone. But this seemed different.

"It's ok," he said, feeling, one breast then the other, as if giving them equal attention.

"Don't," she said, and attempted to sit up on the blanket.

He pushed her back down with one arm. Then he lifted her tee shirt, right up to her neck and roughly yanked her bra down over her breasts. He was breathing hard and touching her all over. "Come on, you like me, don't you? You came out here with me, didn't you?"

Quickly, what was thrilling became frightening. "No, I don't want . . .," she began to whimper. "Please."

'It's ok, shh.' Marc covered her mouth with his own. This time he put his tongue back so far in her mouth that, flat on her back like that, she gagged. He pulled away. "Hey, just relax, will you?" Suddenly, he seemed impatient, angry. He turned and she saw him take something out of his back pocket; she realized it was a condom. She put her hand to her exposed breasts feeling her heart beating.

Her shorts came off easily. They were athletic shorts that all the girls on the volleyball team wore, and she had decided to wear them tonight for the game in the park. The shorts were red jersey. Elastic top. No zippers. He pulled them down. The underpants came next, which ripped.

"No, don't," she said. "Stop." She added: "Please." She tried to get up from the blanket, but he pulled her back down. His arm was strong, muscled. "Too late," he said casually, as if she had just missed a train.

There was an intake of breath. The pain was sharp but swift. She looked up and above them saw stars before she squeezed her eyes shut tight so that that she would not cry.

"Shit," he said after. "Look at this. There's blood all over my Buckeye blanket. Look at all this." Her shorts were red. The Ohio State blanket was red. The wet blood looked black in the moonlight. Marc Teller shook his head in disgust, pushed her off the soiled blanket, balled it up, and went to the car. "Damn." He threw the blanket into the back seat. "That's great. That's a good blanket. I think it's ruined now." He added in an accusatory voice: "You never told me you were a virgin."

Shakily, she put on her torn panties and shorts, holding herself for balance along the front of the car before she got in. He slammed his door, starting the car before she was even inside. He looked straight ahead as he drove back to the park. "I mean, how was I supposed to know?"

Betsy Randall told her rapist that she was sorry.

Chapter 9

Happy Birthday to Mitzi

"Bye," Lily called, waving as her mother and sister drove off. "Love you." She stood on the corner in front of the SWIC studio, watching as the car headed toward the expressway. It had been a wonderful few days for the three of them: sharing a hotel room, shopping along Michigan avenue, a comedy club where they laughed hard because they needed to, and perhaps because the girls were slightly drunk. Megan, at nineteen, was not asked for her ID when her mother ordered the first pitcher of beer. Betsy shook her head: "Your father would not approve."

Lily loved seeing Megan, with whom there had never been even mild rivalry. Growing up, Megan used to leave her own bedroom each night to snuggle, and the sisters would fall asleep holding hands. Later, Megan was an adventurer. She did things in cars with fast boys and smoked weed in high school. Lily never told on her. Megan's grades were barely good enough to get into a state school, but she was wily and smart.

Seeing her mother and sister pull away, Lily got teary. They had such a good time. Maybe too good a time, she wondered. Was she talking too much about how delicious the pizza was, laughing too hard at Megan's jokes? Lily saw her mother stealing looks with Megan across the table in restaurants, a tilt to her head. Was Lily trying too hard to prove that she was doing all right? The trouble with being a good girl was that people always suspected you were hiding something, repressing some secret darkness covered up by the happy self you showed to the world.

***

Lily looked forward to seeing her new friends; there was comfort in what they had all been through, a common denominator that cut across more traditional barriers. "My darling girl," Mitzi called from the office when Lily entered the studio. There was another class just getting out. "There's cake. Have some before our class starts. You're early."

"My mom dropped me off," Lily said. "Happy birthday."

"Echh. Who wants to celebrate?" Scowling, Mitzi swiveled in her chair to meet Lily's hug. "At least my husband had the good sense not to throw me a party."

But there was the cake, white crème and raspberries, a woman's shape. Only the bottom half was gone. "Rosie the Riveter," Mitzi said. "But she's a kickboxer. The legs have already been eaten."

Lily took a paper plate and neatly cut off a piece near the edge, mostly frosting. "I saw the birthday posts this morning," Lily said. "You were all over."

The night before there had been a profile of Mitzi Solomon on the ten o'clock news. In the interview Mitzi made an effort to appear modest and grateful while accepting the accolades. But in her older age she was no less angry, after years listening to women's stories of fear and abuse. Mitzi did not like to think of herself as a man-hating feminist, but entering her seventh decade, she was not going to be sensitive about labels.

She liked some men, but had truly loved only one, her second husband, Ira, whom she had married when her boys were teenagers. Ira, who never had children of his own, was a friendly, non-authoritarian presence who took the boys to ballgames and concerts, who lit up when she walked into a room.

My Ira, she would say. Her Ira, only fifty-two when his heart gave out one Sunday evening while he was watching 60 Minutes. Mitzi had stood in the doorway of the den, waiting to tell Ira that it was time for dinner, the brisket was already cut. She did not notice right away how Ira was slumped in the chair. An anterior interventricular break of the left coronary artery. The Widow Maker. Mitzi thought she was much too young to be a widow.

Ira left a pile of money to Mitzi and the pile became much larger when she invested in a stock with the improbable name of Google. She met her third husband, Benjamin Berg, soon after Ira's death. Very soon, in fact. Benjamin had been Ira's golf partner and trusted financial advisor. Knowing how very rich Mitzi was, the first thing Ben did (before he asked her out for dinner and to a concert to see Carole King) was write up a plan to protect her assets. All of them. From any man who would later come into her life. Himself included. Benjamin Berg was an honorable man. He was also a recent widower, who had loved his first wife before she was taken from him by a cancer that ran its course before she even began chemotherapy.

Partnered by grief, Benjamin and Mitzi found solace in each other.

***

"My dad texted this morning," Lily said. "He asked for your phone number. I don't know why." Lily licked frosting off a finger. "I think he wants to ask you about me. How I'm doing. He knows I spend a lot of time at SWIC."

Mitzi took a business card from a basket on her desk and wrote a number on the back. "Tell him to call this one. At night. Any time after seven. I'm up late." She added: "And how are you doing, my darling?"

Lily shrugged. "I think, pretty good, actually."

Soon the other women started coming in for class. Mitzi offered them cake. "I think you're pretty good, too" she told Lily. "Have more cake. You cut yourself only that tiny piece."

Mitzi got up from her chair and stretched. "Eat up. And fire up. Let's go!" Mitzi, at seventy years old, has had three marriages, two sons, a curable breast cancer past the five-year mark. Now some of her friends were starting to get sick and dwindle. Become widows. But for her, there was work to be done. She and Benjamin Berg give away lots of money, mostly to philanthropies supporting women. And more than just being very rich, Mitzi Solomon was a Chicago icon in the women's movement. She kept her connection by teaching one self-defense class in each session. Some years ago, she appeared on the television show Undercover Boss. There was still much to learn.

Recently she read an article about a start-up in San Francisco. Someone had invented the SkunkLock, a bicycle lock that emitted a noxious gas when anyone tried to steal a bike by cutting through the U-shaped steel lock. "Try to steal a bike. And end up smelling like the skunk you are!" the inventor promised.

Mitzi laughed when she read the description of SkunkLock, talking about it with Benjamin over coffee one morning. "Can you imagine?" she asked. "Honey, do you think we should invest in this?"

Chapter 10

After Spring Break, Anaya Pran Smells Something Is Up

A t seven o'clock in the morning, the very first day after spring break, Anaya came into the lab, looked down her nose at the counter and took a breath. "Jesus, Dr. Lerner. It smells like someone puked in here."

"Good morning," Howard said. "Is that the first thing you say to me after your honeymoon?" He added: "Did you and Vera have a good time in Vegas?" He hadn't expected Anaya to come in quite so early.

"It was wonderful. When we were camping, we got up every day at dawn to see the sunrise. Guess I got used to it. Rise and shine. You're here earlier than usual." Anaya looked around, sniffing audibly. "Did you have a good break? Get a lot of work done without everyone wanting a piece of your time?"

Anaya and Vera had spent a few days on the Strip before hiking in the desert. Vera was from Mexico City, in Iowa on a graduate scholarship in design. Her 'duration of status', that is, the length of her F-1 certification covered the time she was registered full-time as a student. There followed a sixty-day 'grace period' to exit the United States during which Anaya proposed to Vera Perez.

Vera was a talented jewelry maker who crafted intricate chunky silver rings and pendants. All the women in Howard's family had at least one of Vera's pieces. Now, newly married, Vera would be able to apply for citizenship.

Howard nodded. "What about your time in Vegas?" Vera might enjoy the glitz, but Las Vegas didn't seem something Anaya would choose.

"Totally cheesy," Anaya said. "But I loved it. The impersonators, especially. Dolly Parton? Oh my god! That woman was so great." Anaya was practically gushing. "You know, the food was also surprisingly good." Anaya was a foodie whose specialty was the cuisine of her native India. Although she also loved pork.

Suddenly Anaya turned toward a sink, sniffing. "But really. Ecch! Why does it stink in here?"

Howard looked around. There were few others in so early. And he had just finished wiping a spot he missed under the counter. "There are some notes I've been taking on the mycotoxin research results from the Vinton farm. Why don't you go back to my office to read it now? I'll finish up cleaning here."

Anaya looked puzzled. "Notes about what?"

"I meant to tell you. Betsy and I thought that you and Vera had a very nice wedding," Howard said, apropos of nothing. Usually, he didn't talk much in the lab if he was working on something new. He liked that about Anaya. They were very suited to work companionably in silence. "We really enjoyed seeing your family again. Looks as if retirement agrees with your dad." He added: "I was sorry that I didn't get to meet anyone from Vera's side."

"No, she was sad about that. My family loves Vera, though. More than me, I think sometimes."

Without confusion or apparent angst, Anaya had been 'out' almost all of her young life. Out in the most ordinary way. Her traditional Indian family had never known what to make of their brilliant, assertive, lesbian daughter. As Indian immigrants, they had only anticipated the brilliant part.

And yet, Anaya was so implacably confident that there was nothing to do but accept her. Her parents and sisters came from New Jersey to attend the wedding. Saris and all. Anaya wore blue and Vera wore a silver lamé sari with silver bracelets snaking up her muscled arm. Anaya said that Vera's family would not be attending but joked that they'd be singing "Who's Sari Now." Vera's Mexican family was complicated by divorces, estrangement, and poverty. In Iowa, Howard and Betsy and their girls had been family to both Anaya and Vera for the last few years.

"Anaya," Howard said before she opened the door." I might have discovered something." He cleared his throat, lowering his voice, sounding almost conspiratorial. "I mean, something exciting. It's in my notes. Handwritten. I didn't want to put anything on the computer. Things could get…" Howard whispered: "…complicated."

"Ohhh. Dr. Lerner. Sounds very underground." Anaya began some good-natured banter, but Howard interrupted.

"It might very well be," he said seriously.

"You're kidding, right?" Anaya had worked with Howard long enough to know when he was joking. Which was infrequent since his daughter's attack. Anaya missed the old Dr. Lerner. To Anaya, Howard Lerner was not only a wonderful scientist, but also her mentor. Her own father was adequate, but distant. Her own father didn't get her at all. "I'll read it, Howard. No pressure." Sometimes Anaya called him by his first name, especially if she thought she had the upper hand. Joyce Corning didn't approve.

"You will be surprised," Howard said. "But I don't want you to discuss this with anyone," Howard added. "Not even Vera."

Anaya looked puzzled. Not that Vera showed any real interest in the work at the lab. Vera was squeamish. And she was also an animal lover. Piglets were smart and adorable. Anything that distressed them, Vera did not wish to know about.

"Are we talking national security clearance here?" Anaya wasn't sure if this was for real. Of course there was competition in scientific research. A lot of information was secretive, if not classified. Anaya furrowed her brow: "Dr. Lerner, what were you doing for the week I was gone?"

"It's serious," was all Howard would say. "I haven't exactly been following university protocol. That might be a little concerning for us."

While Howard Lerner was someone who followed the rules, Anaya, who hated both conformity and bureaucracy, was not. "Genius shouldn't be tamed," she had said one time when she had not followed some minor, but very specific, IACUC guideline and Jerry Ketcham had written her a reprimand. Anaya believed that Ketcham felt threatened by her. "I think he's scared of me," she told Howard.

"Of course he is," Howard said. "We all are."

Anaya paused, her hand on the knob, raising an eyebrow, waiting for Dr. Lerner to continue. When he didn't, she filled in. "And this is something that might lure me to stay in Iowa and continue working with you in this poorly paid post-doc? During another deep-freeze Iowa winter?"

This elicited a smile. "The Midwest is a good place to raise children. No fires, earthquakes, or hurricanes."

"Tornadoes? Boredom? Repressive politics? Field of someone's dreams, maybe. Not exactly mine."

"But boring can be a good thing. And climate change? A pandemic? The middle of Iowa might be one of the safest places to live. But I do understand. And this might actually be an interesting opportunity for you. Read the notes," Howard said. "I want to know what you think about this before we go ahead with something that might be foolish." We. Us. Howard was aware of using plural pronouns. He and Anaya together. "Or perhaps illegal."

Before walking out of his office, Anaya said: "What the hell was going on around here while I was gone?"

***

Anaya burst back into the lab after twenty minutes. "Dr. Lerner, wow! This is some crazy shit." Since the wedding, Anaya had a new hairstyle. Her black hair was now tipped with bright orange, brush-cut, standing on end, away from her face. It gave her a wild demeanor, as if she had just risen from flames.

"You're a fast reader," Howard said.

"What are we going to do with this?" She held Howard's notes in her hands, looking down at them with amazement.

Howard felt a sudden excitement, when Anaya also said "we." An inclusive 'we'. He was relieved at having someone to share this with. Who would believe—he couldn't believe it himself—that he, a reputable scientist who was aware of the many dangers of biological agents, would even begin such a dangerous path. All his life, he had been a deliberate and careful person. But since Lily's attack, something was released in him. A desire to do something. He recognized the drive. But towards what? Was he deranged?

Anaya continued. "What you found here. Incredible. The pigs. Ok, I understand that. They just have to get rid of that feed. But in the ground, the spores are still there…" Anaya was running all her words together. "I mean, they spores are there. They don't go away."

She was not telling Howard anything he did not already know. Then: "But what's more important…" she paused, her dark eyes shining. "Oh, my god." Her hand went to her forehead with a slap. Like in those commercials for V-8 juice.

Howard noticed that Anaya's nails were manicured with white-tipped points; and she was wearing a wedding ring, a silver band with intricate designs. Vera must have made the ring. Perhaps the rings were exchanged at the wedding. The ring was beautiful. Howard didn't usually pay attention to these things.

"Oh, my god, Doctor Lerner! What this means? What this could be used for?" These were not actually questions. Anaya had read his comments and suppositions, all the more difficult to decipher notes he had added in the margins.

"Yes," Howard said. "That's what I was explaining…"

Anaya interrupted him: "I got it! I know. I got it!" She was standing close to him in a conspiratorial way. He wanted to hug her, but had always refrained from anything physical, especially with female students. "Whew." Anaya let out a breath, shaking her head. "So, I'm in Vegas over spring break watching female impersonators and you're here in Iowa all by yourself, doing these experiments and…vomiting?"

"Yes," Howard said again. "Quite a lot, actually."

She had many questions. Most of them Howard did not yet have answers to.

He knew only that the formula, an extremely simple combination, caused this highly unusual reaction. The spores were plentiful and could last in their dehydrated state for a very long time. Like Anthrax. Yes, the spores could last years.

Decades, even. And only a very few of the tiny strands, when mixed with the chemical cleaner, elicited the response.

"What are we going to do?" Anaya asked.

"I'm not sure."

"The thing is, you're right. This is not exactly a bioweapon," Anaya continued. "It doesn't kill anyone." He realized she was figuring it all out as she spoke. "I mean, it sort of could be considered in a bioweapon category. Imagine—a whole enemy army, throwing their guts up?" Anaya went on. "They'd have to dig deep pits. It would give a whole new definition to trench warfare."

Howard was both relieved and unsettled to have Anaya as a partner. No, this wasn't a crazy idea after all. He had carefully explained the results in his notes. What chemicals produced this strain. And the highly unusual consequences of its inhalation.

"But if I'm thinking what you're thinking, this would be used for something else entirely," Anaya said. "Am I right?"

Howard nodded.

"Yes. A weapon used for self-defense." Anaya paused. "For anyone who is in a dangerous situation." After a few seconds, she calmed down, looking at him straight on.

"Yes," Howard said.

Then Anaya spoke gently to her mentor. "This has everything to do with what happened to Lily, doesn't it?"

Howard nodded.

"What do you want to do?" she asked.

"I don't know."

"Well, first we have to figure out a delivery system,"

"Delivery system?"

"So someone could safely use this," Anaya said. "A woman could…as a method of self-defense…the liquid would be required to activate. But very little is needed. That's good. Concentrated…" Anaya was running all her words together again, her mind going faster with a plan, one that she envisioned but was not yet clearly able to articulate.

"Yes, you understand…"

"I'm very smart," Anaya said without a hint of irony. "Of course, I understand."

"We'll work on this, Anaya. But I don't want you to tell Vera," Howard said. "I feel bad about that. I don't think married people should keep things from each other, I haven't told Betsy because…"

Anaya interrupted: "Does Joyce know?" Howard's office door was open. Anaya peeked out to see if Joyce was in the hall.

"No. I was alone all week doing this. I didn't even tell Betsy when she got back from Chicago with the girls."

"She'll know," Anaya said.

"She who?"

"Joyce," Anaya said. "Joyce knows everything. You can't put anything past Joyce."

"True."

"And you also know that Joyce is a good girl. Follows all the rules, just right."

"That she does," Howard said.

"But, you know, there's a part of me that thinks she would not get in our way. After what happened to Lily?" Joyce had a righteous side. But she loved Howard's daughters. Anaya continued: "And that scumbag her daughter is married to? Royce? He's hit her, you know. Royce hit Caroline."

"I didn't know," Howard said. How was Anaya privy to that information?

"I overheard a phone call," Anaya admitted. "Her daughter was on the phone with her, crying."

But Joyce was not someone to ignore protocol. The National Scientific Advisory Board. The Institute for Animal Care and

Use committee. "I don't know about telling Joyce," Anaya said. "She wouldn't like to go behind anyone's back with this."

Howard nodded. There were a lot of backs to go behind.

"Shit, it's a wonder we can get anything done at all in science. There's so much chicken-shit accountability. Yeah, like you really think we should run this one by Jerry Ketchum?" Anaya snorted. "Shit. Because what this might be, used for…" Anaya stopped herself in mid-sentence. "Holy shit!"

Howard nodded again, adding: "Anaya, you can stop saying 'shit' now."

He had explained it all in those detailed notes. Not only the procedures he had followed and the results that had ensued. But also the hypotheticals. The activations of the spores had implications beyond his simple experiment. Just writing it down made him nervous.

"I want to test the strain myself," Anaya said.

"You do?"

"Yeah. Sure. I want to try it."

Howard started to protest. Instead, he said simply: "Thank you."

"I could start today," Anaya said, her face aglow. She looked so young and healthy and bright that Howard began to tear up with gratitude.

Anaya continued: "I'll help you set up. I don't have classes this afternoon. Or meetings. I don't think. I'll check with Joyce. I could get the lab ready. Maybe begin when people leave for lunch…"

Howard was musing. "Are you sure you want to do this? Now? Today?"

"If not now, when?" Anaya said.

Howard looked at the clock. "So, at noon?"

"Damn, I was going to go out and pick up some barbecue at Hickory Park."

"Well maybe you should wait on that?"

"Just kidding. No use wasting money on lunch if I'm only going to throw it all up."

"Okay then."

Anaya was quiet for a moment, her lower lip extended as she was lost in thought. Then: "Something else I'm thinking. I want to tell Vera. She can help us. I'm thinking of something she can do." Anaya's hand went to the silver pendant she wore around her neck. One of the early pieces crafted by Vera.

Howard nodded. "If you think…"

"I am. She can make something. Vera is really quite a genius."

"I thought you were the genius," Howard said, smiling.

Before she left the room, Anaya gave him a playful punch to the shoulder. "So, let's get cooking, Mr. White."

By eight o'clock people started to come into the building. Howard heard music coming from an office down the hall, students greeting each other outside a classroom. Joyce was at the front desk, already having made coffee in the break room.

Anaya and Mitzi. Soon Vera. He realized that the more people knew about spores, the more real it became. But it was only after Anaya closed the door and went back to her own office that Howard got her joke: Get cooking, Mr. White. Both he and Betsy watched the entire season of Breaking Bad on Netflix long after everyone else. The comment gave him pause. Were they going to start a partnership that could get them in that kind of trouble?

***

No grass growing under her feet. That very night, Anaya told her wife. Anaya's idea was to use Vera's expertise in creating a jewelry design, an accessory, as a vehicle for the delivery system. That's what was needed: a delivery system. Vera had listened, open-mouthed, as Anaya explained their plans. "So do you understand what I'm asking?"

"I think so," Vera said. Holding one finger to her lips, she added: "Is this legal?" Vera was more cautious than Anaya. Well, anyone was. But now they were married, and Vera was loyal. Also, she couldn't be deported back to Mexico. "I will do whatever I can to help you," she told Anaya earnestly.

Chapter 11

Joyce Hates Royce

After Anaya left, Howard went back into his office and saw Joyce, already at the door. "I brought you something, Dr. Lerner." She stopped and sniffed in the hall, but didn't say anything about a smell. "I know it's kind of silly, but I got a chuckle when I saw it in one of the gift shops. Larry told me I ought to get it for you." She presented Howard with a little bobble-head of Porky Pig. "It's appropriate for the office, don't you think?"

"Thank you, Joyce. It certainly is." He made a show of making room on the edge of one of the bookshelves. "How was your trip?"

Joyce and her husband Larry had just come home from taking the older grandchildren to Disney World over Spring break. The lines were long, but the weather was glorious, and they indulged the children with junk food and souvenirs and spent a great deal of money. The grandchildren were just the right age, still young enough to abandon themselves to magic. Larry was a good sport, even though he observed that everything was a rip-off. At night, the children swam in the hotel pool until they wrinkled and peeled. The water was so chlorinated that at the end of the vacation the children's hair had a greenish hue.

Disney World was fun, Larry agreed, although adding that once was enough. He preferred renting a cabin on a lake and taking the kids fishing. Joyce felt bad since she promised Caroline that someday they would take her daughter, Nora, too. Oh, well. Someday was far away. Who knew where they'd all be someday?

She wished that Caroline and Nora could have gone with them to Florida, but didn't ask. At only two years old, Nora was really too young for Disney World. And Royce wouldn't like it. The other grandchildren were old enough to go off by themselves and to stand in lines. "In a few years, we'll take Nora with her cousins," Joyce told her daughter. What she really wanted was to get Caroline, who seemed increasingly anxious lately, away from Royce.

Joyce Corning was a Christian and a Republican, but in recent years, this connection had become puzzling. She had never talked politics much and so had not told her church group that she had voted for Barack Obama. Twice. That first time she found it thrilling, alone in the voting booth, using the lever to close curtains, then filling in the empty circle next to his name. She pressed that pencil hard.

She and her husband were registered Republicans, as her family and his had been. They were small-town people, who believed in working hard, helping your neighbor and keeping the government out of their business, although she wasn't sure what that entailed. Her job at the vet school mandated the filling out of many government forms, and Dr. Lerner's research was mostly funded by governmental agencies. She liked and trusted Dr. Lerner who treated her with respect and often talked to her using the same scientific terms he used with his graduate students.

When she was a young girl and first started working, she typed some of the professional papers and grants. Later, she still read some of Dr. Lerner's applications and had questions about the research. Now, computers had turned the faculty into their own secretaries, but strangely, it was even more difficult to get people together for a meeting. She was as high up on the professional ladder as her job would take her, an administrative assistant. No longer called a secretary—although that is what she still called herself.

Everything was both easier and more complicated these days. Next year she would retire and spend time with the grandchildren before they were all off to college. Maybe even take a few classes at the university herself.

Joyce had married Larry Corning when they were just a few years out of high school; she had not graduated from college, but she believed in science, in global warming, in evolution, in farming conservation that preserved the rich, Iowa soil and didn't pollute the water and—many of the things the so-called 'progressives' believed. She might be anti-abortion. A fetus was a baby. You couldn't kill a baby because its life was an inconvenience. Still, she recognized that this might not be her decision to make.

On every other social issue—even the legalization of marijuana—she supposed she was really becoming a liberal. On gay marriage, she had 'evolved'. Just like Obama. At first, it just seemed like the silliest thing, two men marrying each other; two women walking down the aisle. But eventually she realized that was because no one was used to it. Then, when Iowa was the first Midwestern state to pass marriage equality, she was proud. And because she respected Anaya, Dr. Lerner's post-doctoral student, Joyce was happy when Anaya announced that she and her partner, Vera, were getting married. Vera was a nice woman and a calming influence on Anaya. Joyce wished that her Caroline could find herself such a stable person to spend her life with.

Joyce accepted that everyone she knew had guns. Larry grew up hunting, after all. But she certainly didn't like that Royce, her youngest daughter's husband, had so many of them. Even though she was going to retire soon, she was indeed glad to be back at work and not think of the problems in her own family. Dr. Lerner was a familiar and welcoming presence. "Didn't you once take Betsy and the girls to Disney World?" she asked.

"Years ago," Howard said.

"It was pretty wonderful," Joyce said. "The kids had such a good time."

"Well, I guess once was enough for me." Howard smiled apologetically.

"That's just what Larry said," Joyce replied, the glitter of fantasy still in her eyes.

***

Joyce and Larry's house, on an acreage a few miles outside of Story City, was often filled with grandchildren and hockey helmets and tutus and basketballs. It seemed as if Joyce had spent her whole life going to dance recitals and soccer games and having Sunday potlucks, and perhaps there was something more to life, but she never felt that she had anything at all to complain about.

Because Joyce was a Christian, she did not see herself as a hateful person. In fact, she didn't have to work very hard at all on the forgiveness and mercy and love-thy-neighbor part of church teaching, because those values pretty much defined her.

Except for her son-in-law, Royce.

Her daughter's unhappy marriage caused Joyce pain, a tightening-in-the-stomach kind of pain. She felt her body alignment change when his name came up: Royce. "You're making a mistake," Joyce wanted to tell her youngest daughter many times. Her other daughters had married perfectly fine men who could keep jobs, who went to their children's sports events and never got kicked out for yelling at the coaches.

Royce Diamond. He was—Joyce saw it right away—an abusive man. In part, Joyce blamed herself for not ever saying anything. But it was not her way to interfere.

Royce never kept a job for very long, because his temper often got the best of him, and he felt compelled to tell someone off. He was the type of person who never accepted blame. Everyone was too stupid to see it his way. Recently he worked for a tree-trimming service out of Des Moines. It was dangerous work involving climbing and chain saws. Joyce had fantasies of accidents that were sure and swift.

Joyce had known it was going to be awful, even before Royce had gotten so drunk at his own wedding that he and Caroline almost missed the plane that would take them to Jamaica for their honeymoon. Dr. Lerner and his wife were at the wedding, and Joyce was deeply embarrassed at the behavior of her soon-to-be son-in-law. What would the Lerners possibly think?

Two years ago, when Caroline had a baby, a girl, Dr. Lerner said that was a good thing, intimating that some men might be tough on a son.

A man like Royce, Joyce added.

"No, no," Dr. Lerner was apologetic, explaining that he also preferred having girls. "I mean," he added. "Some men might be more comfortable having daughters. I was never the kind of guy to throw the football around."

"Well, Royce could do that, at least," Joyce said sourly.

Royce and Joyce. The fact that she and her son-in-law had rhyming names was upsetting. It felt intimate.

Royce Diamond. The name even sounded like the mean, cheating guy in a country and western song.

***

On their wedding anniversary, Royce Diamond told his wife Caroline that she was fat. They had been married for four years, and it was true that she had not lost the baby weight following the birth of Nora two years before. Caroline had planned to have another baby, but even she—so late to arriving at any rational and mature conclusions in life—realized that another child in her situation would not be a good idea.

They lived in Des Moines, in a modest ranch-style home near Merle Hay Mall. Caroline worked at Kohl's, and Royce had been employed almost two years at AHT, Arbor Heights Tree service. It was dangerous work but paid well, and there was a family insurance plan. It was the longest he had ever held a job, but recently he was having trouble at work. The boss was an asshole, Royce said. That spring, AHT hired two Mexican workers. Royce said that the men were illegals, but he didn't know that for sure. His main complaint seemed to be that the men just worked too damned hard.

Their house in Des Moines was small but well located to Caroline's job and a block from a Montessori day care where Nora was happy and flourishing.

On the Friday night of their fourth anniversary, Caroline got a babysitter, one of the teacher's aides at Nora's preschool, and made a reservation at an expensive downtown restaurant. She dressed carefully, a new dress she got at Kohl's with her employee discount. The dress was dark blue, with a scalloped hem, right below the knee and showed off her legs, which were still shapely. It was a little snug around the waist, but it was low enough to show cleavage. Royce liked cleavage.

She had saved for this special night out, but she had qualms. Nothing was going the way she planned. Royce seemed to want to pick a fight with everything, she said. She was determined to be upbeat and chipper, although she talked too much when she was nervous. Which she often was.

Caroline wished Royce would put on a nice shirt; she had left one, newly pressed, hanging on the bedroom closet doorknob. But she knew enough not to ask him to change. He had already had two beers after he came home from work. He showered, at least. And put on a clean tee shirt. And he still looked handsome enough when his hair was slicked and wet; despite the intake of beer, he was muscled from his job.

It was almost seven. The babysitter was going to arrive any minute. Royce stood in front of the refrigerator looking at the beer. "Shit, there's only this crap." Despite his rough manner, Royce was a beer snob.

"Well, you bought it, Royce," Caroline said. A few weeks before, Royce had hosted a poker game with some of the guys he knew from his previous job at a muffler shop. There were still several cans of Old Milwaukee in the door of the refrigerator.

"Well, I didn't expect that I'd be the one drinking it," Royce said. He looked at her with what she called his 'devil eyes'. When they were dating, she thought this look was sexy. But lately, she saw in his eyes the hooded anger of someone in a police mug shot.

She twirled around in her new dress and asked Royce how she looked, hinting that when they came home, taking it off, there would be a surprise.

Royce opened a beer, took three loud slurps and poured the rest down the kitchen sink. Then he crushed the empty can and threw that, too, into the sink with a clang. He put one hand under his chin and looked hard at his wife as if surveying a property. "I don't know, hon," he said at last. "Honestly? I think that dress makes you look fat."

***

In Joyce Corning's backyard, blueberries and raspberries grew plentiful enough to be frozen for jams and pies all year long. Joyce was taking a fresh blueberry pie, Larry's favorite, out of the oven when caller ID reflected Caroline's cell phone number, but when Joyce picked up the phone all she heard was gurgling, like someone underwater.

"Caroline? Is that you?" The steaming pie sat on the counter. The crust was perfect; little drops of shiny berry oozed out of the slashes across the top.

'Oh, mom." Caroline began to wail uncontrollably.

"Caroline. Where are you?"

"I'm in a parking lot at the mall." More sobbing.

"Where's Nora?"

"She's in her car seat. Right behind me. I've been driving around for an hour, and I finally got her to sleep." Caroline began to cry softly. "Oh, Mom."

"Take a deep breath, Caroline."

"Mom, can I come home?" The question was clear. Without knowing, Joyce knew. There was a part of her that, although scared, felt relieved. She didn't ask where Royce was.

"Of course, you can come home," Joyce answered. This, despite the fact that her youngest daughter's home was with her husband. The house had belonged to his alcoholic mother who killed herself by falling asleep while smoking in a La-Z-Boy. Insurance covered the damage to the house, which was significant. Royce then became the second alcoholic homeowner, although after Nora was born, he did his smoking outside.

Caroline said something else before she started to cry again. "What, honey? I can't understand you," Joyce said.

More crying.

"Just come home," Joyce said. "Are you all right to drive?"

"I don't have diapers," Caroline said.

"We have diapers."

"Are you going to tell daddy?" Caroline asked.

"Well, of course, I'm going to tell your father," Joyce said.

"It's over. I am going to get a divorce." She had said this before.

"I know you are," Joyce said. She had said this before as well.

***

Sometimes it takes just one thing to begin the motion, the one thing that goes over the limit, that final straw, the one that breaks the camel's back. Royce had called Caroline names before. He had even hit her a few times since they were married. Not hard, really. It was always in the middle of a fight where sometimes she gave, although not physically, as good as she got. She egged him on. The arguments escalated until he was chasing her around the kitchen table, pulling her by the hair, pushing her up against the wall. She never told anyone.

But lately he had been acting meaner, so she was careful not to provoke him. That morning, a shelf in the dining room came down and the crystal wine glasses that had been his mother's, broke on the wooden floor. It was odd, thinking of his mother having crystal wine glasses at all when what she drank was beer, right out of the can. Royce, who didn't care much about decorating, insisted that those glasses be displayed.

The shelf had not been attached securely to the wall. Nora could have been hurt. That was the first thing that Caroline said to Royce when he emerged from the bedroom in boxer shorts, his hair flattened with sleep. He looked at the mess; then, without saying a word, he went over to Caroline and slapped her full in the face with his open hand. Nora, still in her pink footy pajamas, looked on, upset by the noise, the broken glass, her mother holding her face with her hand. Nora started to cry. Royce ignored her, looking murderously at his wife. "Clean it up," he said before going back to bed.

"This is not the first time," Caroline said to Joyce. She took a deep breath. Now she sounded almost defiant. "But it's going to be the last time he does this to me."

Finally, Joyce thought. At last.

Chapter 12

April: Royce Has An Unpleasant Encounter

"You like this song, Muffin?" Through the rearview mirror, he saw Nora smile. An oldie his mother used to play and dance around the house when she had a buzz on. "Gimme, gimme good lovin', ev-er-y night..."

"Gimme, gimme," Nora said from the back seat. She had dressed herself that morning. Many of her clothes were still at the house, left over from Caroline's discounts at Kohls. Nora had on an orange dress and chose orange barrettes. "Daddy, I match," she said when Royce brushed out her hair. She was so smart. The big-girl bed with the side-bars was still in her room. Her room. His house.

It was his house after all. Caroline's name was not added to the deed when they moved in two years ago and it was he, Royce, who had repainted and ripped out the old carpets after the fire. Even so, Caroline still complained that the house smelled like smoke.

The house was his free and clear, paid in full, because even though his mother had a string of crappy jobs, she had lived there with an assortment of boyfriends for, like, thirty years. The house was where Royce had grown up. His house.

Royce's father had never been a part of his life. Some other men were, but didn't stay long. The longest to stick around was a nice guy who fell off a ladder cleaning out a gutter. Dead at fifty. Then his mom really amped up the booze along with a string of men she met in bars—or sometimes in AA—and brought home with her, like shelter dogs. Royce had little to do with his mother in the last years, although his own drinking was fairly significant.

There was a half-sister somewhere. Maybe Arizona. And some loser cousins who were in and out of jail, mostly for dealing drugs. It was not a family history anyone would be proud to claim. Royce felt defensive that, at his wedding to Caroline Corning, he had so little family in attendance. His mother, skinny and sober for once, looked jittery and out of place among Caroline's hearty clan: her sisters and their stuck-up husbands and their perfect kids. Royce liked Caroline's old man well enough. Larry was a regular guy. They went hunting sometimes. But Caroline's mother, Joyce, was a bitch, the quiet type, who would stab you in the back.

It was his house. His family home. If Caroline thought she was hiring a lawyer and getting half the equity, well, she had another thing coming. He would sue for shared custody. And then she wouldn't be entitled for child support, right? If the custody was shared?

Anyway, there was no blood to get out of this stone. Fired from his job despite spring being one of the busiest seasons in the tree-removal business, Royce blamed it on the Mexicans. The way they worked without complaint, chattering to each other in a language he could not understand. But he knew they were talking about him.

The boss told Royce: "I'm really sorry, but I'm going to have to let you go." Only two weeks' severance, and there was no reason why he was being fired. Royce didn't complain because he hated the job anyway, but he knew it was the Mexicans. Probably hired really cheap. They were everywhere. On the roof. On the roads. Working their brown asses off.

Royce could collect unemployment for a while. He had a plan. Put a kitchenette in the finished basement. There was a separate entrance, and he could rent the basement out as an apartment. He also had a stash. $10,000 that his mother left from an insurance policy when she worked cleaning offices at State Farm, now in his name in an account he had kept secret from Caroline.

Shared custody was the way to go. He loved Nora. His daughter was sweet and agreeable, not like her nagging mother. Nora adored her daddy. And Royce liked the way he felt when he was with her; he liked the way other women looked at him when he was taking care of his little girl. Being a good daddy was definitely a chick magnet.

He drove up to the vet school to drop Nora off at his mother-in-law's office. His almost ex-mother-in-law. He didn't want to see the old lady but managed to act respectful, kissing Nora goodbye in front of Joyce, ruffling her hair. "Now be a good girl for your Grandma," he said, smiling for show.

Joyce didn't even look at him. Bending down, she hugged her granddaughter. "Nora Bora. How's my big girl?"

"Good," Nora said solemnly, taking a thumb out of her mouth with a pop.

Royce placed a bag with Nora's things on Joyce's desk with a bit more force than necessary. "Bye, Muffin." Nora waved, blew him a kiss, and stuck her thumb back into its comfortable position. God that kid was cute.

Royce started to walk out, then stopped, showing how polite he could be, to hold open the door for a woman who suddenly appeared behind him, waving to Joyce: "Bye now. Thank you." The woman in front of him was short and curvy; Royce took an admiring look at her ass in tight jeans. In the parking lot, she went over to a crappy car parked right next to Royce's truck. He watched with squinted eyes when she opened her car door. "Hey, watch it," he yelled.

"Excuse me?" The woman had straight black hair, almost past her shoulders. Dark eyes. Pretty.

"You hit my door," Royce said. The truck was a Chevy, candy-apple red. He had just gotten it washed that morning. Nora loved to go through the car wash with him, so practically every time he had her, he got the truck washed.

The woman gave his truck a casual once-over. "I did not hit your vehicle," she said. She had a scornful air that set off something in him. Also, a slight accent. Shit, the Mexicans were everywhere.

"Yeah, I'll be the judge of that," Royce said, walking over to her.

She stepped closer against her car, the open door a barrier between them. "Just take it easy, mister."

"No, you take it easy," he said, not exactly sure what he meant by that. He thought he'd heard the doors scrape. He squatted to get a better view, feeling his chest tight. The door of his truck looked smooth and shiny, the chrome, gleaming. He squinted, looking with a hard gaze, to see something that might be there.

"Just move on out," the woman told him, straightening her broad shoulders. Shit, a little Mexican and for sure a dike as well.

***

Assured by Ayana that Howard Lerner's discovery would incapacitate, but cause neither significant nor lasting harm to the recipient, Vera soon had a notebook filled with sketches of silver pendants. She devised one with two small containers under a hinged bezel; one socket held a tiny bit of spore, the other could hold a few milliliters of liquid. The pendant, not metal alone, was made water-tight with a flexible plastic shield. That was all that was needed. Vera worked on perfecting the spring action which, when activated, would combine the two agents.

The owner of the pendant—which could be attached to a key chain or worn on a chain around the neck—had only to hold her breath, flick the hinge, then press a small button with her thumb. Flick. Then press. An agile thumb was all that was needed.

"You're a genius," Anaya had said when Vera explained how it worked.

"But holding in breath. That is essential," Vera warned. "I am not sure yet how far the spray goes."

Leaving the lab that afternoon, Vera Perez wore the pendant around her neck, spring-loaded, and ready to go. It was a display of artistic vanity. The working design was completed, and she was proud. But of course, no one had used it yet.

She had spent the last hour with Anaya and Dr. Lerner showing them the result of her labor. After weeks of working every day, the device was perfected. The artistic design was of a woman's head, with lots of filigree. The woman looked fierce, her hair flowing in silver braids, her mouth opens seemingly to emit not a scream, but a roar. Anaya had cut out photographs of goddesses. Furies. The pendent needed to be on a chain long enough so that it could be held and pointed in the right direction.

Vera would have preferred something tamer, less obvious. Perhaps an abstract design. Or the head of a woman, more goddess than fury. But Anaya's vision prevailed. Having read Greek mythology, Anaya recalled that Athena, goddess of wisdom and war, had a shield to represent a power to protect. Athena's shield included the head of Medusa, whose frightening visage was said to turn her onlookers into stone. Of course, it would be difficult in modern times for urban women to walk around with a protective shield, so a necklace or a key chain would have to do. The turning-to-stone part wasn't going to work, either. But Vera herself had not tested the desired result.

Vera's pendant was designed so that when a woman felt danger was imminent, she could use the thumb of one hand to activate a catch (flick) that was as small as the on-off button on the side of an iPad. Then, still using the thumb, the wearer would flatten the catch (press) that would combine the two substances, wet and dry. The result was not a strong aerosol spray like Mace, but a slight emission wafting briefly into the air and, if the pendant was held close enough to the face of the offender—Vera was not sure how close—inhaled. A poof. A breath. The release was targeted and immediate. There were some caveats. The inhalation would not work if the attacker came from behind. Nor if he were further away than a couple of feet.

Tonight, she and Anaya were planning to do one more test. Well, Anaya was. That girl was a perfectionist. Or maybe a glutton for punishment. How many times had Anaya tested the strain in the past few weeks? Vera was concerned that her wife was becoming bulimic.

But now, her attention was directed to the man following her when she came out into the parking lot whose truck was parked, way too close, next to her car. He was muscled with the beginning of a beer belly and a square jaw, a still handsome man but going to seed.

Vera had male lovers before Anaya. She never liked the macho ones. The few Latino men she dated were actually sweet and doting. But they were disappointing in a way she could not articulate. Sex with them seemed somehow empty and uncomfortable. Their bodies, and their smells did not feel right to her.

But unlike Anaya, she had not always accepted that she was gay. There were a few awkward experiments with other women after she left Mexico. Then fue amor a primera vista. Love at first sight. Anaya swept her off her feet. Yes, that would be the better expression in English: swept off her feet. They had met in a gay bar in Des Moines and found out they both lived in Ames, only forty minutes north. "Great," said Anaya. Then, that very night, Vera was swept off her feet.

***

"Hey, watch it," the man yelled, pointing to the side of his truck.

He seemed upset about her possibly dinging the door.

Vera kept the door to her car slightly open but stepped back so he could have a better view. There was no apparent damage to the passenger side door of the truck. "There is nothing," she told him. It would be harder to ascertain damage to her car, an old Honda Civic with hail damage and scratches along both doors.

The man didn't move. He stood in between the cars, chewing the inside of his cheek as if he was about to issue a proclamation. "Why don't you go ahead now," Vera added. "I see nothing there." She did not like this man.

"Don't tell me when to go," the man said, sounding ominous.

"Just move on out," Vera told him.

"Move on out? Who do you think you're talking to? A cowboy?" Again, he scrutinized the passenger side door of the truck, taking his time, lightly rubbing over the door with his fingers as if feeling for a scratch.

"I would like to leave," Vera added. She gestured with her left hand, then grabbed the pendant, holding the tip pointing directly at him; her right hand firmly held her car keys. Her nails were the bright red color of his truck.

"Yeah, me, too," the man said. "You don't think I got better things to do than…"

Vera interrupted: "Look, stop making something out of nothing. No one damaged your precious truck."

Royce came closer to her, leaning down, making a show of carefully inspecting the door again. "Bitch," he said quietly.

"What did you call me?"

"Hey. You got good ears," Royce said, looking directly below her neck. "What else you got on you that's good?"

It happened all at once. Vera took a deep breath, held it, and raised her hand toward the man's face; then she popped the spring release on the slim, silver pendant. Flick. Then press. Still holding her breath, her heart beating fast, she scooted sideways into her car, shut the door.

As she pulled away, she saw the man holding his side, leaning over the truck's fender, his back suddenly hunched in a spasm. She was at the wrong angle to get a clear look from her rear-view mirror, but at a safe distance, finally taking a deep breath, she stopped her car and turned around over her left shoulder to see the man there in the parking lot, heaving.

That truck would have to be washed.

***

Still shaky, Vera was having a glass of wine and stirring spaghetti sauce on the stove when Anaya came through the door. "Smells good, hon." Anaya began sorting through the mail, mostly junk; there was a catalogue that featured some cool hiking equipment. They planned a trip through the Badlands at the end of school, but their recent project interfered. Anaya went on: "We should eat early. I don't want to eat too heavy because you know, it'll all come up later and..." One more test on the product tonight before and Howard and Anaya would be ready to go.

"It came up already," Vera said.

"What came up?" Anaya put the mail down on the counter. "What are you talking about?" Anaya knew how averse her wife was to throwing up. Vera had never, ever, drunk enough alcohol to make her sick. And in their discussion about who should become pregnant, Vera was the one who brought up morning sickness, even though she was the one who wanted so badly to have a baby. No way Vera would ever do a trial run, making herself vomit to test the strain.

"Well, there was this angry guy in the parking lot when I left the building; he kept insisting that I hit his car." Vera tasted the sauce and added a splash of red wine. "He was such a jerk."

"Oh, my god," Anaya said. "This afternoon?"

"Yes. He was saying goodbye to Joyce in the office and, I think, dropping off his daughter? Then in the parking lot, he was acting weird. I was kind of scared of him. I don't know," Vera smiled mischievously, "Maybe I just wanted to try it out."

"You set it off?" Anaya was incredulous. There was a flush to her cheeks. "It worked?"

"Oh, yeah, baby!" Vera tasted the sauce. "Mmm, s'good."

"Wait. Wait a minute. You actually tried it? By yourself? On someone else?"

"Anaya, it does not take more than one person. That's the way I made the piece. It's user-friendly." Vera stood in front of the pot with a wooden spoon in her hand. "Wasn't that the whole point of my design?"

"And it went off?"

"It went off perfectly. Flick the latch. Then press. We sure practiced that enough times. Actually, it was easy."

They had practiced enough times. But always with safe substances. Any liquid able to make a spray with spores placed in the adjacent compartment.

"Jesus, I need a beer," Anaya said. "Or maybe a whiskey. We have any hard stuff?"

Vera went to a cabinet and took out a bottle of Templeton Rye. "You want ice?"

"Hon, you know who that guy was?" Anaya asked. She sat, dumbstruck, at the kitchen table. Do you know who you did that to?" Vera shook her head. "That's Joyce's son-in-law! The one who's married to the daughter who moved home? Caroline? I've seen him before. They're getting divorced."

"Well, she should," Vera said.

"What?"

"Divorce him," Vera said. "He is an awful man."

"Echh. Royce." Anaya took three long swallows and poured herself some more from the bottle that Vera put in front of her. "Shit, Joyce really hates that guy. She doesn't usually say much, but she's been so upset. When Caroline moved home, Joyce was asking Howard about lawyers."

"Well, she should," Vera said.

"What?"

"Hate him." Vera took out the pot for spaghetti and filled it with water, adding a couple pinches of salt. "Because that guy is a real asshole."

"I can't believe you did it," Anaya said, shaking her head. "You actually did it."

"I did!"

"Hon, I'm so proud of you."

Vera sat down at the table with her glass of wine and filled a small bowl with almonds. "So now what?"

"How many pieces are ready to go?"

"Four right now are finished. The mold is set. I have enough silver for ten more. Plus or minus. I could have them all by the end of the week. By the time you and Dr. Lerner want to take them to show the lady in Chicago. Also, there is the one I just used. It's on the worktable, ready to be reloaded." Vera looked down at her left hand, decorated only by her wedding ring. "I don't know why I just decided to get a manicure the other day, but my hand sure looked nice when I did it."

Anaya nodded, sucking on an ice cube. She was feeling a little tipsy. "It's good. It's all good."

"And you have enough spores?" Vera asked.

"There's always enough spores," Anaya said. "I told you; we only need a couple of strands from each one. We can produce enough to make a whole lot of bad guys throw up for years to come."

"Is that what we want to do?" Vera asked.

"I think so."

"Well, there are a lot of them," Vera said, raising an eyebrow. "You know: bad guys."

***

Mitzi was in her bedroom when the phone rang. She still had a landline at home, one in every room. Including some of the bathrooms. The caller ID said Iowa. The man introduced himself as Howard Lerner, Lily's father, and Mitzi told him, yes, she had been expecting his call. "Lily has told me about you, Dr. Lerner."

"My daughter thinks so highly of you," Howard said. "You've helped Lily's recovery more than you know. My wife and I are very grateful."

"I adore your daughter!" Mitzi said enthusiastically. "She's a wonderful girl!" Mitzi was beginning to think of Lily as the granddaughter she never had, her two sons producing sons of their own, now four boys altogether, ages six to twelve. She loved the grandchildren, but after every visit to her home, something got broken. The boys threw footballs in the dining room. Toy racing cars scratched the glass coffee table. The boy stereotypes were played out in her family as predictably as Chicago winters.

"Thank you," Howard said. "Her mother and I think so, too."

"Just a wonderful girl!" Mitzi repeated. On her lap was Meow, an aged cat with many physical ailments. Meow was fourteen years old, comparable to Mitzi's age of seventy. Cat years were not the same as dog years. Meow, however, was nowhere near in as a good shape as her owner. Deaf and arthritic, Meow occasionally urinated outside the box. The veterinarian said the cause was anxiety and prescribed Prozac. Mitzi didn't know how Meow could possibly be stressed, living in a penthouse apartment on Lake Shore Drive, eating Fancy Feast and occasionally fried chicken livers. Meow also had a cat door with open access to a landscaped balcony facing Lake Michigan.

Howard took a deep breath and began the reason for his call. No, it was not only about Lily. "I know you share a number of devices with the girls in your self-defense class." He stopped and corrected himself. "The women, I mean. Lily told me about what you do in class."

"Yes…" Dr. Lerner was not a fast talker. Mitzi, who often stopped herself from jumping in, filling in words for people who seemed to be searching for what they wanted to say, waited for him to go on.

"I, uh, well I think I might have discovered something…"

Mitzi listened carefully, letting him go on. It took her a while to get the gist of why he was calling. Lily had told her some things, but said her father would further explain. Ok, Mitzi thought: explain. She didn't have patience with deliberate talkers.

It was an antiperistalsis agent, Dr. Lerner said, going on in some detail with the scientific terms. There was also a delivery system. He had done a number of trials. Trials. He added: "But I haven't tested this as a method for self-defense. That is, in any scientific sample. I know what you do teaching the class, and I'm not sure I want to imply that this might be used in any adventurous…"

Mitzi, running her hand over Meow's soft fur, interrupted him: "In my line of work, life is always an adventure."

Howard finally said—well, it wasn't even exactly his idea—but he had this wonderfully, smart, graduate student who was, in fact, adventurous. Her name was Anaya. He would like to come to Chicago with her and show Mitzi what he was working on. He made it clear that he was not interested in profiting from the project he believed would be of interest to her, helping in her line of work. "I don't want to sound like I'm above making any profit from this. I mean, I believe in capitalism."

"Well, that's good," Mitzi said encouragingly.

"But financial gain is not a motivation."

"Nor mine," Mitzi said, though she happened to be sitting in a bedroom with art on one wall that was worth as much as four years tuition for both of Howard's daughters. She was being truthful. Money was not her motivation for the work she did. In point of fact, it never had been.

"You have access to women who could use this product," Howard said. "For myself, I'm a scientist. I don't want to go into the self-defense business. For me to go through a process of getting all of this approved, perhaps first a grant, then getting a patent, the FDC—this would be very time-consuming, and I'm not sure successful."

"And some of us don't have that much time," Mitzi said cheerfully. Seventy. How could she be seventy? Frequently. In bed at night, she counted up the years she had left, which made her anxious. Lying beside her, Benjamin, snoring softly, seemed to have no trouble at all falling asleep. Her husbands rarely did.

"In fact, for me to be connected with this, might not even be a good idea. Getting something approved at a university is always a very slow process…" Howard began. He had been so excited. Why was he stalling now?

Mitzi added: "Yes, universities must move slower than Congress."

"Academics are careful people," Howard said. "Scientists especially. And grant money is becoming more and more difficult to come by. There are always obstacles." He thought of the dour and precise Jerry Ketcham as he said this. Howard assured her that there were not lethal consequences, even when someone was exposed perhaps accidentally to the substance he was describing. "But the product does have the potential to become a powerful deterrent. When Lily told me what you do in your classes at SWIC, I thought that you might be interested."

"Oh yes, I am," Mitzi assured him. "I have a line of self-defense products that I promote. Some can be ordered online. Others I sell at the studio. We'll see how this goes, yes?"

"Oh, thank you…" Howard stopped, not knowing how to address her.

"Call me Mitzi," she said, picking up on his hesitancy.

"Thank you, Mitzi," he said. "I have more work to do, but I'd like to come to Chicago with Anaya. Just show you what this is about."

"I'd like that very much," Mitzi said. "When? Spring is lovely in Chicago. Let's set a date. Let me get my calendar." After she hung up the phone, she thought: Bashert. Fate. Yes, this was meant to be.

Chapter 13

May Day (Howard)

The first of May was celebrated by socialists as International Workers' Day, honoring the eight-hour workday. Having nothing to do with socialism, Iowa children deliver baskets to their neighbors on the first day of May, usually paper cups filled with candies and flowers, sometimes dandelions. Lily and Megan used to visit the neighbors up and down the block with their gifts.

May 1st was also Betsy's birthday. Howard, busy in the lab almost every night, told his wife that he would be home in time to go out to dinner and arrived before six with a bouquet of tulips that he picked up at the grocery store.

For many years, they had stopped buying birthday presents, a relief for Howard who agonized over traditional gifts. Once he purchased an expensive silk scarf in turquoise and pink which Betsy wore only on subsequent birthdays, finally admitting that she didn't like the colors. Another time he bought her a leather jacket, which she returned, telling him she wasn't really the leather-jacket type. Ultimately, she released him from the obligation of buying her birthday gifts. "Just come home early and we'll go out to dinner," she said.

There were times when he almost told Betsy why he was at work every night in the lab. Never in all his married life had he kept anything from her. But Betsy seemed preoccupied since Lily's attack; he didn't want to add to anything that might cause more stress. He would wait and be patient, and the woman he knew would come back.

The month before, Betsy made an appointment with a woman who worked primarily with victims of abuse. Howard agreed that this might be a good idea for her to see a counselor, even though he didn't understand why it had to be someone with this specialty. Betsy was still upset, and so was he. Didn't they have reason to be?

Betsy wore a black sweater and a necklace with an intricate silver pendant designed by Vera Perez. Sitting in a back booth at the restaurant, they both had martinis, and the waiter said, "Good choice," when Howard ordered prime rib.

"This is nice," Betsy said, taking his hand across the table when Howard blurted out, "I have something to tell you, Bets." Betsy's eyes widened; she let go of his hand but was silent. "Last summer…" he began telling her about the farmer in Vinton, his distraction in the lab, the accidental discovery, the experiments first with the pigs, then himself when she was away to see the girls for Spring break. How he finally included Anaya. And her excitement about his discovery. And the role Vera was playing in this adventure. "I didn't expect any of this," he said, leaving out the trip he and Anaya were planning to see Mitzi Solomon in Chicago.

Betsy remained still. There was only the din of conversation at other tables, silverware clanking, and some background music that was not loud enough to be annoying, "Are you angry with me, Bets?"

"No, never, Howie," she said, shaking her head. Then: "I just wish you had told me." There were tears in her eyes. "Why didn't you tell me?"

"Oh honey, don't. I wanted to protect you. After all we've been through. And I didn't want you to think I was crazy."

Betsy laughed. "Howard Lerner, you are the least crazy man I ever met."

"But you don't think this is really—well—I don't even know what to say. I mean, the ability to make someone vomit. It's like a joke, don't you think?"

"But it's not, Howie. I mean, it's not a joke."

"No," he said. "It's not."

"Do you remember that liquid?" Betsy asked. That the pediatrician gave us when the girls were little."

"Ipecac?"

"I never had the occasion to use that," Betsy said. "The girls were both good. Hardly got into anything, not like some other toddlers."

"They don't recommend that any longer. Syrup of Ipecac. It's actually dangerous to induce severe vomiting if a child swallows something poisonous." He began to describe the immobilizing effects of severe anti-peristalsis when the food arrived. "Looks good," he said as the waiter placed a plank of prime rib before him, one rare pink slab already cut.

"Enjoy!" the waiter said cheerfully.

Talk of anti-peristalsis had not affected Howard's appetite. "The thing is, what I discovered is very simple," Howard went on. "And basically harmless. And yet, it could be used as a very powerful deterrent in self-defense."

"Like Mace?" Betsy reached over and, without asking, took a small piece of meat, putting it on her salad plate.

"Well, this would work better, because it's easier to control. More focused toward the attacker. Afterward, there's not a mist that lingers in the air. So, there's less of a chance of push-back. The woman who feels in danger can basically hold her breath for a very short time when the spray takes effect. Less than thirty seconds." He did not tell her what happened with Royce and Vera in the parking lot.

"But is this going to get you in trouble? You and Anaya?"

"I don't think so," Howard said. Then he added: "I don't know. Maybe. Anaya wants to take over. And you know when she sets her mind to something. Anyway, I'm happy to let her."

"Does Joyce know?"

"No. She's so close to retirement. I don't think we have to get her involved."

"Involved?" Betsy asked.

"Well, I mean, you know…" Howard stuttered a moment.

"I do?"

"You know, how Joyce is…"

"No, how is Joyce?" Betsy asked, raising an eyebrow. She understood the occasional friction between Joyce and Anaya. Betsy liked them both. More than liked. She loved Anaya like a daughter, but also highly respected Joyce, who put the well-being of others—always—before her own considerations. Betsy understood that Joyce had a reliable moral compass while Anaya's swung more freely.

"Joyce, well, she might get upset," Howard said. "You know, there's filling out all the regulatory forms, protocol. There's that. She's pretty exacting. I mean, that's what's made Joyce such a great secretary all these years."

"I think I'd like another glass of wine," Betsy said, letting out a deep breath.

"Honey, don't worry. You know me. I wouldn't do anything…well, against the law."

"And Anaya?" Betsy asked, raising an eyebrow.

"Betsy—Anaya wouldn't either. She really has a good head on her shoulders."

"You know, she can be very impulsive, Howie. I'm just saying."

They ate for a while in silence.

"I think of what happened to Lily every day, " Howard said, not wanting to appear dramatic. "I wouldn't risk our future. But you have to know, I've been obsessed with this. Not only the assault. But how Lily might have protected herself. I've fantasized about her having a gun, of blowing that bastard away. Or some kind of punishment. I think about it often. I know it's not healthy."

"She's doing all right, Howie." Betsy reached across the table for his hand. "That defense class she goes to? The women she met there? And Mitzi? She's been such an inspiration to Lily."

"I know. I know. She's doing all right." He paused: "Still."

"Just two things, a spore, and a disinfectant, mixed together?" Betsy asked. "That sounds too simple. How could it work like that?""

"Some things in science really are simple," Howard told her. "Egyptians knew about compounds produced by bacteria and fungi." He went on: "An old folk remedy was a poultice of mold applied to open wounds. This was way before Fleming." Betsy nodded, an attentive listener. How lucky he was to have a woman who was beautiful, smart, a life partner so unequivocally by his side. "So, what do you think? Does it sound too weird? Dangerous?"

There was a long pause. Betsy chewed her lip. Then: "I'm excited about this," she finally said. "Well, especially if Anaya takes it over."

"Really?" He looked carefully at her. He was grateful. She knew that. But did he tell her enough? Too often he was lost in his work. Everything about her seemed welcoming and opened to him tonight: her clear, blue eyes; her hair, a shade darker now than when she was young, was an ash-blonde that fell in soft waves around her face; the shimmer of Vera's silver necklace. "And Vera's so creative, you know. She invented the design."

They split a chocolate mousse for dessert. "What's the worst that can happen?" Betsy asked. This was a question she occasionally asked when Howard shared his worries about the children aloud, the strange noise of the water heater, or the state of the world. She had a tiny bit of whipped cream on the side of her mouth which Howard found endearing.

"What's the worst that can happen? I don't know," he said. "No one is ever really prepared for the worst that can happen."

"I mean, you and Anaya couldn't go to jail, or anything, for this?"

"Jail? No, of course not."

"Or your career? Could anything happen that would jeopardize your work?"

"I don't think so."

"You don't think so?"

Howard shrugged. "Well, Anaya, I think, wants a new challenge. She says they're never going to catch this guy. I tend to believe her. And I'm not writing this up as research in any way, Bets. I'm not asking for money from anyone. I'm not applying for a grant." It occurred to him that he was enumerating all the professional things he was not going to do. He was not exactly clear on what he was going to do. Besides possibly bequeathing the project to Anaya."

"Ok," Betsy said. "I was just asking."

When they got up to leave, Howard noticed that Jerry Ketcham, the university's Vice Provost for Research was sitting with a group at a round table in the back of the restaurant, looking rapt in conversation. Well, as rapt as someone like Jerry Ketcham was able to look. The men at the table were wearing suits. The one youngish woman was plain and unadorned. Perhaps they were interviewing her for a job. Not wanting to make eye contact, Howard quickly turned his head, following Betsy out.

Later that night, in the darkness of their bedroom, she told Howard a secret, too: what had happened when she was in high school. She described the night, her confusion and pain, the water in the quarry shimmering under the moon. What was his name? Mike? Mark? The brothers. She couldn't remember. Sometimes she wondered: Did that boy, now a grown man, even understand what he did? Did he have a family? Or even a teenage daughter?

"Oh, love," Howard said in a whisper. "Oh, Bets." They held each other for a long time before falling asleep.

May Day (Anaya and Vera)

"Well, what would you want to do next year?" Anaya asked. "I mean, if it wasn't up to me. If you were alone."

"If I were alone, I would be crying without you," Vera said with some seriousness. "Why would I want to be alone?"

"Not that you would want to be alone. But if you were alone. I'm talking hypothetically."

"I don't know those scientific terms," Vera said. Anaya sighed. Despite being a romantic, Vera was often a very literal person. It was dusk, and they were sitting on the deck of their small house, sharing a beer, passing it back and forth, though Vera had taken only a few small sips. "Do you want me to get you one of your own?" Vera asked. "I've had enough."

"No, let's go in. I'm hungry." They had been talking about plans for the following year. Vera had her graduate degree. If they stayed in Iowa, she could probably teach part-time and rent a studio space downtown to make her jewelry; Anaya would be welcome to stay for at least another year in Dr. Lerner's lab. On the other hand, there were tempting possibilities. One in Arizona. "We would be close to your family in Tucson," Anaya said. "And the weather would be better."

"That is not such a good thing," Vera said.

"You hate the winters here."

"I mean, being close to my family," Vera said sadly.

"You might give them a chance," Anaya said. "It's not exactly as if my parents are the most enlightened people. They accepted you. They loved you."

Vera shrugged. She had met Anaya's mother and father only once before the wedding, and although there was a lot of nodding and smiling, the talk was stilted. Anaya's parents were as foreign to her as she must have been to them.

For supper, Anaya made her delicious samosas and a lightly spiced Tikka Masala. Vera was gaining weight in this relationship. "It's all muscle," she explained to Anaya. "I'm bulking up." Vera was broad-shouldered, a little thick around the middle, and very strong. She might have given Royce what he deserved, even without the spray.

"You are so good to me," Vera said later when Anaya settled in next to her on the bed.

"You're good to me," Anaya said, kissing her wife on the shoulder. She covered them both with a beautiful quilt, gold and silver and blue and purple, which her mother had made from old saris.

In bed, they watched a movie where a wise Rabbi gave a speech to survivors about rebuilding their lives after World War II. "Do not let anything destroy your capacity for love," the Rabbi told the congregation. "He reminds me of Dr. Lerner," Vera said.

Anaya narrowed her eyes at the screen. The Rabbi was older than Howard, with a broad, fleshy face and sad eyes. "Well, he does in a way. I can see that. He sounds wise, too."

Vera sighed. "Maybe we should both convert to Judaism."

"Really? Anaya asked, turning to her side, ready for sleep. "Isn't it enough for us to be Hispanic Indian Lesbians?"

May Day (Joyce)

The first day of May and all the tulips were in full bloom in the Corning's front yard. Red and gold tulips, Iowa State colors. Larry Corning was a fan, but Joyce thought football was a violent and silly pastime. Sillier still were people dressed in cardinal and gold and drinking beer in the morning out of the trunks of their cars. Larry and his fishing buddies were usually among them. Like her changing politics, Joyce kept these thoughts to herself.

This night she made a meatloaf, a green salad, and twice-baked potatoes, but only a half for each of them. There was no pie to be had, no dessert at all. Larry was unhappy about this but admitted that all three of them could afford to lose a few pounds. Caroline, living with them now, was going through a terrible time. Some people lose weight when they go through a divorce, but Caroline used food as a stress reliever.

Joyce wanted to help her daughter as much as possible, to keep her motivated and on the right course. Caroline was able to transfer to the Kohl's store in Ames, but she had to work Saturdays and occasional evenings. Joyce was happy to put Nora to bed now that she and Caroline lived with them. Nora was such a sweet little girl. Joyce knew that if Nora had been a boy, both Larry and Royce would have encouraged him to play football.

Every other Saturday, Royce came to collect Nora at the Corning's home when Caroline was at work. Joyce did not invite him in, and so Larry brought Nora to the door. "Hey, Muffin," Royce always said, scooping the child up into his arms. "How's my girl?" He could have been any divorced father, happy to see his daughter. But watching from the kitchen window as Royce drove his shiny red truck down their gravel drive, Joyce knew otherwise.

Also, something at work was unusual. Joyce was bothered but didn't quite know what it was she was bothered about. Anaya, always independent, was in Dr. Lerner's office often. A lot more often than she used to be. And whenever Joyce came by, both Anaya and Dr. Lerner stopped talking so abruptly that Joyce (who did not think of herself as a suspicious person except, of course, when it came to Royce) was taken aback. And also feeling left out. As if she interrupted something. What was going on? This confirmed her decision that she should retire within the year.

But the decision coming the way it did made her feel sad.

May Day (Mitzi)

The celebration of Cinco de Mayo started early at Pepe's, the Mexican restaurant across the street from SWIC where today there were half-priced tacos and margaritas. After class, Mitzi asked Laura Murphy into her office before she changed and headed out. In her navy-blue shorts and white tee shirt, Laura looked like a high school girl, sweaty after gym. "How are you doing, sweetheart?" Mitzi asked, closing the door to her office. The class all knew about Laura's stalker and Mitzi wanted to follow up.

"It's still going on," Laura said. "I have security at school. And I'm staying with a friend. Not at my apartment. Jeez, I am a dope," Laura said, confessing she should have known better. She was almost thirty-five years old and had been single for a long time. Usually, she was cautious, researching the men she met online. "You know, maybe I told you this before. He—his name, George Murphy—he told me that it was a sign that we had the same last name. Murphy. It was a sign according to him that we were meant to be together. I mean, Murphy is a pretty common name in Chicago. I thought he was joking."

They were alone in the office, a room of soothing grey and white; orchids bloomed on the windowsill. Outside the office door, they could hear people leaving class, their voices raised, laughing; the women were always louder leaving the building after a self-defense class than they were coming in.

Laura Murphy swallowed with difficulty, her eyes brimming with tears. Auburn curls framing a heart-shaped face; her eyes were a honeyed hazel. Laura looked so young. Thirty-five? Forty? How are women of these ages supposed to look? Mitzi thought.

"I'm sorry," Laura said. "I'm really ok. The girls in the class—they're all younger than I am, but they've sort of taken me in. Lily, especially, is wonderful. And she's even the youngest, I think. In a way, she seems wiser than I am. But we're all friends! Like now—we're all going out to Pepe's. Oh, god, but with that guy—George Murphy—I feel like such a fool. How could I have let myself...I kind of knew."

"Laura. Your intuition was telling you something. Women need to listen more to these voices inside themselves," Mitzi told her. "That voice that says 'something is not right'."

"I really thought I'd be married by now, have a family. I love my kids. My first graders," Laura said.

"There is nothing wrong with wanting to be with someone. Or wanting a family."

Laura took a tissue off Mitzi's desk and blew her nose. "I have a picture of him," she said, looking at her phone. "That was one of the things he did that puzzled me. He took pictures of us. You would think we were on a date having a great time." Laura brought up the photo: a smiling couple, leaning their heads together over a pepperoni pizza, clinking bottles of beer. "I showed this to Lily and the others. But I don't know if you've ever seen it."

"That's him?" Mitzi asked. George Murphy, a non-descript, slightly balding man of middling age, had a shy smile. He looked like someone eager to wait on a customer in a Best Buy. "Do not blame yourself," Mitzi said sternly, still looking at the photo. "You did nothing wrong."

"I sent him a text. I used the boyfriend excuse. But I was firm. He didn't even respond to what I said about a boyfriend. It was as if I didn't even tell him no. I repeated it. It was as if he knew I was lying. He simply refused to acknowledge it."

"Lily told me that you took out a restraining order?"

Laura nodded, the flush now gone from her face "Well, I hadn't responded to him, and he didn't stop. He just didn't stop." Her voice rose. "A few weeks ago, I'm coming out of the building, and I see him standing by my car in the school lot. I must have told him where I taught. Or he looked through the registers of the Chicago public schools. At first, I didn't recognize him. I just saw a man by my car. He knew my car because I drove it when we met, and he walked me back to the car after we left the pizza place."

There was a knock on the office door; Mitzi padded barefoot across the room of gray, plush carpet. "Hi, sweetie. She'll be right out," Mitzi told Lily. "Give me another five minutes."

"Oh, sure. I'm sorry," Lily said. "We didn't know if she was still in there with you."

Laura continued. "We have a cop, you know we have someone who polices the school; he's called a 'community resource officer.' A very nice older man. I don't even know his real name. The kids call him Officer Smiles. He's there, I guess, for protection. But also to show the kids that a police officer is your friend. Officer Smiles."

"I like that, Officer Smiles." Though Mitzi thought it sad that a police officer was needed in an elementary school.

"I asked Officer Smiles to accompany me to my car because I felt threatened. We go out and George is there, and he waves, friendly; he sees I'm there with a cop, but he just goes right on as if there's nothing wrong at all and says he thought we'd go out across the street for coffee. Officer Smiles looks at me like, 'really? You're scared of this guy?'"

"What did you do?"

"I thanked Officer Smiles, got in my car, and drove away. I didn't speak to George Murphy. Not a word. I tried not to even look at him. That night he started texting me with threats.

Leaving me ugly phone messages. Said I had no gratitude for all he did for me. That I was a crazy old maid and would never get a man because I was such a bitch. Then the next day he sent me flowers." Laura looked at the windowsill at the orchids. "He sent roses."

Laura told Mitzi that she has looked into buying a gun. But she was afraid of guns. The idea of having a gun made Laura sick.

It is one of Mitzi's dreams to be a savior; her favorite book was The Catcher in the Rye, which she first read so many, many years ago, and reread a number of times. Her favorite part is where Holden imagines catching innocent children as they plunge off a cliff. Mitzi's desire to protect was awakened when she first read the novel. Again, when her sister was brutalized, and again and again with every self-defense class she teaches, toward the women she gets to know and yearns to protect. She wants to make a promise: No one will hurt you; I will give you the power and the skill to make you strong.

"I am so glad you took this class, Laura," Mitzi said.

"Well, me too!" Laura seemed enthusiastic. "All of us are taking the next session, too. Lily, Alida, Maryanne and me. Really, we have so much fun together. I don't think any of them mind that I'm older."

"Please! Age is just a construct," Mitzi said. Although lately she wasn't sure she totally believed that herself. After Laura left, she watched out the window as Lily and the girls headed across the street to Pepe's.

Chicago weather was unreliable, even at the beginning of May, but it was a warm evening as Mitzi headed out of the office that evening and walked to the train. It was dusk, and a pale light hung over the city. Mitzi walked and walked; no one gave her a second glance. Older women are invisible. She was even more invisible because coming from the class at the SWIC studio, Mitzi appeared a gray-haired woman wearing a pink sweatsuit, a backpack and black orthopedic shoes. She walked fast and far, and, at a certain age, vanity gave way to comfort.

Her hair was not exactly gray. More like silver. Her hair started turning soon after she was a young divorcee. She didn't color it at that time because she didn't have the money, and silver hair had been attractive on a petite young woman with big blue eyes. Ira, her second husband started calling her "The Silver Fox," and it stuck.

She almost named her first studio that. Then thought the name sounded too much like an upscale clothing boutique. Strong Women in Chicago. SWIC. That was a better name.

Now, walking along the crowded street, she suddenly felt power in the realization that no one knew who she was. No one knew that this old lady in a sweat suit was rich enough to afford a penthouse on Lake Shore Drive and a condo in Palm Springs. No one knew she was a black belt, a kickboxer, a cancer survivor. No one knew Mitzi Solomon was the Silver Fox.

May Day (Lily)

"I'm starving," Maryanne said. "Of course, I'm always starving." She giggled nervously, finishing off the last chip before the waiter took away the basket. He brought out skillets of sizzling fajitas and a bowl of guacamole with fresh lime. They had a booth for the four of them: Lily, Laura, Maryanne, Alida. They would not be friends under ordinary circumstances, but a bond has been forged.

Maryanne who had been attacked by someone impersonating a policeman who pulled her over and raped her in her very own car, is sitting against the wall, facing the door of the restaurant. Maryanne has some difficulty breathing if she cannot see an exit, a way out. She still lives at home with her widowed mother and brothers. No one ever mentions the rape.

Next to her is Alida Salgado, the nanny who fought off her attacker so fiercely that she broke her hand; Alida is the most accomplished at this hybrid martial art, which at SWIC includes punching, kicking, and full-contact Karate. The family, who has employed Alida as a nanny since the birth of their son, believes that she saved his young life. In gratitude, they are paying for a trip this summer for Alida to visit her family in Guatemala.

Lily. Laura. Maryanne. Alida. Strong women in Chicago; though Maryanne is the least strong. After the attack, she was able to transfer to a day job at the post office, but the anti-anxiety medication she is taking does not seem to do much, except make her hungry for comfort foods: ice cream, potatoes, pasta. Since the attack she has gained weight. When she is steady on her feet, the kick she employs in self-defense could be powerful if she were only able to focus.

Lily sometimes wants to ask Maryanne about the rape, but she does not. Did he do it to her right there in the car? Was she badly hurt? Lily replayed her own attack many times but could not imagine how he would have been able to carry out an actual rape in the bathroom stall. How could he have gotten off her tight jeans, to position himself to get inside her?

The four of them were a support group, and they didn't need to talk about the details to help each other. Maryanne, who seemingly had the most horrific experience, was also the most fragile. Alida the toughest. Wherever she came from in Guatemala was a brutal place, one she described with crime so rampant that her father slept with a machete beside the bed. Laura was oldest but she didn't seem so. She was fun, and there was something so youthful about her. She was the kind of elementary school teacher who probably made all the children in her class feel special.

After dinner, Lily, Alida and Maryanne walked Laura Murphy to her car, hugged goodbye and then took the brown line to other parts of the city. On the train, Lily texted her mother: Happy birthday to the most wonderful mother in the whole world. I love, love you. Lily didn't add that it was almost dark, that she was on the El and would walk alone the two blocks to her apartment when she got off before her friends.

On the train, Alida and Maryanne sat across from Lily, both giggly, slightly tipsy from too many Margaritas, but Lily remained on high alert, her hand around the smiling-cat key chain with the sharp ears. The spikes stuck out between her fingers, like brass knuckles, cute but menacing. This was a new purchase since her class. Be prepared, Mitzi had said. Lily was. Alida and Maryanne chatted on, oblivious to their surroundings. Lily looked around the car, feeling confident in her accomplishments at SWIC. The train rumbled on.

More than four months had passed since the attack, and Lily was pretty much resigned that her assailant would not soon be caught. She wondered if her attacker came into the bathroom at Union Station to rob or to rape? That little fucker. That sicko jerk! Lily sometimes echoed her sister's words during self-defense drills in class.

A group of teenagers in hoodies came on at the next stop and strolled to the back of the car, laughing and jostling each other. Lily sat up straight. Throughout her recovery, Lily continued to picture her attacker, although initially that was painful. She had spent a lot of time going through file after file of unflattering police mug shots: guys with pocked skin, sweaty sheens, creepy smiles, and still she remained at a loss to pick anyone out. What if her attacker had been Black? Then she would have had an even harder time attempting to differentiate. She wondered: was that racist?

Her attacker was white, that she was sure of. His hair was matted and straight and brown. He was thin. He was not a teenager. Not older than thirty. She had been close enough to see the dangerous look in his eyes. Close enough to smell him. But after a few afternoons at the police station, looking through photos of sicko jerks, they all started to look the same.

On the train, a middle-aged guy in a baseball cap and a dirty work shirt sat in front of the girls, manspreading across two seats. He stared at Lily, his mouth ajar. Boldly, Lily met his stare until he looked away.

Chapter 14

June: Road Trip

Because it was June and perfect weather, Anaya and Howard took the northern route, even though that made the trip to Chicago about half an hour longer. Highway 20 outside of Dubuque had picture postcard scenes of rolling hills, dotted with white farmhouses. It was the middle of the week, still early in the season, so tourists had not yet clogged the road around Galena.

Anaya insisted on driving although she was not used to the silence of Howard's Prius. He thought Anaya drove too quickly and passed too frequently on the two-lane roads, but he didn't object. Everyone drove faster than he preferred.

The silver pendants, spring-loaded and ready, were in the trunk in a canvas shopping bag, each wrapped in tissue paper and separately boxed, like presents. Vera had purchased a few dozen grey velvet boxes from a jewelry consigner. One device was filled only with water in a clear, plastic box labeled 'For Demonstration Purposes Only'.

After a few hours in the car, Howard suggested a bathroom stop. "And maybe something to eat?" Howard was happy to see the sign advertising breakfast served all day.

"Do you think we need gas?" he asked. "There's a station across the street.

"I don't think you ever need gas in a Prius," Anaya said. "Maybe you can fill it up when you turn this one in for a newer model." Pulling into the parking lot of The Ox-Bow Inn, designed to look like a rustic cabin, she seemed suspicious although there were plenty of cars. "I just hope they have pie."

The door had a welcoming tinkle, and the restaurant smelled like bacon. A woman behind the cash register was arranging little figurines in a glass case. She looked over her shoulder and smiled. "You folks sit yourselves wherever you want. Someone will be right along to serve you."

Anaya led Howard to a booth by the window. They made an unusual couple, Dr. Howard Lerner and Anaya Pran. He looked like what he was: a middle-aged university professor needing a haircut. He had left while Betsy was still in bed, so sleepily kissing him goodbye, she did not notice that he was wearing black socks with his sandals. Also, that he had an irregular shave.

Anaya looked like Anaya: startling and bold. This month, her hair was white blonde with a few inches of natural black at the roots. She was wearing hiking boots, jean shorts and a tight black T-shirt. Long, silver earrings in the shape of cyclones, came almost to her shoulders. Vera made them as a present the last time the Iowa State Girls' basketball team won a conference title.

"Be right back," he said, before sitting down.

"I'll wait to order."

The men's bathroom smelled like fermented fruit. Relieving himself at the urinal felt so good that he sighed. Washing carefully, scrubbing up to his wrists for twenty seconds the way he did in the lab, he examined himself in the mirror and saw that he had missed quite a large patch when he shaved that morning. Dark stubble remained along one side of his chin. When he came back to the table, Anaya poured his coffee and passed the cream. "You missed a spot, shaving," she said. "I didn't see it when I was driving."

"I just saw," he said, feeling the growth along his chin. "Is it too noticeable?"

"Well, I noticed," Anaya told him.

"I wasn't going to shave at all this morning, then thought I should, to make a good impression." Anaya raised an eyebrow. "On Mitzi Solomon," Howard went on. "I didn't want her to think that I'm some crazy scientist." Anaya looked at him with affection. "Dr. Lerner, no one is less crazy than you."

"That's what Betsy says." Howard ordered scrambled eggs, bacon and pancakes; Anaya, grilled cheese and a slice of strawberry rhubarb pie. They ate slowly, talking in a desultory way, comfortable in each other's company. "I'm going to miss you when you go to another job," Howard confessed.

"I'm going to miss you, too," Anaya said without a bit of her usual sass.

"Life goes on," Howard said.

"With or without us," Anaya said.

Back in the car, Howard became so sleepy that he nodded off before the Rockford exit; Anaya listened to an NPR podcast about the decimation of ocean coral. Light filtered in between Howard's half-closed lids; leaning against the window, he felt the sun, warm on his face. In a half-dreamy state, Howard imagined the flicker of silver pendants. Anaya drove about ten miles over the speed limit, thinking about the prickly coral, how it was needed to protect the ocean's treasure and how man seemed to be making such a mess of the natural world.

***

"Lily doesn't look at all like you." That was the second thing that Mitzi Solomon said when she opened the door to her office and saw Howard. The first was that there was always traffic in Chicago, no matter what the time of day, and you just had to go with the flow or, as she pointed out, the lack of flow. "You can never say for sure when it is exactly that you'll arrive. You have to be very Zen about it if you live in the city."

Howard, still rattled by Anaya's driving, thought that Mitzi was not someone who was very Zen about anything. Mitzi ushered them in, and Howard and Anaya sat next to each other on a gray couch; Mitzi served them spiced tea in beautiful floral cups and set out a plate of little pastries covered in powdered sugar.

"No, she doesn't look like me," Howard agreed. "Lily looks like her mom. I guess she's lucky about that."

"Not at all. You're very attractive. For a man." Mitzi herself was as he imagined: short and slim, bird-bright, eager. She chattered on: "In fact, Howard, you remind me of my second husband. Ira was a man anyone could be comfortable with. He died too young. Fifty-three years old." She shook her head at the injustice.

"I'm sorry," Howard said.

"And you, my dear…" Mitzi turned just as Anaya bit into one of the pastries; sending a puff of powdered sugar across the front of her black tee shirt. Undeterred, Mitzi went on. "You are gor-g-eous! A beautiful woman warrior. May I ask: were you the model for the pendant? Lily showed me a picture on her phone. Now that I meet you, I think the image resembles you quite a bit."

"I don't think so," Anaya said "My wife…she cast the impression. But I don't believe she was trying to replicate me."

"Well, you have a fabulous look," Mitzi said warmly, reaching across to pat Anaya on the knee. "Fabulous! I love your hair."

"Anaya has been my right-hand woman," Howard said. "I couldn't have run the lab without her. But she'll probably be leaving after the summer." He managed a sad smile.

"To go where, may I ask?"

"I have some interviews set up," Anaya said. "Though Dr. Lerner would like me to stay another year." She looked at Howard and smiled. "And maybe I will. If he makes me an offer I can't refuse."

Mitzi leaned over, lowering her voice: "I can. Make you an offer. I mean it. If you ever want a change of pace, want to move to Chicago. I'd hire you in a minute."

"Thank you." Anaya brushed the powdered sugar off the front of her shirt. "These are delicious."

"Take another. My housekeeper made them. They're Polish. Kolaczkis. I think that's how you say it. I'll give you some to take home." Mitzi looked straight at Anaya: "I'm not kidding. Not about the Kolaczskis. About working here with Lily. She's young. She's going to need a strong woman who can help. I have big plans."

"I'm flattered. I could use a change from academia." Anaya sighed. "You know there are so many rules and regulations with science. And everything takes such a long time. It's stressful."

"There's stress here too, but it's better when you're the boss. If you have the resources to call the shots," Mitzi said seriously. "Lily told me all about you. How successful and smart you are. A PhD and everything. Your parents must be so proud."

Finding his voice, Howard interjected: "They are."

"Well, I did plan on leaving Dr. Lerner's lab sometime soon," Anaya said coyly. "But who knows? Maybe I should consider going in a different direction."

The fan on the air conditioning shut itself off and the room was still. Mitzi looked straight into Anaya's dark eyes. "Darling, I am dead serious about you working for me. I'm in the process of setting up a legacy here." Mitzi leaned closer. "Chicago is an exciting city. Very diverse. Your wife? She would want a shop of her own? I could set that up for her. I own this entire building. The whole damned thing." She gestured with one hand pointing toward the ceiling. "Three floors. There's a big space on the top floor that would be perfect for an artist's studio. It was a shirt factory once upon a time. Empty now. No problem. And I'm telling you, the West Loop is happening. And I could make it happen for you."

Howard looked back and forth at the two of them. He was quiet, taking it all in. It seemed as if Anaya had finally met her match.

"We will definitely talk," Mitzi said. Then abruptly: "Ok, Let's see what you got for me." Howard reached for the box on the floor in front of him, opened it and took out a small box. "Oh," said Mitzi. "Gray velvet. Lovely. I like that it matches the couch. Who would have planned that?"

"Here it is," he said, unwrapping the treasure and holding the in the palm of his hand. He realized for the first time that the head of the woman on the silver pendant did, in fact, resemble Anaya Pran.

***

"Would you really want to leave and go work for Mitzi?" Howard asked Anaya as they left the studio.

"Leave your lab?"

"Not only me. The university. Academic life." He had been surprised by the interest Anaya had shown in Mitzi's offer. "All the work you've done to come this far."

"I love science. You know that, Howard. The challenge. Discovering things. There's a creativity in science that's always been exciting to me."

"But…"

"But in academia you can't do what you want. I see that more now. There's the tedium of writing grants, getting everything approved, of being blocked by bureaucrats, by diminishing budgets, by politics and stupidity. Sometimes I feel as if they're squeezing the life out of what I love."

"I understand," Howard said, sighing.

"I mean, you know how much I appreciate the freedom you've given me. And the respect." Approaching the car in the lot behind the studio, Anaya went toward the driver's side without even asking if Howard would like her to drive his own car. "Do you have Lily's address in the GPS?"

"Sure." Betsy had set it up before they left, but in truth he still didn't know how to use it. "What about Vera? Would she want to move to Chicago?"

Vera was with them, deep into this. Howard was not sure he would have even gone as far as finding a delivery system. It was Anaya's energy and Vera's talent that drove the project. Betsy knew what they were doing but Howard had decided against revealing specifics. Was he beginning something that could put his scientific career in jeopardy? The possibility began to gnaw at him.

"Vera is more adventurous than she seems. Tougher too." Anaya was thinking about the parking lot outside the Vet school and Vera's encounter with Royce, the most deserving trial run. As if she were reading his mind, Anaya said it plainly: "You can be finished with this if you want. You won't be involved. It's all good."

She did not tell him about the call she received before the trip from assistant provost Jerry Ketchum, his request to see her. She did not reveal that she had signed off on the permission forms that had come out of the assistant provost's office for the past few weeks without Howard's knowledge. Anaya decided that if her boss didn't know certain things that he would not be held accountable.

She had been cool on the phone with Jerry Ketcham, informing him that she would be out of town until after the July Fourth holiday. She would try and see him when she returned. It was not entirely a lie. Chicago. Then a job interview in New Jersey for a job she no longer thought she wanted. A few days added on to see her family. For whatever he was after, let him wait. Jerry Ketcham. Anaya noted that his name was ironic: "Catch'em. Catch who?" she said to Vera. "That guy has his head so far up his ass that he couldn't see to tie his shoes."

Chapter 15

Looking for trouble

M itzi practiced so many times that she now was deft herself at releasing the safety catch, confident about how close to stand in front of a person who might do harm. Easy enough for even a person of a certain age who would find it difficult using fine motor skills. There is a desire to prove herself. Would she be able now at her age to thwart a real-life attacker?

Mitzi offered to purchase as many pendants as Vera Perez was able to produce. Another shipment was coming soon, another tool in the arsenal of self-protection, incorporated into the lectures offered in the SWIC self-defense classes.

Howard requested that, since his discovery had not undergone clinical trials nor been vetted and approved by the rigorous standards of university scientific procedure, the source of the pendants not be advertised. He also wanted to protect Anaya, who didn't seem to think she needed any protection at all.

As a result, the product was available only through Mitzi Solomon and there evolved a not-so-secret society. It is a kind of code to ask for 'the spray'. Dr. Lerner's name was not mentioned. Nor was the laboratory in Iowa where the mycotoxins were discovered. And where many more spores remaining secured in locked storage. The contaminated feedlot at the Vinton farm had been cleaned up. The pigs there now were happy and thriving.

***

Mitzi arrived home at her building on Lake Shore Drive around seven in the evening. The lobby is a safe sanctuary: ferns and white lilies and light; two pink love seats arranged in a cozy corner.

"Good evening, Mrs. Berg!" The doorman greeted her with genuine warmth. Mitzi had once given him the Taser Strike-Light which he kept on a shelf below the front desk. She is generous with tips at Christmas and has helped his daughter apply for a SWIC scholarship at a community college where she studies criminal justice.

"Hi there, Carl. Nice night."

"Are you in for the rest of the evening then, Mrs. Berg?"

Solomon. Allen. Horowitz. Berg. Too many names for one lifetime. When husband number two, Ira Horowitz, died so young, she went back to Solomon, the name of her birth. Much as she was happily married to Benjamin Berg, Mitzi decided not to change her name again. Although the apartment lists Benjamin and Mitzi Berg: 28A, she did not protest. Pick your fights, she believes.

"No, Carl," Mitzi said. "I'll be going out again in a little while."

"Oh? Would you like the car bought around then?"

"I don't think so."

Carl raised his eyebrows but did not ask. An elegantly dressed couple emerged from the elevator and the man held the door open until Mitzi entered; the smell of gardenia permeated the car when the doors closed.

There are only two apartments on the penthouse floor, the space between them a common area, which Mitzi's sister Grace decorated with gilt mirrors and candelabras. Benjamin calls this vestibule The Liberace Waiting Room. The new residents across the hall are a young couple of indeterminate citizenship who never actually appear to be in residence.

On this Friday evening Benjamin was out of town, driving to a visiting day tomorrow at his grandchildren's camp in Wisconsin, a trip for which Mitzi is thankfully given a pass. Alone in her beautiful home, she has been looking forward to this time. So why did she plan to go out once again?

Looking through her closet, she carefully chooses the perfect clothes and lays them out on her bed: elegant black silk pants, a yellow cashmere sweater set. She goes to her jewelry box and picks out a double strand of Mikimoto white south sea pearls. Then to a shelf for a purse: a Gucci small chain bag in pebbled red leather, whose interior has so many pockets as to render it useless to any woman searching for a lipstick. The purse was a gift from a daughter-in-law. Mitzi suspected it is a knock-off.

Mitzi headed into the kitchen to open a can of Fancy Feast Grilled Chicken and Cheddar, her cat's favorite. Lately, Meow eats only a small portion of what Mitzi lovingly spoons out for her. "Meow, meow, meow," Mitzi coos, massaging the animal's arthritic legs. "You finished already, my baby girl?" Mitzi plucks a bit of moist cat food from the dish, rolling it into a tiny ball between her fingers. "One more bite?" Meow turns her head scornfully, mouth clamped tight. Sighing, Mitzi places the cat down on a fluffy rug next to a window; the lights of the city blink below.

***

Mitzi's mother used to threaten: "You're looking for trouble!" This was a warning to children in a city apartment too small to contain their exuberance, given by a tired mother much annoyed by the tumult. Mitzi herself had never been a stay-at-home mom. She worked her whole adult life at different jobs to support her children; then, with her wealthy second husband, she founded Strong Women in Chicago. Now there were SWIC studios all over the city. Free counseling. A full-time fund-raiser and benefit-planner.

The work was necessary. Why should a public-school teacher like Laura Murphy be afraid every waking day? A girl like Lily Lerner, so good and guileless, subjected to such evil? Sweet, trusting Maryanne tricked into letting a man with phony authority into her car? Mitzi admires brave Alida Sagado and understands how protecting a child can turn a woman powerful beyond her imagination. Even protecting a child who is not your own.

Mitzi's sister Grace was raped when she was about Lily's age. Beaten in the lobby of her apartment house, the first place she lived on her own after college, her first try at independence. The apartment was in a good neighborhood. Her mother always said: Don't look for trouble. Grace would have died had a neighbor not taken the trash out to the incinerator late at night and screamed when she saw legs sticking out from under the stairway. In a coma for a week, Grace remembered nothing. But there were unseen scars.

That was so many years ago. Miriam Ellen Solomon, the feisty oldest child of Nathanial and Esther Solomon, was Chicago-born and -bred. Her father owned a paint store. Her mother was a housewife whose full-time job was pestering her children to better themselves.

Always a rebel, Mitzi dropped out of college and married a handsome acting major who only played the part of a faithful husband. Now in her seventh decade, she is still a rebel, ready for a new adventure.

Mitzi keeps a list, the dates, names, and addresses of the pendants she begins to distribute. She has a feeling Laura Murphy might be using hers soon. As a result of being in the business for so long, Mitzi understands how a restraining order seems to amp up the anger of the abuser, and Laura was afraid.

It is close to nine o'clock by the time Mitzi is ready to leave the apartment. She wears little jewelry. No diamonds. Her pearls are actually very valuable, insured for thousands of dollars, along with her other jewelry. But who mugs someone for pearls? Mitzi has attached the pendant to a key ring she will hold in her hand. Press, then flick, she whispers.

On her way out, she waves to Carl in the lobby who looks puzzled when she tells him that it's a beautiful night and she's going for a walk. He nods: "Have a good evening, then Mrs. Berg. And you be careful, now."

***

The beginning of a Chicago summer, slightly breezy, and so the yellow sweater set is just right. Then she walks and walks. Mitzi can walk for miles.

On a dark side street, Mitzi feels herself on high alert. A group of young guys are sitting on a stoop, two drinking from cans in paper bags. They watch the older white woman in cashmere and pearls walk by, so out of her element, it's as if they are seeing an exotic tropical fish swimming down the sidewalk. "Evening, Ma'am," one of them says, politely. Mitzi nods and walks on.

Hours later, exhausted, disappointed, relieved, her feet hurting, she calls an Uber and within minutes a woman in a white Mazda pulls up to the curb. Mitzi, used to a car service, gets in the back seat and breathes a sigh of relief. The young driver is chatty, friendly, offering a bottle of water. "Glad I was right in this area. I bring home a nurse from the hospital, she's a regular customer of mine, after her shift. But you shouldn't be walking around here by yourself at night.

Mitzi asks: "Don't you ever worry, having strangers come into your car every night?"

The woman shrugs. A bright sun tattooed on the back of her neck scrunches into a yellow line. "Nah. I've only had a few bad customers. Mostly drunks. I hate when they throw up in my car."

"Of course," Mitzi says. "That's disgusting!"

The driver catches Mitzi's eye in the rear-view mirror. "Late on the weekends. That's when the trouble begins. But I'm usually home before midnight. Like Cinderella." She adds: "Why are you out, walking around by yourself so late? I mean, maybe it's none of my business. Sorry."

"That's all right," Mitzi says. Why indeed. An old lady with her Gucci and pearls, a silver pendant on a key chain held in her right hand. Flick. Then press. She has practiced so many times with the dummy, both alone and demonstrating for the class. Did she really believe she was going to use it tonight? Or, like her mother used to say, was she just looking for trouble?

At home, in front of her apartment house, Mitzi gives the Uber driver a generous tip and then asks her to stay for a few minutes just to talk. There is something she wants to give her.

Chapter 16

Save the Date

"Here it is," Laura says, holding the silver pendant in the palm of her hand. It is attached to a key chain, although there are no keys on the sturdy chain. "Mitzi gave it to me after our last class."

The others lean in to see. Anyone looking over at the group would think Laura was someone recently engaged whose friends are craning their necks to admire her diamond. The four of them—Lily, Laura, Maryanne, Alida—are sitting together in a coffee shop on a rainy evening.

The police have not found Lily's attacker. Nor Maryanne's rapist. Nor the man who came after Alida Salgado with a knife in the playground as the toddler cried alone in his swing. Laura Murphy is the only one with an ongoing story. And also the only one who knows the identity of her perpetrator.

Laura has taken herself off all social media, but George Murphy continues in his quest. The restraining order gives her no solace. But after meeting with Mitzi, she feels strengthened in the companionship of these like-minded new friends. The story of George Murphy, an improbable stalker, fascinates the other three and is a topic for much discussion.

"It's really so pretty. Like a piece of jewelry." Maryanne, a dainty eater, finishes her lemon cake, slowly savoring the last bite. "I love it!"

"Me, too," Lily says. "I know that the jeweler wasn't happy at first with the design of the woman's head."

"Really?" Alida says. "I think it's perfect. Perfect!"

"Well, maybe the designer thought it was too, you know… realistic." Lily is thinking of Vera Perez. "Like: here's an angry woman."

"So angry! And she's gonna make you sooo sick," Alida says. "That's what I like."

The women laugh.

"And every piece is the same?" Maryanne asks.

"Yes. It's actually a mold." Lily is the only one besides Laura who has her own pendant, although they have all practiced as Mitzi demonstrated in class. There is a safety feature to prevent someone from accidentally activating a release. A catch has to be flicked and then pressed. For practice, the women in the class chanted: flick, then press.

"Here's mine." Lily takes her piece out of a backpack and puts it around her neck. The pendant is on a long, silver chain. "I wanted to have it totally accessible."

"Yeah, good idea," Maryanne says, her eyes growing wide. In truth she is a little scared. She wonders if she would ever be calm—or brave—enough to use it.

"Most of the pendants are given out already. And Mitzi kept one for herself," Lily says. "But more are ordered. They'll be coming soon." Vera Perez is working over-time. "And don't forget. Each piece after it's used, can be refilled."

Alida turns to Laura. "So what are you planning to do?"

It is Lily who suggests that Laura set up a meeting with George Murphy as "a way to say goodbye."

Maryanne gasps and puts her hand over her mouth, like a damsel in distress in an old movie.

"We'll all be there," Lily says decisively. Then to Laura: "We'll cover for you."

Cover for you. It seems funny that she is using that phrase. For all of them, the police have not been successful. The last time Lily met Officer Lois Lane from the Chicago police department assigned to the case she learned again: Nothing. Nothing. Nothing. The lines around her neck have healed. Lily is no longer dreaming of metal doors closing behind her, trapped in cubicles with an angry man who smells like garbage. She is strong.

The four women take out their phones, check calendars, and save the date.

***

What happens the following week is unexpected. Lily is talking on the phone to her sister as she walks up Lawrence Avenue to Mariano's to meet her girl gang: Laura, Maryanne, and Alida. They are going to be there as support. This is the day that Laura has arranged to meet her stalker.

"So you think you're going to stay in Chicago?" Megan asks. "Dad is ok with that?"

"He's going to worry no matter where we live," Lily says. He just worries all the time. He's always been a compulsive worrier.

"True. When we were kids and going anywhere on our own? He always thought we'd be kidnapped or something. And now, after what happened to you? I think he's still sort of a mess."

"That makes me feel terrible," Lily says.

"Hey, it's not your fault what happened. Don't take that one on, too. He'll be all right."

A guy with hipster stubble is standing in front of a truck idling in a loading zone, smoking a cigarette with lazy insolence. He looks Lily up and down as she approaches, then smirks when she meets his gaze. The pendant around her neck bolsters her self-confidence.

"Hi there," he says slowly. Lily does not answer but neither does she avert her gaze. If he had added "Nice day" or "How ya doing?" she would not respond. She would have walked on, continuing the conversation with her sister. Instead, with only a few feet separating them on the sidewalk, he asks in a fairly conversational tone: "So baby, how'd you like to sit on my face?"

Lily stops in her tracks, facing him, her shoulders squared. He blinks in surprise. "No, I wouldn't," she says evenly.

"Lily? Who are you talking to?" Megan asks.

Taking a step closer, Lily continues to stare him down. An older man sitting in the passenger's side of the truck is also smoking a cigarette, the window open on his side. He laughs and shakes his head. "Hank, what you starting up for, man?"

Lily begins to shout: "Do you know how I feel when you say that to me?" Her voice rises again: "Do you know how I feel when I hear that? Do you? Do you?" Saying this, she steps close so that the man rears back, rocking against the curb.

"Whoa!" He holds up his hand, a barrier against her rage. "Hey, calm down, lady, ok?"

"Lily who is that?" Megan asks. "What's happening?"

"Yeah. Hold on, don't hang up." Lily says to her sister. Then turns back to the man. "When you say something like that," she begins, yelling so loudly that others walking along the sidewalk stare. Spittle flies out of her mouth as she screams in his face. "When you say that—when you ask me if I want to sit on your face," she repeats, adding, at the very top of her voice register: "It makes me…it makes me want to vomit!" There is emphasis and some pantomime on the last word. Lily sticks out her tongue and pretends to wretch. Enjoying the appearance at least of crazy, she goes on. "Pervert! Pervert! Pervert!"

"LILY?"

The guy in the truck throws his cigarette in the street. "Hank, get in the truck," he says. He isn't laughing any longer. "Come on. Let's go," he says, raising his window.

The younger man—Hank—appears shaken. "Hey, I'm sorry," he says finally. "Ok?" He keeps his eyes locked on Lily but starts walking backward, feeling with his hand along the side of the vehicle. "Take it easy," he says.

"Men like you make me want to scream!" Lily said, holding her phone aloft as if to hit him. And then, scream she does. A mom with toddlers in a double stroller walks by, giving Lily a wide berth. The street seems quiet. The light on the corner flashes the pedestrian WALK sign.

"Lily? Lily? What's happening?" Megan is yelling into the phone. "Are you all right? Answer me."

Lily stands there and watches as the truck pulls away into the traffic. "Nothing, Meggy. I'm okay. Just some creep on the street. I told him off."

"Oh my god, sure sounds like you did."

***

Lily is only a few minutes late, but she sprints the last three blocks, comes into Mariano's, and sees Alida at a corner table waving to her. Maryanne and Laura have not yet arrived. The upscale grocery is new, catering to the changing demographic of families who want to live in this gentrifying part of the city. Despite Chicago's reputation as dangerous, it is also a place of coveted neighborhoods. The family whom Alida works for recently completed a million-dollar renovation on a home within walking distance to the store. Alida lives in the finished basement with her own kitchenette, bathroom, and cable TV. She has never lived in a place so nice. The family is very good to her, and she adores the toddler she has cared for since he was a newborn. In her country Alida was the youngest girl, doted upon by older siblings, and she had never had the opportunity to be the caregiver.

Today, sitting next to Alida in a stroller is her charge, a curly-haired toddler in a highchair, gumming a biscotti. "Say hello, Simon."

"Hola," the boy says.

"Hola yourself," Lily says, catching her breath. "Does he speak Spanish?"

"Agua," says the boy, holding up a red sippy cup.

"That's about it," Alida tells her. "We're working on numbers, too." She turns to him: "Uno, dos, tres..."

"I'm going to get some coffee," Lily says, wiping her brow. The line is slow. When Lily returns to the table, Laura and Maryanne are there, cooing and clucking, making a fuss over the little boy who looks from one to the other, delighted to be the center of attention.

"You are the cutest baby. I could eat you up, I love you so," Maryanne says, mixing together Maurice Sendak with her own longings. She takes his sticky hand, pretending to eat him. "Nummmmy, num num." Simon giggles, coyly hiding his face in his shoulder. "Gimme your paw. Gimme that little paw." Maryanne tickles a palm.

Laura is purposefully unrecognizable, wearing a baggy, blue work shirt, no make-up, and square, black glasses; her curly auburn hair is concealed under a ball cap. "Travelling incognito?" Lily asks.

"Travel how? What does that mean?" Alida asks. "Incognito?"

"Like in disguise," Lily tells her. "So she won't be recognized."

"Oh, I never knew what that meant, either," Maryanne says. "I've heard that word before. Good to know."

"Until he gets close," Lily says. "George won't know who you are. Even then he might not. Maybe until you speak. Hey, are those real glasses?"

"Yeah. I didn't put in my contact lenses." Laura looks at her phone. "He'll be coming down the block in like ten minutes." She takes off her hat and tucks up her hair again, making sure every strand is covered. "God, I'm so nervous. My heart is pounding."

Incognito. This was Lily's idea. Maybe George's running into his unrequited love on the street, and seeing her now, he might realize that she is not so special. She can be anyone. Lily read this in an article online about dealing with stalkers.

"It's cool. Don't be nervous. You'll have us as backup," Lily says. Then they all laugh. "I know. Backup. That just sounded ridiculous, didn't it? What are we, a SWAT team?"

"A SWIC team," says Maryanne who loves being part of the group. All her life, she was the quiet one in the back of class, not a stellar student, but she never gave the teacher any trouble. And here she was now, at a table with the popular girls.

Outside Mariano's, stationing themselves in such a way that they won't appear to be together, all will have a clear view as George Murphy comes up the block. Phones are convenient props. Lily and Maryanne stand strategically apart from Laura and pretend to be engrossed in whatever is on their screens. There is no recognition of the other. Alida sits on a bench in front of the store, Simon in the stroller by her side; her job is to record the interaction on her phone.

Laura again voices her hesitation. "What if he doesn't show up today?"

"We'll come back tomorrow," Maryanne says. "I can get off work early again."

"He'll show," Lily says with confidence. Then, turning to Laura: "You're ready."

***

George Murphy, leaving the Social Security Administration building where he has a job as a disability benefits specialist, will be out by 4:45. Promptly. George's work is bureaucratic and predictable: filling out forms, correspondence, and answering questions from anxious callers about their entitlements. He has worked in this same job for almost a decade. Except for stalking Laura, his other routines are unremarkable. Since his mother died the year before, George walks after work the few blocks east to pick up a ready-made dinner at Mariano's grocery, usually meatloaf or chicken pot pie.

"That's him." Laura spies George Murphy half a block away. She is surprised at his unusual gait, a shuffle more than a walk, shoulders slumped, defeated. The teacher in her wants to instruct: stand tall, pick up your feet. Laura is embarrassed in front of her friends that she has actually gone out with this man, this schlumpy, sad sack of a stalker. In the movies, a dangerous man, a person you might have to run from, often has something of a sexual cachet.

The sidewalk is crowded outside of Mariano's, people coming into the store, like George, grocery shopping after work. Laura watches as he waits at the light, then crosses in a throng of people. "There are too many people around," she whispers urgently to Lily. "I don't know if this is going to work."

It's ok," Lily assures her. "You're going to talk to him. Face to face. But first act as if you're surprised to see him."

"Oh, I'm so nervous."

"Deep breath," Lily says, coaching her. "Deep breath."

On her corner, Maryanne is taking her own deep breath, her lips pursing with each exhale. Ready with her phone, Alida sits with little Simon on a bench near the front entrance of the store, offering him animal crackers.

As George comes toward them, Laura is close enough to examine him with some clarity. He is odd looking. Not ordinary as she first thought. There is something prim about the way he holds himself; the thinning hair on top of his head is sprayed into an unyielding comb-over. She recalls how he cut his pizza into child-size bites and the fastidious use of his napkin, dabbing after almost every bite. Why does she remember this now?

"George?" Suddenly, she calls out to him in such a commanding voice that he startles. He stops. Blinking. Not sure who is calling his name. "Why George Murphy, hey there." Laura tries to sound—as she has practiced under Lily's tutelage—surprised, confident, casual.

"Yes?" he says hesitantly. Apparently, the ploy works. He does not even recognize Laura. His beloved. He stands there, puzzled. All these weeks of stalking and he doesn't know who she is. Of course, he doesn't know who she is. In his demented mind, she is his other half, his perfect mate, the object of his affection. The photos he has seen of her on Facebook (before she dropped out of all social media) are of a pretty, smiling woman with a head full of reddish curls. The purpose of today's interaction, with coaching from Mitzi and Lily, is not so much to scare him off, but to demystify the connection he has with her.

"Hi, George. It's Laura." She adds, her voice catching, but still strong. "You remember me?" She has practiced a wide, open-mouthed smile, her tongue out as if she is surprising someone at a birthday party. Then madly, she scratches her chest as if she has fleas. This too, is practiced.

"Hi. What are you doing here?" he asks. Pausing: "Laura." His voice cracks, like a teenager.

"Oh, you know, shopping for groceries. It's a great store, don't you think? A little expensive. But you know, quality counts. Isn't that what they say? What you put into your body is just as important as what comes out. Haha. That's a joke. I like the potato casserole here. But too much of it, I guess." She puts a hand to her stomach. "I must've gained at least ten pounds since I saw you last…" Playing this part, she is manic, almost gleeful, rubbing her stomach, scratching her face, touching herself all over, and laughing. Under her baggy work shirt, she is padded, covered by a grey tee shirt, also several sizes too large. She continues scratching her chest. Then, like a monkey, an armpit.

George stands, dumbstruck at this interaction.

Confidence builds when she gets going with the charade. Years of being in front of a classroom, reading stories to children, and acting things out, help in this role.

Laura continues with fast talk. She tells him she's had the same boyfriend. Remember Jimmy? She told him all about Jimmy, didn't she? Does George want to meet him? She's having a party. A pizza party. Does George like parties? She knows he likes pizza. Ha, ha, ha! Remember once they went out for pizza? Pepperoni. She prefers mushroom. Does he still cut up his pizza with a knife and fork? She likes to eat hers by picking up the slice. But that's what makes menus. Or horse-racing. What's that expression anyway? Or—haha—pizza.

The blather continues until she is interrupted. "I'm sorry…" George begins, but she never gets to hear what he is sorry about.

"Oh, that's all right. I'm sorry too," she replies, talking over him.

"You know, some things work out for the best. Some things just can make you sick, you know?" Her anger is rekindled at what he has done, despite how pathetic he seems standing before her. This poor schmuck becomes again her dangerous predator. She has anger too about the money she spent on a private detective to follow him, to find out his habits. Where he shops when he heads home after work. She is a school teacher and this was money she could really use, money she had been saving for a down payment on a house. Fuck you, she thinks but does not say aloud. From someplace deep inside her, Laura musters up the courage to direct her hand toward his face.

***

Perhaps George Murphy thought she was going to slap him, this strange woman whom he loved so. He takes a step back and starts to block his face with his forearm. Flick. Laura takes a deep, deep breath, holds it, and also steps back, but a beat later than she practiced in class. Then press.

It works. It really works. She watches George's face, surprise, turning very quickly to confusion as the first spasm hits so suddenly. She watches as George throws up in one violent heave, soiling not only himself but spraying her on the front of her work shirt. Shit. Shit. She backs away yelling: "Oh, my god!" Oblivious to her dismay, George groans, curling into himself and falling to his knees on the hard pavement outside the supermarket. A shopper walks by, covering her mouth.

Alida comes to the rescue and leads Laura to the bench, offering burp cloths and wet wipes from the diaper bag. "Pobrecita, oh dear, oh dear." Then Alida begins a tirade directed at George who is still on the ground: "What's the matter with you? You are disgusting. If you sick, go to the street like a dog, not dirty up some poor girl with your filth!"

Chapter 17

July 4ᵗʰ Independence Day

The Fourth of July was not one of Howard's favorite holidays. Fireworks were dangerous. When he was a boy, he saw a teenager at Jones Beach get his fingers blown off reaching into the sand to retrieve a cherry bomb that he believed was a dud. Then there were the parades and the patriotic militarism that always made Howard feel lonely.

Later, with a family of his own, there was the manly expectation to barbecue, about which he was not confident. When he and Betsy were first married, he started the grill with charcoals and lighter fluid—again dangerous—and then, even with the purchase of a gas grill, there was the timing; it was presumed that he knew when hamburgers would be ready, but in truth, he did not.

So, there he was with Betsy, happy in Anaya's and Vera's backyard, eating Indian food, roasted eggplant and classic tandoori chicken wings on the grill, expertly tended to by Anaya who was drinking beer after beer and still confident about the timing of her meal.

Howard and Betsy were the oldest guests, but he felt enlivened to be in the company of so many bright young artists, lesbians, and international graduate students. Vera had set up a croquet set, and the ball made a satisfying thwack as it was hit across the lawn. Some Chinese graduate students stood off in a corner talking in their own language, louder than they ever did at the university.

Some of those in attendance knew that Dr. Howard Lerner had recently received an award for his distinguished scholarship in Porcine Stress Syndrome (PSS). The year before, he and Anaya had isolated the recessive gene that caused malignant hyperthermia in the exudative muscle of pigs. Someone in the scientific community suggested that perhaps the specific gene might even be named for Dr. Lerner.

In a couple of weeks, he and Betsy would be taking a vacation, going to Europe following Howard's award ceremony at the European Pig Innovation Group (EUPIG) in Brussels. Howard was a rock star in the world of swine. But no one in the pig-producing countries in Europe had heard anything about Howard's other significant discovery. And perhaps it would be best that they never did.

***

It was hot but with surprisingly little humidity and few mosquitoes for a July evening in Iowa. The night was beautiful. Maple trees lined the backyard of Anaya and Vera's modest rental, so the busy road behind the house was not even visible. Daylilies flamed orange in front of the trees. The guests had brought over drinks and desserts: lots of beer, pitchers of white Sangria, and cupcakes with red, white, and blue sprinkles; Betsy made a strawberry cheesecake and decorated it with tiny American flags. Two of the graduate couples had brought their babies.

"Love the food, babe," Vera said, biting into chunks of slow-roasted lamb, marinated in a puree of tomatoes, onions, turmeric, and ginger. Anaya's famous fried potato snacks were served on the side. Anaya had spread out a buffet of Indian specialties on a picnic table, effortlessly arranging everything to be ready at the same time.

"Love you, babe," Anaya responded kissing Vera full on the lips.

"You're a little drunk," Vera said.

"More than a little." Anaya chugged the last of her Kalyani Black Label, an Indian beer she bought at the international grocery. "I'm drunk on power." She raised a fist over her head and cheered: "Strong Women in…" she stopped and laughed heartily: "wherever!" She gave another whoop-whoop for good measure.

The croquet players looked up, mallets in the air. An infant in her car seat awoke and began to cry, "It's ok. You don't have to yell, hon," Vera said to Anaya.

"You…" Anaya looked deeply into Vera's eyes: "You are my hero. My heroine. Whatever. You are the one who made it all happen."

Vera Perez had been working pretty much nonstop creating specially ordered jewelry. Mitzi Solomon was paying her and doling out the pendants free of charge. In the meantime, Vera was making a very nice living indeed. She and Anaya had bought a new car and some expensive camping gear. If Anaya took up Mitzi on her offer to work at SWIC, they would be living in Chicago—rent free—in one of the lofts that Mitzi owned in the West Loop, and Vera would have her own artist studio. Vera loved the idea but thought that Anaya would be giving up too much, having come this far in her academic career.

"I'd like to make a toast," Anaya said suddenly, holding up a barbecue fork against a backyard sculpture that also served as a gong. "Toast! Quiet! Toast!" She banged the sculpture, three metal rings of concentric circles, made by someone in Vera's art collective. "Listen up! Listen up, you all!"

Vera caught Howard's eye, sending a quizzical glance.

"To my wonderful, creative wife, Vera, whose art makes women strong and brave," Anaya proclaimed, hitting the gong again.

"And to my mentor and inspiration, Dr. Howard Lerner, whose academic brilliance gave women a special gift: independence from fear!" Gong!

"And to America, the land of opportunity, the home of the free and land of the brave!" She hit the gong three or four times before Vera took away the barbecue fork. No one knew exactly what Anaya meant by all the references—or seemed to care. Anaya's toast sounded inspirational and patriotic, so those holding a glass aloft, cheered and drank up. When it got really dark, the party headed out to see the city fireworks sponsored by the Jaycees.

***

The Fourth of July was Joyce Corning's favorite family holiday. There was not the tension of Christmas, deciding what gifts to buy and how much to spend. The grandchildren already had so many expensive electronics and fancy gadgets. The Corning's Christmas of years past, when her own girls were young, seemed simpler and more spiritual. But maybe that was nostalgia. Maybe Joyce only remembered the past as a less complicated time. She also liked Thanksgiving, but that entailed so much work. Cooking and clean-up (although her girls did help), the television blaring football, the grandkids over-fed and cranky about being cooped up indoors.

July Fourth was paper plates and corn on the cob; Larry was with his two sons-in-law at the barbecue pit he built by himself one summer; everyone liked burgers and hot dogs. Her daughters brought sides dishes of slaw and potato salad. And still pie. Lots of pies. All the Corning women made exceptional pies. Except banana cream, which wasn't a big favorite with anyone except Royce. And now no one had to worry about that any longer.

Royce was not in attendance this Fourth of July, and everyone seemed just fine with that. Even Caroline, who was relaxed for once, not tense about whether Royce would drink too much and get nasty. Nasty always followed drunk with Royce.

It made Joyce sad that one of her daughters was now a divorcee, and her youngest grandchild would be one of those children who came from a broken home, but Joyce was growing accustomed to that, practiced in telling her church friends that her daughter was getting divorced and living with them again.

But even this change in her home life did not preoccupy Joyce as much as the unusual things going on at work. She tried to tell Larry about it, but he didn't exactly understand. For one thing, Vera Perez had been coming to the lab frequently. Going into Dr. Lerner's lab. Joyce raised the question to her husband: "Why was that?"

Sometimes Larry would say "Vera?" and look puzzled when he was reminded that Vera was Anaya's wife. And yes, Anaya was married to a woman. Joyce was proud that she was able to say wife so casually, the way Anaya herself did all the time.

Now sitting with Caroline on a backyard glider, they watched Nora play with her older cousins in the creek where

Larry had circled boulders together to make a wading pool. "There's something going on. I don't know what they're working on, but it does seem awfully hush-hush," Joyce said. "And Anaya's doing some of the paperwork that I usually do."

There was a farm over the hill and a development of new houses which could be viewed from the Corning's front porch, but the backyard was just about as it had been a hundred years ago. Pine trees. Wildflowers along the edge of prairie grasses. A gentle creek where the kids caught frogs. The deer were a problem. But watching them from the kitchen window as they walked gracefully through the timber was also a blessing.

"Mom, there's always government papers that you have to sign off on. You've complained about the regulations before," Caroline said. "Why is this different?"

"Well, Dr. Lerner always depends on me to check everything before we sign and remind him of the due dates on his projects. That's just it. I'm not sure what his last project was about. I wasn't privy to any information." Joyce sounded almost huffy about it.

"This pie is my favorite," Caroline said, "Blueberry lemon. Yum." She scraped the empty plate with her fork. "Did you make this one, Mom?"

Joyce nodded. "Anaya, she's in charge of the project. Dr. Lerner told me to go to her if I had questions. But questions about what exactly?"

Caroline stopped, her plastic fork in midair. "Mother, are you jealous?"

"Why would I be jealous?"

"Of Anaya?"

Joyce thought about it. She was not someone who got either easily offended or jealous. "No, I don't think I am. We've worked together before: Dr. Lerner and Anaya and me." She paused: "All three of us. I mean, Anaya's always been willful. But she's very smart. And Dr. Lerner has always given her responsibilities that he never gave the other post-docs. But no," Joyce shook her head. "We work together well."

"So what is it, then?" Caroline asked

Joyce shrugged, searching to find the words for her feelings of unease. "I kind of feel left out of things lately," she confessed. She found Caroline was so much easier to talk to since Royce was no longer in the picture.

"Left out?" Caroline asked.

"Maybe a little. I really don't understand this latest project. I mean, seems like they're done with it. But they've not said anything about presenting or publishing new research. Or if there's grant money involved." Joyce stopped and shook her head: "Or what Vera, you know, Anaya's wife, has to do with it. Vera's not a scientist. She's an artist. A jewelry maker. It's not as if she's coming in all the time to meet Anaya for lunch. I don't know. And Anaya has taken it upon herself to sign the paperwork without running it by me. It all seems kind of unusual. Like they're working on something that they want to keep secret…"

Caroline's eyes got big. "Well, mom, do you think they're spies?"

"Caroline, don't be ridiculous." Joyce finished off a slice of watermelon, saving the rind for Larry's compost. "I suppose I should be grateful to have a little less work at this point in my life before I retire. Not concern myself with all the forms filled out each time we buy a box of paperclips." She sighed, looking over the grandchildren splashing in the water, the older ones making a loving fuss over little Nora. "It's just peculiar. That's all I'm saying."

***

The Fourth of July can be an uneasy holiday in Chicago; the sound of fireworks on a hot summer night is easily confused with gunfire. Of course, in Chicago, it sometimes is gunfire. But Mitzi Solomon was hosting a party on the roof of her building and the fireworks would be seen from a safe height.

Her wealthy friends had gone to their lake houses for the long weekend; Benjamin and Mitzi's kids were home in suburbia with families. This party was for SWIC teachers and students, a special celebration in honor of America's independence and Mitzi's new project. Everyone at the party knew someone—or at least someone who knew someone—who made use of the—what were they calling it? They asked: Have you heard about that… You know. Used for self-defense. Most people didn't know how exactly it worked. A spray. But, yes, it worked.

"Sweetie, girls. My sweetie girls," Mitzi said, approaching Lily, Maryanne, and Laura. Laura did not mind being called a sweetie girl by Mitzi. Nor did politically correct Lily object to Mitzi's use of Spanglish when asked: "Where's your amiga?" Alida was in Colorado with Simon and his family for the holiday.

"How's the food?" Mitzi asked.

"So good," said Laura. "Really delicious." Laura had lost weight since the travails with George Murphy. But she has heard nothing from him. Nothing. The SWIC offensive worked. Or maybe seeing her up close and not the girl of his dreams shook George Murphy out of his fantasy. Laura took another helping of coconut shrimp, fried to perfection and dipped in a honey glaze which was being offered around by one of the smiling, young servers.

Laura has not gone on another dating site. And declined even when a friend wanted to fix her up with a co-worker. Recently she found that she didn't really mind being alone. The summer would be a time of rest and recuperation. Perhaps she would become one of those kindly, old-maid school teachers, someone who asserted that the kids she taught were her family.

She smiled now, thinking of her kids. Even though it was July, she was looking to go back to her classroom. To the children. The kindergartners would be moving up, and she wondered which one of them would be in her class. Sometimes a mom would request Laura Murphy for their first grader. The school was not supposed to honor those requests but sometimes did. Ms. Murphy was known for her kindness, for her special way with even the most troubled child. Kindergartners came in as babies, some not even knowing their colors, unable to spell their names. By the end of first grade, most were reader-ready, even the slowest ones who showed little promise.

"Yummy." Maryanne was relishing a second helping of corn soufflé served in a tiny cup. "I want this recipe."

"I don't think this caterer gives out his recipes," Mitzi said. "Not that anyone who hires these fancy-pants caterers does any cooking themselves."

"I love to cook," Maryanne said. "And eat." Maryanne owned a pendant but then loaned it to a woman who used to work with her at the post office, a sad woman who was in an abusive relationship, as far as Maryanne could tell, although she still couldn't tell much. Even with all she had gone through and her new smart friends, Maryanne remained innocent. "This is so pretty up here," she said looking out from Mitzi's balcony. "It's like a fairyland."

"Do you?" Lily asked Mitzi. "Cook?" They were friends, seeing each other at least three or four times a week the last few months. But although Lily knew and admired much about Mitzi, her strength and spirit, her values—Lily didn't know much about the life she had away from her passion for SWIC and the women there.

Mitzi looked thoughtful. "I used to. Husband number two. My Ira. He loved my brisket." She smiled. "Easy. Lipton's onion soup mix," She said quietly, giving out the secret.

Mitzi was struck by the sense of longing she felt after all these years, just saying his name. My Ira. Not that number three, Benjamin Berg, wasn't perfectly nice and politically well-suited. And yes, she cared deeply for him, grateful especially at this time of her life. Two out of three isn't bad, Mitzi would say, referring to her husbands. Lucky in love was sometimes lucky enough.

She had been married to Benjamin Berg for more than two decades. Longer than her first and second marriages combined. Years passed so quickly these days, like calendar pages flipping to show time gone by in old movies. "What year was that?" Mitzi and Benjamin often ask each other, referring to vacations, weddings, and dinner parties. Then they did the math. Twenty years ago sometimes seems like recent history. She couldn't remember who was in the movie they saw a few months before, but she could remember all the words to the songs from her teenage years. She missed the girl groups: Martha and the Vandellas. The Ronettes, The Supremes.

July Fourth so many decades ago, there was a war whose purpose and reason made sharp divisions across the country, just like today. Sons did not speak to fathers. Generations marched; some avoided the draft any way they could; others went off to fight; mothers cried no matter what. Families were torn asunder. Race riots. Plane hi-jackings. Bombs made in basements by revolutionaries, white kids who had grown up in the suburbs. Those were neither better nor simpler times.

In Mitzi and Benjamin's life these days there was more sickness, more deaths. Benjamin was older than she, but still in pretty good shape. But the clock was ticking. She tried to acknowledge gratitude in a found moment of every single day.

At this stage of life, there was always loss. More days than they cared to count, she and Benjamin were going to funerals and paying respect at shivas. She herself was feeling a little run down, attributing this to lack of sleep. Now she was often up in the night, her mind spinning with excitement about the project.

Mitzi had a cough that was keeping her awake, too. A cough coming from a place deep, deep down. Sometimes in the night, she coughed so hard, her ribs hurt. When she felt the cough coming on, she moved to the spare bedroom so as not to wake Benjamin. He wanted her to see a doctor, but she dismissed his fears. A summer cold had turned into a tickly cough that sometimes spiraled out of control. Lots of people had colds this July. She didn't have time for doctors and would not admit to him that sometimes she was afraid.

The view from the roof was stunning. A seat on top of the world. A loud explosion, then color. "Oohhh. Here it comes," Maryanne said as the fireworks began. Everyone on the roof looked up across the water. The first round exploded in the night sky, and strings of colored jewels slowly floated and disappeared into the lake; cascade after cascade of white diamonds, red rubies, and white pearls. "It's like a fairyland," Maryanne repeated. And everyone agreed that it was.

***

On the Fourth of July, Vice Provost for Academic Research Jerry Ketcham sat in his cool basement playing a video game, eating Doritos, and drinking a beer out of a frosty mug. He knew when the phone rang that it would be his wife calling from the lake and he debated not answering, but since he told her that he was staying home because he was sick with this terrible cold and he certainly did not want to infect her entire family on their summer vacation, he finally he answered on the fifth ring. "Hi Doreen," he said, sniffling.

"Where were you?" she asked.

"Where was I?"

"I mean it took you a while to answer; were you taking a nap?"

"No," he said simply. "I was in the bathroom," he said. The woman would not stop until he offered a suitable excuse.

"How are you feeling?"

"Not so good," he said, coughing, which began just for show and then developed into something authentic.

"I'm sorry, hon. We all do miss you," Doreen said.

He doubted that this was the case. Doreen was at the lake house she owned with her two sisters. When the three women were together, the inane chatter was nonstop, and he was annoyed by her more than usual.

The summer house was a modest A-frame on one of the many lakes in Minnesota, handed down to Doreen and her older sisters, willed to the three of them after their parents had died with the stipulation that the house would remain shared in the family for at least two additional generations. One generation now had their own additions, some of whom camped on the property, making the last decade of July Fourth family reunions filled with noisy young children and, for Jerry, almost intolerable. He was happy to use the excuse of a summer cold, which possibly was his allergies acting up as they usually did every summer. "I bet the weather is nice up there," Jerry said.

"Oh, it's been a beautiful weekend. Just right. A good breeze in the evening when we're all sitting out on the deck, the mosquitoes don't seem so bad this year, but Diane bought these candles anyway and we put them all around on the deck when we ate out there."

"Did the kids water ski?" Jerry and Doreen had married late in life and their own girls were teenagers, sullen and dismissive. Doreen's sisters were already grandparents. Doreen went on for a while about how there weren't enough life vests for them to use and take out both boats and how they were about to go into town but then LaMonte Collins, their neighbor's father-in-law, had two extra in the trunk of his car that he brought over... At the end of the life-jacket story, Doreen asked Jerry if he was drinking enough liquids, just as he was getting up from his chair to open another beer.

"Miss you, hon," Doreen said before they hung up. Jerry told her to enjoy herself, assuring her that he'd be fine alone for the next few days. He went back to his video game, where he was involved in building a new civilization by controlling the troops under his command, but the phone call had interrupted his momentum.

He was bothered by a recent phone conversation with that Indian woman who worked with Howard Lerner in veterinary pathology. The nerve of her. The nerve! Speaking to him as if his request to meet was putting her out, checking her calendar to see when would be convenient for her, saying she'd have to get back to him. He wanted to reprimand her then and there, but that was not his managerial style. He prided himself on equanimity. And careful attention to detail. Of course, one had to be careful these days when suspecting irregularities. Anaya Pran was a woman. And an ethnic minority. And, he suspected, a homosexual. The trifecta. Certainly, he should be careful about even the whiff of impropriety in any accusation he made.

He suspected that something was going on in that lab. But what? He was not sure that Dr. Lerner himself knew entirely what was happening. Jerry Ketcham respected Howard. Now, that man was a solid scientist who played by the rules. The rules. Dr. Lerner brought in a lot of grant money, even in these fiscally conservative times. Jerry checked and rechecked the forms that had been sent over the past six weeks, but it seemed that neither Dr. Lerner nor his secretary, Joyce Corning, signed off on any of the paperwork requested by the IACUC.

Feeling a tightening in his chest, Jerry Ketchum swallowed some Tums and followed with a beer chaser. He didn't trust that Indian woman, who thought she was so great, acting as if she were Dr. Lerner's partner rather than a graduate student. Ketchum thought it presumptuous, to take advantage of a world-renowned scientist and perhaps besmirch the reputation of this fine research institution. No, he didn't trust that Indian woman at all.

Chapter 18

Six Chicago Stories
Hot Time, Summer In the City

How easy it is for something to catch fire. Who could keep up? There wasn't advertising. Nothing was for sale. Yet that unusual silver pendant was the most coveted of summer accessories. There were pictures on social media of women having drinks with friends, a hand held aloft against a cheek, holding an ornate piece of silver jewelry, and the head of a frighening woman, her mouth a wide howl.

Homicide rates for Chicago remained stable—which is to say, unacceptable for a civilized country. After the July Fourth weekend, there were more than one hundred gun fatalities. It was not established that there were also more than one hundred incidents of foiled attacks initiated by women who were cautious and wily. A few of the women were feminist adventurers, pioneers in the art of self-defense. Perhaps some of the men did not deserve what they got following a misogynist slur, but some women had just simply had enough.

Police officer Lois Lane heard the rumors and initially discounted them—as rumors. There were rape cases to investigate and the victim's unit was still busy, with files open, and DNA samples in the labs. So many crimes were still unsolved. Yes, Officer Lane heard rumbles, and stories coming out of the women's self-defense classes at SWIC. There was something about a new product in the self-defense arsenal, able to temporarily incapacitate any aggressor. There were stories of women who had used it. Was it just a rumor? Officer Lane didn't hear all of the details, but she was certainly paying attention.

One night she followed a call to a parking garage outside Rush Memorial Hospital. An emergency room nurse named Sandra Voycovitz had finished her shift and was headed home when she was accosted by a man with a gun. Officer Lane was on duty nearby, got to the scene, and saw a man groaning on the concrete floor of the parking lot.

The suspect's name was Jamaal La Crosse. He was a repeat offender in his middle thirties, in and out of prison since he was an adolescent. Mostly drug offenses, burglary, and car theft. Never for anything as serious as rape.

The victim, Sandra Voycovitz, was not hurt. In fact, she had confiscated a gun and handed it over to Officer Lane when she arrived at the scene. "Body fluids," the nurse said matter-of-factly, looking at the mess on the ground. This story was just one of the many that came to Lois Lane's attention that hot Chicago summer. What was that old line about being eight million stories in the naked city? That was New York. This was Chicago. These are six of them.

1. Julia Roberts: Pretty Woman

Julia remembered how she ached down there. How in the morning there was blood, and it burned when she peed. Inside, she felt cut. She sat, looking for a long time at the red smear on the toilet paper. On one thigh there were purple bruises, the distinct imprint of a thumb and four fingers.

A lingering sadness hung around for months after; a slight nausea rose in her throat before a meal, even when she was hungry.

The party for her twenty-third birthday had been at the apartment of a friend, but the numbers grew, and others kept coming; she didn't know everyone who was there.

Julia knew who he was. Kind of. Once he had been with some of her friends at a bar. They called him Jackson, but she didn't know if that was his first name or his last.

There was a birthday cake: chocolate coconut, her favorite. And vodka shots. She had enough to make her so dizzy that she retreated to a back bedroom and fell upon a pile of coats on the bed. It was early March and still cold; there were many coats. She was lucid enough to know that she shouldn't be sick on all those coats, so she rolled off, onto carpeting that had seen better days. The rug smelled like feet.

It was probably what they call a black-out. She didn't remember how she got to his apartment. He must have driven because when she reached consciousness, she realized he couldn't possibly have taken her on the train in the condition she was in.

Her friends told her later that he offered to drive her home. The party got out of hand and someone in the building threatened to call the police. Sure, like with all the serious crime in Chicago, the police would even respond to a complaint about a loud party. Still, everyone started to leave.

She knew that he didn't drive her home because she woke the next morning on a strange couch, no blanket, cold leather against her skin. She had a pounding headache. And it burned when she peed in a stranger's bathroom.

Julia Roberts had some things in common with her almost-namesake. She was tall and had a generous mouth with big, white teeth; some people found her attractive, and some thought she had a horsey look.

Pretty enough, but she was also smart and ambitious. She graduated from De Paul with an accounting degree, immediately landing a job that would enable her to pay off the student loans before she was twenty-five.

Trying to cope with anxiety after what had happened—although she couldn't exactly remember what—she began to see a counselor affiliated with SWIC. It was there that she met Lily Lerner and became the owner of a beautiful, silver piece of jewelry, once used by a woman named Laura, an elementary school teacher in the Chicago public schools, who said she didn't need it any longer. Julia was instructed on how the defense worked. Stand no more than an arm's length from the target. Point. Hold your breath. Flick, then press.

Tracking him down wasn't all that difficult and she didn't understand why it took her almost four months to begin. Brent Jackson. Jackson was his last name. He lived very near her, by De Paul, only a few blocks away. There was no reason for him not to take her home that night, home to the apartment she shared with college friends. Perhaps she saw him from time to time, taking the same train.

Early that steamy Saturday morning in July, she walked down the street with some urgency and found the address, an old building, three floors, with a courtyard, geraniums in stone planters by the door. His name alone was on the buzzer. The apartments in this neighborhood were expensive. Julia wondered if he lived there by himself.

Three buzzes. No one answered right away. Then, just when she was about to leave, a sleepy, slightly annoyed: Yeah?

"Package," she said. "I need you to sign." Maybe hearing a woman's voice dissipated suspicion. He buzzed her up.

The lobby was old but well-kept. Black and white tiles. A dark wooden banister. She went up the stairs and entered the hall, she saw him already standing in front of 2F, the door ajar. Shirtless, he stared as she walked to him. "Where's the package?" he asked.

"I need to talk to you," she said.

He held his head to one side. "Do I know you?"

"Do you?"

"You're friends with…Sorry, I forgot your name." He was ordinary looking: brown hair, sandy stubble, and a compact, muscular body.

Moving closer, she noted that he was shorter than she was, at least three inches. "My name is Julia."

He invited her in, even though he was in boxer shorts, and it was nine o'clock in the morning. "I don't understand," he said. Did he not recognize her?

The toilet flushed down the hall. A woman wearing a blue robe appeared in the doorway. "What's going on?"

"Sorry, honey," he said to the woman. "Did the buzzer wake you?"

The woman shook her head. "I was up." She didn't venture further than the hall, her arms crossed in front of her chest.

Julia walked a few steps into the apartment. In the small living room, there was a black leather couch and a flat-screened

TV that took up almost an entire wall. "I'd like to talk to you," she said. "At my birthday party a few months ago…" Clearing her voice, she stood to her full height. "March. It was March 8 to be exact. My birthday."

He furrowed his brow in concentration. "I think I was really drunk that night," he said, giving a little cough. He seemed embarrassed. "I'm sorry. I don't think we made it home."

"We made it to your apartment." She looked around. "You took me here." There was nothing familiar except for the couch, and the cold leather against her skin. She spoke distinctly, clearing her throat, which seemed to be tightening. "That night, I was drunk, I passed out, you took me back to this apartment and you raped me." There was no mistaking the emphasis on the last three words.

The girl in the hallway gasped and covered her mouth. "Brent!"

"No—o—o," he said. "We were both really drunk…"

"You were not so drunk that you couldn't drive."

"Yeah, and lucky that the cops didn't stop me. Look I offered to take you home. You didn't even know where you lived…You couldn't even tell me. I was really drunk," he said again. "So were you." His ears were reddening.

"I was drunk, but I didn't hurt anyone," Julia said calmly. "Are you saying that you're no longer responsible for what you did because you're drunk?"

"I'm sorry," he said, his mouth a tight scowl. "But I didn't do anything."

She looked at him evenly. "Then what are you sorry about?"

The girl in the hallway said his name again, a question this time: "Brent?" But she hung back, not coming to his defense.

"Because you think I might have done something," he said. His eyes grew big and sad as if he felt sympathy for her. "That I might have hurt you."

She noticed that the kitchen counter was littered with bottles. "You might have hurt me? That's what I think? That you might have hurt me?" Maybe a few months ago, she would have believed that. But a few months ago, she would not have made the decision to find out where he lived. She would not have tracked him down and come to his door on a weekend morning. Taking a step towards him, she held her breath, and extended her arm. She held an object in her hand. "You might have hurt me?"

The girl in the blue robe repeated: "Oh my god, oh god!" Though Julia noticed before she left, that when Brent Jackson fell to his knees, sick and retching, the girl did not come to his aid.

Julia ran quickly out of the apartment, her heart pounding as she turned the banister in a leap, flinging open the heavy front door. It was already hot and humid early this morning in Chicago, but the air felt fresh and clean.

2. Lynnette Zaring: Your Order Is Ready

She liked the wait staff, but she did not like some of the guys in the kitchen, chopping, mixing, standing over steaming vats, and scrubbing the pots. The dishwashers at La Bouche were mostly Hispanic guys, doing a crummy, minimum-wage job; piles and piles of dirty dishes just kept coming, and they were both frazzled and bored. Their flirting was annoying but harmless. Who knew what they might have been saying to each other in another language? She didn't care.

However, Hector, a sullen French chef with nicotine-stained teeth, was actually threatening. He would be in the pass window for the girls to pick up their orders, taunting them with dirty talk. He made lewd movements with his tongue. Kissed the air. Once he leaned over and pinched Lynnette's breast while she was helpless, balancing her tray.

She complained to the manager whose solution was for her to stand back away from the window when she got her plates. "Hector just likes the girls," Pierre said. Pierre was not French, but a sixty-year-old gay man from Indiana with the disposition of an angry toddler. He stamped his feet, yelling when things did not go his way. Which was often. Pierre implied that Lynette was Hector's favorite. "He likes you," Pierre said, making it seem as if the lecherous cook was simply an admiring boy on the playground, and perhaps she should be flattered by the attention.

The food in the restaurant was over-priced, and much of it micro-waved into submission. When Hector accosted her one night as she came out of the woman's bathroom, grabbing her there, she decided to quit. But not before a friend of a friend who was mugged in a CVS Pharmacy parking lot loaned her an unusual piece of jewelry.

Late Tuesday, a slow night, she came close to the window as Hector passed her two plates. "Hey, bebe," he said, smiling a wide, evil smile, showing his yellowed teeth. "How's my pretty bebe?" He kissed the air, then made soft, groaning sounds.

Instead of taking her plates, Lynette smiled and kissed the air back at him.

For a brief moment, he looked confused, pausing, framed in the pass window in front of her. The sounds of the busy kitchen continued behind him, the scrape and clatter of dishes.

"Here you go, Hector," she said, extending her arm. It would be easy to get another waitressing job in Chicago. She was young and pretty and strong. She was tired of this fancy-pants restaurant where the customers stayed too long at a table, talking and talking. She could make more in tips at an Olive Garden.

She took a deep breath and held her hand out. Flick, then press. She stood back from the window before Hector heaved, vomiting across both plates: a mushroom Bolognese and the evening's special, a root beer braised pork shank with goat cheese polenta, Swiss chard and finished with a pine nut gremolata.

3. Chantelle Clarke: Those Are Bad Boys

She was ten years old when one of her brother's friends put his hands down the back of her pants, saying he was just checking to see if that bootie was real, she was growing so big, so fast, so fine.

She was twelve when one of her mother's boyfriends walked in on her while she was doing her business in the bathroom. The lock on the door was broken; he said, sorry, but then he just stood there watching her with a toothy smile as she hurriedly pulled up her pants.

She was fifteen when another of her brother's friends took her to an abandoned apartment and threw her down on a dirty mattress. So fast. Rough hands. Zip. Groan. Gone.

Bad things happened with other boys. She did not get pregnant which sometimes worried her because maybe she never could and what if one day she met someone and fell in love? But that scenario did not seem likely. She thought of herself as dirty goods, used; it didn't matter who was next on top of her.

After high school she got a job in a fast-food restaurant and every day, to and from the train, she walked by a SWIC studio and wondered what went on in there, noticing that the mostly white girls who came out were laughing and happy in each other's company.

One afternoon she was looking in the window when a silver-haired lady in a pink sweatsuit was coming out, and Chantelle was brave enough to ask: what were those girls doing in there?

And suddenly there she was: a scholarship student at SWIC and the star of her self-defense class. Mitzi, the woman in the pink sweatsuit was a nice white lady. She took Chantelle into an office and pointed to her reflection in a full-length mirror by the door. "You're adorable," the woman said. "Just look at yourself!"

One day, Mitzi gave Chantelle a pretty piece of jewelry on a long chain and explained how to use it. "Those boys," she said. "They are doing bad things to you. You don't have to let them."

The woman was kind and strong-minded. She reminded Chantelle of her Grandma Beez, even though Grandma Beez had been so big that she could have put this little white woman under one of her giant bosoms and swallowed her up. Grandma Beez offered Chantelle hope and comfort every time Chantelle crawled into bed with her in the middle of the night, scared of the dark, scared of the noises in the hall, scared of what the next day at school would bring. But Grandma Beez was gone now. Dead of a heart that attacked her as she sat in a chair watching television. That's how Chantelle found her after school one day.

No one had ever given her jewelry before. "It's yours. You can keep it. And have it refilled whenever you need to," the silver-haired woman said. "Just come back to the studio and we'll refill it so that you can use it again if you have to."

Flick. Then press. This was followed by a technique Chantelle learned in one of the self-defense classes. No one in the neighborhood ever quite figured it out how a swift kick in the balls could make a guy so sick. Mostly, they just left her alone.

4. Denise Nutty: Smile!

Denise kept the special silver pendant in her purse. It was pretty, but too large to wear at work at the dental office, dangling from her white uniform as she cleaned someone's teeth. It belonged to a woman Denise knew at church who loaned it out to her and told her about the five, long blocks she had to walk home from Bible study.

Denise was a Christian who prayed all the time, something she really enjoyed because the world out there was increasingly secular; sometimes she felt embarrassed that her love for Jesus figured so strongly in her everyday life. She thanked Him before every meal, even before a muffin and a cup of coffee in Starbucks; she prayed on her knees at night, reviewing her day and giving thanks for everything that could possibly be a blessing. God in his grace was with her right there, personally, in everything she touched. When she accidentally dropped her cell phone in the toilet, she saw it as a sign that God wanted her to get a new cell phone.

So yes, she was lucky to have a job where she could openly pray at work. She had a new job with Dr. Kenneth Epley, a dentist whose family went to her church. Dr. Epley advertised himself as a 'Christian Dentist'. She had wanted to leave her other job where she worked with three other dental hygienists, and not one of them, in her estimation, a spiritual person.

Aside from being a Christian, Dr. Epley was not an appealing man. His skin had a strange pallor under the fluorescent lights, and he was a heavy mouth breather—although his breath was usually scented by wintergreen.

Also, he talked too much. Especially for someone whose conversation was one-sided toward people captive in the chair, mouths open with suction drains and stuffed with cotton. Dr. Epley talked about ordinary things: the weather, his children's athletic endeavors, and an upcoming fishing trip. Denise heard the same dull stories many times a day.

It was just the two of them in the office. She had a white uniform that was a size too small. Dr. Epley bought her three uniforms and three pairs of white pantyhose when she started working for him. At her other job, she just wore a smock over her regular clothes that she had to pay for herself. Dr. Epley told her that the white uniform made her look professional. In fact, he was complimentary almost every day.

She thought it was odd that he sometimes closed the door when he was with a patient and asked her to prepare the other room. She noticed that it was always when he was with a young woman patient.

Sometimes Dr. Epley asked her questions that she felt were a little personal. He asked about her boyfriend, and when she told him that she didn't have one, he asked what she liked to do for fun. The way he said 'fun' made her a little uncomfortable.

Dr. Epley offered to file down her pointy incisors free of charge. It was strange for her, being in the chair, but he acted perfectly natural, not even talking too much as he worked over her with his minty breath.

After work, she and Dr. Epley always prayed together, on their knees, in his office. Framed photos of his family were on every wall. He had four blond children and a plain wife with blond bangs cut straight across her forehead. She had a very wide smile revealing exemplary white teeth.

One evening, right after they finished praying, but while she was still kneeling, her head bowed in reflection, she was shocked to feel Dr. Epley behind her, his hands on each of her arms, his breath along her ear. Startled, she reared back, almost knocking him over. "Oh, sorry, Denise. I was just trying to help you up," he said. His normally pale face was flush, his eyes glassy.

She had been at the job less than a full month. Not even long enough to accrue any vacation time. As she got up, she turned, looked down at the bulge in his pants, and gasped. He had touched her in an inappropriate way. Definitely touched her. And excited himself.

"A man has certain needs," Dr. Epley began...

"Please," she said. "Don't."

"I need you," he said urgently. "I would never hurt you. I respect you." The words tumbled from him.

"Dr. Epley..."

Looking straight at her, he seemed to be somewhere else: "A woman must quietly receive instruction with entire submissiveness. God does not allow a woman to teach or exercise authority over a man, but to remain quiet..." Then he grabbed her hand and drew it to him, moving himself against her, moaning as he started to tremble.

From Timothy? She didn't recall what exact chapter or verse. He held her hand tight and with his other hand, deftly unzipped his pants, reaching inside, manipulating himself before taking out a quite large and insistent penis. Denise gasped. She had been with boys when she was a teenager before she found a righteous path. Those times in the backs of cars were never exciting to her, and afterward she felt cheap. Since she had become a Christian, she looked forward to giving her body to someone she would be committed to forever in this world.

Now her open hand was forced upon Dr. Eply's penis, and he was using it to beat a rhythm, up and down, up and down until, rather quickly, he came in a glob across the front of her white uniform. Silently, she looked down in disgust.

"Denise," he said raggedly and released his grip, standing back against the desk as if using it for support. Dr. Epley's eyes were closed and his breathing still labored. She thought he might pass out.

Without a word, she walked across the room, went to the bottom drawer of the file cabinet, and took out her purse. The pendant was in a small pocket of the lining. She took it out, looking at it for a few seconds before proceeding. Turning to face him, she squared her shoulders and cleared her throat. "I don't think I'll be coming back here to work," she said.

Dr. Epley opened his eyes, shaking his head, as if waking from a dream. "Now, Denise," he said, suddenly his professional, boring self, although he was still breathing noisily. "Please, Denise…" he began.

She didn't know what he was possibly going to say. But it didn't matter. Stepping forward, she remembered: An intake of breath, hold, flick, then press. So fast. So fast. Files, envelopes, the computer on his desk she used to set up the appointments with: everything splattered as he gagged and purged. Even the photograph of his family, his bile obscuring their cheerful faces.

"Goodbye," she said politely. Denise was devout but this did not mean she was a fool.

5. Misty Rose: Twofers

Her real name was Mai Young, which could also be a name for a stripper, but she didn't want to use her real name. Her family was traditional, and strict. They had no idea that their daughter was working nights as an exotic dancer to help pay her way through the exercise physiology program at the University of Illinois. The courses for the MA were difficult, involving the advanced study of biomechanics and physiology to prepare graduates for careers in fitness assessment. She was working on a proposal to introduce some of the self-defense classes taught at SWIC into the corporate world.

Mitzi Solomon had given a lecture at the University for the Women in Power conference last fall, telling the story of her first marriage, being left with two little boys, no job, and channeling her fear and anger into a focused determination: Not only to personally survive but to make something that would endure.

Mai was impressed and hung around in the lecture hall so that she would be alone with Mitzi, asking her question after question until Mitzi finally suggested coming down to the SWIC studio to sign up for a class. After they got to know each other, Mitzi presented a gift which Mai took with her every night as she danced at the club, leaving soon after hours. "You might need this at your job," Mitzi had said wisely.

It was true, the dancing was getting to her, but it would be just a little longer before she graduated. The money was sure good. Before going onstage, Mai smoked a little weed just to take the edge off.

The Executive Club was not the Ba Da Bing, but the clientele was not exactly CEO material either. Mostly working-class guys out for a couple of beers and a chance to see the scantily clad 'ladies'. Crowded for a Wednesday evening because it was twofers 'til midnight. Domestic beer only, not liquor. The Club was a popular destination for stag parties, Japanese tourists, and blue-collar guys getting off work. Occasionally, a man came in with his wife.

Even though she was an exotic dancer and took off most of her clothing, she did not do lap dancing or private 'entertaining' which she thought was disgusting. The money was still good. And she found that pole dancing was very good for physical toning. Mai was small, muscled, and well-defined.

Men sometimes came too close to the stage, trying to touch her. There were occasional racial insults as well. References about 'slants'. And questions about intimate parts of her anatomy.

That night, Mai walked to the lot with the pendant in one hand, a duffle slung over her shoulder with work-out clothes that needed to be washed. It was a hot night, and in the dressing room she had thrown on a loose mini-dress that came just to the top of her thighs.

Two young white guys, one tall and one short, both with close-cropped haircuts and dopey grins, followed her out and asked if she needed a ride. She shook her head. "I don't think either of you should be driving either," she said over her shoulder. They both seemed pretty drunk.

"No, we're good. We're good," the tall one said. "Come on, go out with us for a hamburger. We're hungry."

The other added, "You're a good dancer. You could show us some moves." He started a mock pole dance and lurched against his lanky friend, almost knocking him over.

Two ordinary work-a-day guys having a couple of beers at the club. They were teasing her.

"How about some Chinese food?" the tall one said. "Puh-leeze." He made a motion with his hand, fingers imitating chopsticks.

Despite further requests, she ignored them, a slight head-check as she made the way to her car. And then she heard it. "Hey Chinkerbell, what's the matter? Too good for us?"

This evoked a roar of laughter from his friend: "'Chinkerbell!' Man, that's a good one. I never heard that one before."

Inspired, the tall one continued: "Hey coolie. No hambergee. Want to go out with us for some flied lice?"

Although there was no one else in the parking lot, she didn't feel especially threatened. Still. Enough. Mai drew herself up to her full height of five feet three inches and sauntered over to them, getting right in their faces before finishing the joke: "That's fried rice, you plick!"

The tall one sneered, his mouth curled into a snarl: "Bitch."

Mai took a breath and held it. They were standing so close together that all she had to do after activation was swiftly pass the silver head toward them both, from tall to short. Within seconds, it was hard to tell where one began and the other left off. Both let loose, spewing the same ugly sludge.

6. Sandra Voycovitz: End of the Shift

Sandra Voycovitz initiated the defense on someone who actually might have done her serious harm. Following the confrontation, she stood over her assailant and, despite the mess, confiscated his gun. After all, she was an emergency room nurse and well acquainted with body fluids. While he was down, she called both 911 and hospital security; then she went through his pockets to look for identification.

Like many of the other women, she had acquired the pendant because of her night route home after work, a twelve-hour shift at Rush University Medical Center. Three days on, four days off. She and her husband had children still at home, and this meant that there was more time to spend with her family. Sandra loved her job; the fast action of an emergency room left her energized rather than exhausted.

She was pumped that hot summer night walking to her car. The ER had been busy. Some drug overdoses, a couple of gunshot wounds, a cardiac arrest, and a toddler who swallowed a Lego. Sandra had probably helped save a life or two. That happened almost every shift. There was noise. Tears. Some screaming. The mother of the toddler was the most demanding of immediate attention, but the baby would be fine.

Coming upon someone leaning into the busted-out, driver-side window, Sandra yelled: "Hey! That's my car!" A skinny, black guy with spiky dreadlocks looked over his shoulder, surprised to be caught in the act. Sandra surprised herself, calling out to him in the employee section of the parking lot.

He was probably not a rapist. Just a garden variety car thief, someone she came upon quite accidentally who happened to be breaking into her car. A summer night, it wasn't totally dark yet. There were dozens of cars in that row. And he picked hers, an eight-year-old Toyota Corolla in need of a brake adjustment.

The man extracted himself from the car and yelled: "Get outta here, bitch." He sounded tough, but Sandra thought he looked scared. And maybe high. His eyes were pinpricks of fear and menace.

She stood her ground. "That's my car," she repeated calmly.

"You better get outa here," he said, reaching into the pocket of his jeans. "You hear me?" Suddenly, he was waving around a gun.

"Ok, ok," she said. It was the voice she used to soothe jumpy meth heads in the ER. "I hear you. I hear you." He seemed more surprised and nervous than she was. Still, there was the gun. He wasn't aiming directly at her but waving it over his shoulder and up into the concrete beams of the parking garage. Sandra knew how bullets could ricochet. "It's ok," she repeated. As if in compliance, she started to put her hands up, but instead slowly edge her way closer. "It's ok." Then gracefully moving her hand down in front of him, she set it off. Flick. Then press.

He took a breath, looking surprised, as if she slapped him. "Huh?" His hand went to his mouth, trying to hold back. Of course, it was useless. The first splurge splayed between his fingers. Then another. Then another. Then another. "What the f…" Then another.

Sandra looked coldly at the pool on the ground. God, what had this guy been eating? Chunks that looked like undigested meat, a brown mass of something foul. The tips of the man's dreadlocks were flecked with matter.

He was still on the ground, writhing when security from the hospital arrived, approaching cautiously. The guard, a burly older man with tufts of grey hair spiraling out of his cap, put a hand over his own mouth. "Ewewww," he said, looking down at the weapon. The gun, covered in vomit, was not something he seemed to want to touch. Sandra took charge. "Do you have a bag for this?" He did not. Sandra reached into her own purse, taking out tissues, and picked up the gun with two fingers, a pinky daintily aloft.

Two police officers arrived soon after; one was a woman who seemed as interested in the crime scene as in the suspect. There were a number of different identifications on his person, one of them apparently his. A driver's license with his picture:

Jamaal La Crosse. Male. Thirty-five years old. Just looking at him, Officer Lois Lane would have guessed younger. Jamaal La Crosse lay on the cement, holding his belly and moaning. "Sheee-it."

Chapter 19

We Trust You

Howard was not in Iowa, not even in the country, when a letter from the Institute for Animal Care and Use Committee (IACUC) came to Joyce Corning's attention. More information was needed concerning research emanating from Dr. Howard Lerner's lab. Some of the missing specifics were highlighted by yellow marker indicating requests for additional data.

The mission of IACUC was to ensure humane treatment of animals in research; the committee had to approve any activities that involved the use of live vertebrate specimens. Like pigs.

Joyce's heart thumped as she went down the hall to Anaya's office, letter in hand, and saw Anaya leaning over her computer, lost in thought. Joyce knocked delicately on the doorframe. "Anaya, I'm sorry to interrupt. Can I talk to you about something?"

Anaya leaned back in her chair: "Sure. What's up?"

"I don't know what this is about," Joyce said, standing in front of the desk. "Do you?" She handed Anaya the letter with the official seal of the IACUC.

Anaya moved a plastic bag toward Joyce. "Papadam?"

"No, thank you," Joyce said.

"I made them last night," Anaya said. "They're even better the next day. Not greasy."

Out of politeness, Joyce took a chip. She felt comforted by Anaya's lack of alarm.

"This is no biggie," Anaya said casually. "Howard must have forgotten to send this back with the corrections before he left. I'll fill this out and send it in. I heard from Howard this morning," she added.

"The conference is over and now he and Betsy are traveling. They're in Prague now."

Joyce wasn't exactly sure where Prague was. Somewhere near Germany? She had never been to Europe. When she retired, Larry wanted to go to the Black Hills, to Williamsburg, to the Everglades; he had been to The Boundary Waters in northeast Minnesota and wanted to go back. "Are they having a good time?" Joyce asked. "He surely needed a vacation."

"I think so," Anaya said. "We didn't talk that much. Mostly about work."

"Anaya…" Joyce began hesitantly. She finished chewing her papadam, which was indeed delicious. "Can I ask you something?"

"Shoot."

"What's going on?"

"Going on?" Anaya looked intently at Joyce; her black eyes blazed.

Joyce, feeling awkward, cleared her throat and began: "You know, the end of last semester Vera was coming into the office so frequently. And you and Dr. Lerner seemed somehow so secretive. I didn't know what to think." Her bravery evaporating, Joyce trailed off and looked down, embarrassed. "I still don't," she said softly.

Anaya motioned for Joyce to sit down. Then she got up and closed the office door. "Joyce, what did you think?"

"I don't know," Joyce admitted. "For a while there, maybe…"

Anaya interrupted: "Joyce, I am sorry for keeping you in the dark. For both of us, well, all three of us, actually. Vera, too. It wasn't right. We talked a lot about it, Howard and I. He said not to say anything. To protect you."

"To protect me from what?" Joyce sat across from Anaya. Why had she not noticed before how clear and smooth Anaya's skin was? How her dark lashes fringed her eyes. Her hair was back to its natural color, a glossy black. Anaya was a beautiful, strong woman. Joyce understood how anyone, a man or a woman, could fall in love with her. "I didn't know what to think. And you know, how close you and Dr. Lerner always were. Professionally, I always thought. But then…" trailing off, Joyce shrugged.

"Oh, god, Joyce. Did you think that Howard and I…?"

"No. No," Joyce said. Then: "Well, maybe it crossed my mind. When I came into his office once and you were standing so close together and looking at something. Then you were both uncomfortable when I came in. Dr. Lerner was, especially. But then Vera was here all the time. So I thought, no, not that," Joyce said, relieved that the shorthand was understood, that she didn't have to say what she meant aloud.

Anaya held her hand over her mouth and began to giggle. "Really, Joyce."

"Of course not. Even if you weren't…you know, with Vera," Joyce said. "No. Not Dr. Lerner."

"Oh, but me, maybe?" Anaya laughed again. "You could see me be the one who was screwing around?" She seemed in a good mood and not at all offended. Then she got serious: "Oh, Joyce, I'm sorry."

"Sorry for what?" The room was so cold, Joyce felt chilled.

Anaya got up, went to a file cabinet, took out a red folder, and passed it across the desk to Joyce who looked at the folder but did not pick it up. "I'm sorry," Anaya said again. "You know that Howard—Dr. Lerner and I—both trust you."

Joyce noted how Anaya was placing herself on equal footing with the man who was her boss, something that would usually be of some annoyance. But she was being let in on something. "So would this be all right with Dr. Lerner?" Joyce asked. "Sharing whatever this is with me?" She picked up the folder, holding it with both hands against her chest.

"Actually, I think he would be relieved that you finally know. And relieved that I'm the one who made the decision," Anaya said. "Howard doesn't like to keep secrets. And he values you, Joyce, maybe more than you know."

"I feel privileged," Joyce said, blinking a few times to hold back the tears. She sat ramrod straight, as if on assignment. "I'd like to take this back to my desk and read everything if that's all right."

"Thank you," Anaya said.

"For what?"

"Everything. Being here. With us. For being who you are," Anaya told her.

Walking to her own office, Joyce noticed how quiet the building was. The first summer session had ended, and some faculty were on break. She had a grey sweater draped over her chair and put it on. The sweater had been in the office for years. Sometimes she forgot and wore it home at the end of the day, only to bring it back again in the morning. The sweater was plain and reliable and none the worse for its years of wear. Like me, Joyce thought, placing the folder on her desk.

Why was it so cold, especially if classes were out of session? Such a waste of energy. She and Larry had no air conditioning in the old house during the first ten years of their marriage and she hadn't minded at all. At night, with all the windows open, she would hear the crickets and the owls.

Larry was thrilled when they finally had enough money to put in air conditioning and had the old place insulated tight as a drum. "Isn't this wonderful to be cool in the summer?" he'd say, piling blankets on the bed before sleep. But Joyce didn't like the house all closed up, feeling out of touch with the seasons.

In summer you were supposed to be hot. It seemed wrong to be cold in July. Unnatural. Now she made herself a cup of hot herbal tea, sat down at her desk, and began to read. The scientific data included a narrative, written in a more accessible form, with notations from both Dr. Lerner and Anaya. It began with a dated entry from the time the farmer from Vinton came into the Vet school, almost a year ago. Joyce remembered the farmer, how oblivious to protocol he was, walking in like that. Dressed for the part. Joyce knew farmers and most of them would have put on something more presentable coming to town, wanting to talk with a famous scientist. Joyce remembered how she tried to intercept, and Dr. Lerner said, in that kind way he had: "It's all right, Joyce."

She continued reading. There are entries about the discovery of the mycotoxin on the ground at the farm in Vinton, about what happened to the pigs. There were entries about the accidental discovery of the formula, two things mixed together, simple as making Arnold Palmer iced tea, and a splash of lemonade (Larry's favorite).

There were descriptions of experiments during spring break. While Joyce and Larry were walking with the grandchildren along the crowded avenues of Disney World, Dr. Lerner was purposefully making himself sick. All events were dated, like diary entries. There was a description of the method of transmission. There were drawings of jewelry created by Vera Perez. There were descriptions of meetings in Chicago with someone named Mitzi Solomon.

"Oh, dear god. Lily!" Joyce said aloud. Joyce Corning might not know where Prague was on the map of Europe, but she understood what the data revealed about mycotoxins and the resulting antiperistalsis in pigs. And of course, humans.

"Oh, dear god," she said again when she finished reading. She sat for a while, hand over her mouth, staring at the red folder in front of her on the desk. Her heart was beating fast and suddenly she became so flushed that she took off the grey sweater and placed it on the back of her chair.

Chapter 20

Howard and Betsy in Prague

He awoke in a hotel room near the metro, overlooking the red roofs of the Old Town. They had arrived late the night before after a successful conference where Howard was the keynote speaker describing his research in Porcine Stress, a disease that covered disparate symptoms connected with a recessive gene. The disease, characterized by biochemical abnormality, a change in muscle activity, and resulting in necrosis was of serious concern to pork production. There was acute stress in the animal and often sudden death. Fat pigs (well, fatter than average) were more likely to carry the gene than leaner pigs.

Last year, Howard's lab had found a way to isolate the gene and provide an antidote. So far, the results had met with success, and pork producers were grateful. Not known by the science community was research of Dr. Lerner's that was of more interesting significance.

The hotel in the center of the town was too baroque for Howard's taste, but the room was clean, and the bed was comfortable. Howard often found that, after traveling abroad, he came home with a backache. Maybe that was just the long plane ride instead of the beds, but the older he got, the less he enjoyed being away from home.

At eight in the morning, Betsy was sitting in a large, over-upholstered chair facing the balcony reading something on her phone. Howard looked at her through sleepy eyes, his fresh-faced wife, already dressed for the day, her blonde hair swept up in a ponytail. She looked as young as their girls.

He preferred traveling with his wife. Alone, he usually ordered room service, found an English-speaking station on television, and watched the news. "Morning. How'd you sleep, hon?" His voice sounded croaky.

Betsy nodded. Which meant good. "There's coffee. I brought some up from the lobby."

"Wow. I didn't even hear you."

"You were snoring away. Or groaning. I couldn't say which. Were you dreaming?"

"I don't remember," Howard said.

Despite the late arrival to the hotel, they had made love. Howard was brushing his teeth, when Betsy came up behind him kissing his shoulder, looking at their reflection in the bathroom mirror. "I was so proud of you," she said. She had attended his talk, sitting in the back of the room, watching the audience. "I would have been nervous before all those people." On the occasions when she accompanied Howard to conferences—mostly when they were hosted in cities more interesting than Ames, Iowa– she went sightseeing or shopping.

"It's not exactly a TED-Talk crowd," Howard said. "I don't have to be dazzling."

"But you were," Betsy said.

"Dazzling?" Together with Betsy he looked in the bathroom mirror and smiled at the reflection of a rumpled man of older-middle age with a prominent nose. But he had a nice smile. His mother always told him that. Good teeth. And a dimple in his right cheek. His mother explained: "God's finger, showing you were done." Both of his daughters had dimpled right cheeks, and he told them the same thing.

"You were funny. I liked the story about Lily and her first visit to the lab."

"You've heard it before," Howard said. "Probably so have some of the people listening. It's my warm-up."

"Leave the light on in the bathroom, so we can see if we get up in the night," Betsy said.

In bed, she made the first move, climbing over him to turn off the lamp on his side table when he had been preparing to read. "You're not tired yet, are you?" She straddled him and stretched, peeling off her tank top, offering her breasts; then she moved down his body, kissing him along the way. "I want you now," she said.

Howard took a breath. "I bet you say that to all the porcine pathologists."

"Yes, all of them," she whispered urgently, moving back up, kissing his neck. "But especially that German fellow who introduced you," she whispered provocatively. "The one with the comb-over and big ears. He is remarkable in bed."

It was a game they sometimes played, mentioning a most unattractive and ridiculous partner. "I usually do this," Betsy said, rubbing her breasts against his mouth. "It drives him wild."

"Wait," Howard said. "If you're on top, I'll come too fast."

She rolled off and he immediately entered her. She gasped. Missionary position. No foreplay. Nothing oral. But it was the most intense, pure coupling. "I have to stop for a little bit," he said, holding back. He shut his eyes, so he didn't see her face in passion. When he was younger, he used to count backward from one hundred. They had had sex in the months since Lily's attack, but he felt it had been perfunctory on her part; a sadness lingered. "Oh, I've missed you, Bets," he said.

***

"It's still hot." Betsy went over to a desk and uncovered a cup of coffee, milk, and sugar, the way he liked it. Betsy brought it to him and placed it on the nightstand next to the bed. "Do you want breakfast? It's over by nine."

"I could eat," Howard said.

"I just got a text from the girls. Megan is going to Wisconsin this weekend with Samantha. Her parents have a summer house in Door County."

Howard didn't know who Samantha was, but if he admitted that, Betsy was sure to explain that Samantha had been Megan's roommate Fall semester or a girl he had met at least half a dozen times over college breaks, and how could he not know who Samantha was? So he just said: "That sounds like fun."

"Oh, Howie. Listen to this…"

"Bets, let me pee first." The room was airy, a soft breeze coming in off the balcony. But the bathroom had a dank smell. There was no overhead fan. When he was finished, he washed his hands and face and swished around a gulp of the mouthwash the hotel had provided.

"Now what?" He sat on the edge of the bed and took a sip of the coffee.

"And this from Lily," Betsy read: 'Too long to explain, but a great job opp. MS and I met for lunch. Grad school on hold.'"

"MS?"

Betsy looked up from her phone. "Mitzi Solomon. What do you think? Job opportunity with SWIC?"

Howard shrugged. "I don't know if teaching self-defense classes would be described as a great job opportunity." Since the attack, Lily revealed a more assertive stance. He remembered watching Lily as a little girl in the park, cheerfully sharing toys with others in the sandbox. Sweet Lily who never seemed to mind if a more aggressive child took her pail and shovel but simply turned to play with whatever else was available. Howard used to feel anger on her behalf even toward a bullying toddler.

"I don't know," Betsy said. Maybe it's something administrative. You know, running one of the studios? Lily's very organized. Mitzi must have recognized that."

Howard didn't know how many women in Chicago had made use of his discovery. He actually didn't want to know. Anaya was more in touch with Lily and this information.

"Maybe Mitzi wants Lily to assume her legacy. Strong Women in Chicago," Betsy said. "I'd like her to stay close enough to us. Chicago is good."

Howard changed the subject: "What do you want to do today?"

Betsy leaned over in her chair, looking smaller than she appeared in normal-sized furniture, and began scrolling. "There's a walking tour through the Jewish Quarter," Betsy said and began reading: *The Jewish Quarter in Prague, known as Josefov, is located between the Old Town Square and the Vltatva River. Its torrid history dates from the thirteenth century, when Jewish people were ordered to vacate their disparate homes and settle in one area.*

In all their travels the Lerners frequently sought out one thing that identified and restored Howard's roots. These tourist experiences usually resulted in such strong emotions; anger and shame, mixed with such deep, deep sorrow. Despite the cosmopolitan charm of cities like Prague that made the history of the Iowa heartland seem plain as rhubarb pie, he did not ever feel entirely comfortable in Eastern Europe. "That sounds interesting," he said casually. "I'd like to go."

Betsy read: *Terezin is a concentration camp located to the north of Prague. During the Nazi occupation, many residents of the Jewish Quarter were transferred there…*

Howard thought: Monsters. The Nazis became conflated in his vision with all the evil deeds of evil men. He had a picture of Lily's attacker in the stall, larger in his imagination than the scrawny, dirty man she described to the police. He undressed and went back into the bathroom. In the hotel shower, whose water pressure was inadequate by American standards, Howard felt a surge of pride in his heritage. "We're still here. We're still here," he thought as the water trickled down his back. His daughter Lily, a person of quality and integrity, was strong and would be worthy of any job that Mitzi Solomon was entrusting to her.

Chapter 21

Estate Planning

Mitzi had gone alone both times to his fancy office in the West Loop. "How long?" Mitzi asked. Dr. Rakosi, a respected pulmonologist, shook his head looking at her with sad eyes. "I can't tell you that." He was young, in his mid-forties, and had gone to high school with Mitzi's two sons. Rocket Man, Rocky. The Rock. The boys used to have nicknames for everyone. Now he was Dr. Rakosi.

She realized his hesitation in addressing her. Mrs. Horowitz was the name he called her as a high school boy in her kitchen, eating pastrami sandwiches and chocolate donuts before descending down to the rec room. "Call me Mitzi," she had said to her sons' friends. Michael Rakosi was one of the gang of boys in the basement listening to music, playing video games, and watching football. Cheers echoed up the stairs. She remembered him as a sweet, studious boy who always brought his dirty plates up to the kitchen.

"I don't feel sick. Except for this cough," she said now. "I feel pretty good." It was hard for her to admit a flagging energy. "I never smoked, you know. Not in college, when everyone did. My roommate in college was a smoker." Mitzi sniffed.

"Stank up all my clothes. Hah! Probably she was the one who gave me lung cancer."

"We could start you on a regimen…" he began, but Mitzi interrupted: "No!"

There was a pause. Then Dr. Rakosi nodded and explained the forward projection of the metastasis. The cancer was already in both lobes. Small-cell lung carcinoma, stage four: survival rate less than three percent. It was unusual that she felt as good as she did, he admitted. "But you're a tough woman. I read about you all the time."

"I'm not doing that again," Mitzi said, referring to chemotherapy. "Been there. Done it. Enough." The thought of telling her husband and her sons was daunting. Of course, they would want her to do everything she could, everything at all costs. They would tell her how vital and strong she was. Benjamin would beg her to be reasonable. But reasonable was what she had decided many years before. Everyone dies. How did she want to go out? Not bald again, connected to machines, and tubes. This was decided a few years before. She had enough pills, Ambian and Oxycontin, saved up for the end game. She didn't want to fuck it up, half in, half out, lingering and causing everyone even more grief.

Suddenly, she was very tired, tired enough to want to lie down and take a nap. Over by the bookcase in the doctor's office, there was a grey couch very like the one she had in her SWIC studio. She wondered if she and Michael Rakosi had the same decorator.

"I know, it's not a cure," he said. "But sometimes patients with this diagnosis, they want a little more time if they have something they're looking forward to: a wedding, the birth of a grandchild…"

Mitzi interrupted him again: "There is something I'm looking forward to. Something I need to do. And I think there will be enough time to get it started."

Mitzi's new project excited her almost more than anything she had ever done in business or philanthropy. There were a few things she didn't tell her husband. Benjamin didn't have to know everything. Not yet. She was a woman with a mission. If she could protect every woman in Chicago, she would. There was no need to make a profit from this adventure. Not now. Not for her. In the meantime, she had researched the legalities of using an untested substance for self-protection and had already set up a defense fund with a trusted lawyer. Trouble (at least the legal kind) could be avoided. This was good trouble. She couldn't recall who had used that phrase, but she knew it was someone important.

And what could be more trouble than cancer? Those sneaky cells, dormant after the mastectomy for years. Perhaps an errant cell had settled in her lung. Perhaps the cells were fresh and new, energetically reproducing with vigor. She hated the little bastards.

She rose with some difficulty from the chair, pulling herself up with the aid of the armrests. Benjamin was golfing with his buddies at the club. She had made a nice salade Niçoise with the leftover tuna they had had the night before. Lily Lerner was coming over for lunch.

***

Few young women know what they want to do with their lives. Perhaps they are lucky enough to find a job after college and don't have to live in their parents' basement. Or they are able to choose a city with a cool vibe and some friends they can live with without too much drama. How lucky was Lily?

She examined the previous plan. Which included graduate school in a public policy program. The summer working at

SWIC helped fill the gap. She was meeting more and more women whose lives she could help change. Being able to change someone's life. Was that too bold an assumption?

For a while, she would stay in the Midwest. Then maybe go somewhere with a more temperate climate. A city where she could dress for winter without putting on layers and layers of clothing. Though she thought that it was all the layers of winter clothing that saved her life when she was attacked.

Lately she was also realizing that graduate school was not something she was committed to. Lectures, research, and documentation: careful, mundane work. Her heart wasn't in it. And now this: an offer she could refuse, but as soon as Mitzi revealed what she had in mind, Lily knew she would not. Refuse. This was what she wanted to do. She saw her life before the assault, before taking classes, before meeting Mitzi and the women at SWIC, before…Every day she heard more stories.

Like last week. Lily was in the office with Mitzi when a woman came in, still badly bruised, mugged by a teenager who followed her as she got off the train and took her phone. But not before he punched her in the face. "He didn't have to do that," the woman said, her hand shaking as she filled out some paperwork to sign up. She still had to take the same train home from work, she said. Everyday. That's why she wanted to take self-defense classes. "Post-traumatic stress," she said. "Every day when I get off the train, I feel as if I can't catch my breath."

"Of course," Mitzi said. "We hear that frequently here at SWIC." She opened up a drawer and took out a small box.

"What's this?" the woman asked.

"It can save your life," Lily said simply. "Having this will give you the confidence to protect yourself. To be who you were meant to be and breathe freely."

Lily realized that before her own attack, before meeting Mitzi and her girl posse at SWIC, Lily was coasting. Before and after. That's how she thought of it. Before she was happy enough but not, she realized, with purpose or clear direction. Now the direction was coming into focus. She was woke. Woke up. Why would anyone think that was not a good thing to be?

***

The doorman smiled when he buzzed Mitzi's penthouse and announced a visitor. "All the way to the top," he told Lily, pointing toward the elevators at the end of the hall.

"Sweetie girl!" Mitzi was waiting, standing in the doorway of her apartment. "So good to see you. How is it outside? Hot? I love it hot. Are you hungry? I have the table all set on the balcony. Is it all right if we sit outside?"

Lily touched Mitzi's shoulder before reaching down to plant a kiss on her cheek. Not knowing which question to answer, she simply smiled.

The French doors to the balcony led to an outside space that was like a park. Dwarf pines lined the edge of one brick wall; a dense foliage of hostas and cultivated grasses ran along the north side, shaded by a miniature crabapple tree. It was not so hot on the balcony for a Chicago afternoon in July because of all the green space. The table had blue-and-yellow cloth and matching napkins, a vase of daisies, and a basket of salty rolls. "This is so beautiful up here," Lily said.

"Not like the rooftop from the apartment house I grew up in, that's for sure. That roof was more like an asphalt parking lot." Mitzi reached over to a side table and took out a bottle of Prosecco from an ice bucket, pouring some into fluted glasses. "My sister and I used to sneak up to the roof with our friends and drink wine. Cheap wine. Our teeth would be stained red. I don't think our parents ever noticed."

"This roof—you'd never know we were in Chicago. It's more like a country estate," Lily said.

"Good to have money," Mitzi said, taking a sip. "And it's even better to have money that you made from doing good."

"You have," Lily said.

"I also made this salad," Mitzi said. In the middle of the table was the loveliest salad, greens, with tiny, new potatoes, and pink, fresh tuna. "It's already lightly dressed. Shall I plate?"

"Yes, please." Lily accepted the generous portion. "I love salade Niçoise."

"Good to see someone with an appetite."

"You're not so hungry?" Lily said, seeing Mitzi put only half a hard-boiled egg and a small bit of tuna on her own plate. A roll lay untouched, though Lily was already buttering her second.

Mitzi shook her head. Meow jumped up, her furry body draped over Mitzi's tiny lap. Taking a small piece of tuna from her plate, Mitzi placed it under the cat's nose. Meow looked suspicious before slowly opening her mouth and delicately licking it with a pink tongue. "We're both not such good eaters in our old age, are we, sweetheart?" Mitzi asked.

"You're not old," Lily said, narrowing her eyes. "But you've lost some weight, haven't you? I've noticed. It's not something you can afford to do." Mitzi was quiet. "Are you all right?" Lily stopped her fork in midair.

"Like I always say, it's all relative, sweetie girl."

"Relative to what?"

"Everything's relative to everything. What country we are blessed to be born in. Who our parents are. How our kids turn out. If an innocent girl gets attacked in a bathroom..." Mitzi began a coughing fit, which shook her little body with some violence.

Alarmed, Lily leaned forward in her chair, placing her hand on Mitzi's thin arm, feeling through to bone: "Mitzi, are you all right?" she asked again.

"Things will be taken care of. That's what you need to know." Mitzi said mysteriously. "I'm happy about that. You don't know how happy that makes me. Fulfilled and happy. Not to worry."

"I'm not worried," Lily said. "I'm excited about your offer. About your idea. I think my parents will be, too." Lily finished a second glass of Prosecco.

"You have wonderful parents," Mitzi said. Then added: "Did you know how much I love your father? I've told you that already."

"You've had enough husbands," Lily said playfully.

But Mitzi looked serious. "It is important to live a good and useful life. I've done that. You will do that. A meaningful life."

"Of course," Lily said, sensing an urgency between them. Suddenly she felt like crying. Maybe it was the alcohol.

Mitzi reached over across the table and touched Lily's cheek. "You are wonderful and..." she stopped, a wave of fatigue washing over her. The cat was a weight on her lap, immovable. "Oh, sweetie, girl. Excuse me. I think I have to go inside and lie down."

***

Benjamin came in soon after Lily left and found Mitzi in bed. Not unusual, since she was a good napper. Less than twenty minutes and she woke with renewed energy. "Let me close my eyes, for a quick driml," she would say before they went out together for the evening. "And then I'm good to go."

Benjamin himself had not slept in the daytime since he was a toddler. Never on a plane. Or in a hammock, vacationing at the lake. He admired this trait in his energetic wife: the ability to shut herself off so completely right in the middle of the day to wake coherent and refreshed and go back to whatever she was doing. When she had breast cancer years ago, the chemotherapy knocked her off her game. Then the naps were long, and she woke groggy and miserable. He could hardly remember the diminished Mitzi from that time.

But he had been worried about her lately. She seemed to slow down and sometimes, when he was reading the paper and he looked up at her across the kitchen table, he noticed that she was not drinking her coffee, reading and commenting about the injustices of the world as she was wont to do, but staring at the page, her brow furrowed. If she were troubled about something, wouldn't she share it with him? Mitzi was independent, that was certain. But he had never known her to be quite so furtive.

Frequently, papers strewn all over her desk in the study: financial statements, codicils, stock reports; a will with changes made in her own hand. He was familiar with it all because, in fact, he had drafted most of the documentation himself. Benjamin was old-fashioned in many ways and believed that a husband was obligated to take care of his wife.

Although Mitzi never seemed to need taking care of, a third marriage was financially complicated. They both had grown children who were wealthy enough in their own right that money wasn't a problem for any of them. The boys all had homes, savings enough for college for their own children, even a stable retirement, though it was too early for them to consider. There were some families where he supposed that money, no matter how plentiful, was never enough. Bickering. Lawsuits. Their families were not like that.

Also, Benjamin and Mitzi had kept their investments separate. Mitzi sometimes alluded to "when I'm gone" and Benjamin always responded: "where are you going?" But after the cancer, the joke hung in the air between them like a bad smell.

Recently Mitzi told him that she was divesting. SWIC Studios was getting to be too much. She would be selling the SWIC franchise, but would bequeath the studio in the West Loop under a special contract to Lily. Mitzi was smart enough to own the building as well. She had plans, she told Ben. Maybe big plans for that studio.

And now, when she awoke from her nap, so small with Meow curled next to her in their king-sized bed, Mitzi finally told Benjamin about seeing Dr. Rakosi. And the dire diagnosis. She told this to him in a matter-of-fact voice as he fell to his knees by the side of the bed, his head down, crying into the duvet. She reached over to touch his shoulder while he wept. "No, no, no," he cried, shaking his head. "Please, please, no." When he looked at her, she saw his lined face, his puffy eyes, an old man bereft by grief. She also saw the little boy in him who was not yet willing to accept the bad news.

Chapter 22

Chicago: Dog Days of Summer

God, it was hot. One afternoon in mid-August, Officer Lois Lane and her partner, Rico Martinez, were called to a domestic disturbance at an apartment above a Korean take-out place on Lawrence Avenue. The outside door to the walk-up was battered, paint peeling, and solidly locked. A neighbor called, saying that furniture was breaking upstairs, glass shattering, a woman was screaming, the dog was hysterically barking; then it was quiet. The caller in 2E, a young Asian man with a goatee, opened his door to talk to the police as they entered the building. "Those two, above me, they're always fighting, pounding. They were screaming all morning. But this time it was different," he said. There were strange sounds. "Like gurgling." And then he went on to explain how it got totally quiet. There was a thud and footsteps running down the stairs. 2E lifted his eyes to the floor above: "I called because I thought someone might have been murdered up there this time."

They walked up the back stairs. Down the hall, at 3E Officer Lane could hear a dog whimpering. "Police," Officer Lane announced. "Police," she said again. "Everything all right in there?"

Opening the door was a disheveled woman of unfortunate appearance: protruding teeth above a weak chin, a head round as a bowling ball set upon thick shoulders. Yellow bruises, suggesting battle from other fights, were along both of her bare, fleshy arms. On one arm there was a tattoo of a rose. "He's gone," the woman said dully. She was holding a perfectly groomed tiny white poodle. "Shhh, Marie," she said tenderly. The dog continued to whimper.

"You want to tell me what happened?" Officer Lane asked. Her partner, Martinez, new on the force, looked around the apartment and sniffed. He stayed silent, letting Lois take the lead. The one-room kitchen and living room was a mess, a lamp turned over, the broken-screened television was in the middle of the room; the stench was foul, a combination of despair and neglect: grease, garbage, dog shit. And vomit.

"He's an asshole," the woman said. She was cooperative, answering their questions with a resigned weariness. Her name was Rhoda Mersh; she worked nights at the post office; she had been living with her boyfriend, but now it was over. "He broke up with me," the woman said, repeating the phrase with righteous indignation. "I mean he was the one who broke up with ME!"

Martinez took notes as Officer Lane asked questions. Occasionally he paused, putting his nose against the crook of his elbow, as if the smell of his own body could refresh him.

"We're still living together, 'cause he got no other place, but I'm the one paying the rent. So he goes, 'I don't want you seein' nobody for a while. Can you give me that?' Can you just give me that?' And I say, 'No, I can't give you that. Not if we're all broken up, I can't. I don't hafta.'"

"You were seeing someone else?" Lois Lane asked.

"No," Rhoda Mersh said. "But you know, I shoulda been able to. He was living for free off me. The asshole. I told him,

'No, I can't give you that.' So he goes, 'So what about if I give you a fat lip?' Except he doesn't. He punches me every place but. He never liked to hit my face. He always punches along the body."

Lois nodded, as if sure that was a reasonable preference. She refrained from catching her partner's eye.

"I'm sorry it's so hot," the woman said. "The air conditioner is on the farts."

"Excuse me?"

"The AC. It's broke," Rhoda said.

"Off, you mean it's on the fritz?"

"Yeah, that. And I know the place smells bad, too."

Lois agreed. "There is an odor."

"He wouldn't walk Marie even if I was gone for a double shift. Usually, she's house-trained." The woman pointed to a pile of tiny dog turds in the corner which seemed more than a night's worth. "Marie is a good girl," the woman said lovingly. Marie, fluffed and clean and white, with a red bow along the top of her head, seemed ridiculously out of place in her surroundings. "Mmmmm," said Rhoda, snuggling into the dog's neck.

Officer Lane looked with narrowed eyes at a big splat across the wood floor, a blanket half in the mess, covered with what appeared to be vomit. Lots of it.

"Yeah, and he threw up just about everything he ever ate the whole week. All over the afghan, too. My grandma knitted me that afghan." Rhoda gestured to a blanket of gold, green, and brown squares piled in the middle of the room. "Yeah, so like now I have to clean up his mess?"

"Do you want to press charges?" Lois asked.

"Nah. He's in enough trouble. He got some stuff outstanding. And I got him back a good one this time. Didn't

I, Marie?" Rhoda scratched the dog behind one ear. "Didn't I, baby?"

On a table next to an overturned lamp, Lois saw a silver pendant on a key chain. "What do you mean?"

"Yeah, I guess I caused the mess myself. Trying it out. Just wow! But not the beating. He did that. The asshole." Rhoda went over and picked up the key chain. "Guess I'm going to have to get it refilled."

"Can you tell me where you got that…item?"

Rhoda paused and wet her lips. "Yeah. I thought you cops knew about it. It's not illegal, is it?" Rhoda looked down at her hand, seemingly impressed. "I can't believe how it worked. She said it would. She wasn't kidding. Boy, did it."

"Who?"

"Who?" Rhoda repeated blankly.

"The person who said it worked? Who gave it to you?"

"Maryanne. A woman I sorted mail with at the post office. She gave it to me. I'm not getting her in trouble, am I? It's legal and everything? I think, I mean she told me it was. She got it in a self-defense class she goes to. Like a gym. For strong women. She just didn't want to wear it no more. Maryanne, she wouldn't get into trouble, would she?"

Lois assured Rhoda that Maryanne would not.

"'Cause she's a real sweet kid. Maryanne. I mean it's not like she gave me a gun." Rhoda shook her head. "Not that she couldn't have used one, poor kid. A gun. You guys might know what happened. Maryanne was raped. She was raped for real."

"For real?" Officer Lane asked.

"Yeah, by a guy who stopped her car late at night. Said he was a cop. Raped for real. She didn't even know who he was." Rhoda Mersh looked sideways at Martinez who stood still as stone in the middle of the room.

Officer Lane nodded.

"I mean, he wasn't," Rhoda went on to explain. "A cop. He just had a badge or something. And a car with a cherry on the top." Rhoda shook her head. "And Maryanne's a very trusting person." Rhoda sighed. "I guess, I am, too. A trusting person. Letting that asshole still live with me. Thinking he's going to change. And then he's the one who broke up with me! Asshole!"

***

Outside it was sweltering. But even with the bus exhaust, the odor of fried food, and trash, the street smelled better than Rhoda Mersh's apartment. She didn't want to press charges. Well, fine. Lois knew. These women were plentiful, hapless souls, living with the consequences of their bad choices. "Rico, I'm going to drop you back at the station," she said as they got into the car. "There's someone I want to see."

Lois was driving, so the statement was purely informational. Officer Martinez didn't ask. He was a good partner. Quiet. Dependable. Not rattled by drama, of which there was plenty in the Chicago police department, particularly in the summer. "There's a woman's self-defense studio over on in the West Loop. I've been wanting to see someone there," Lois explained.

"Sure." Martinez bent to smell the sleeve of his shirt. "Jesus, Lo," he said. "I think this entire uniform needs to be fumigated."

"Crack a window, will you?"

"So, what's this thing she was talking about? Some self-defense thing?"

"Yeah." As usual, the traffic on Lawrence was slowed to a crawl. "How is Gina feeling these days?" Lois asked, changing the subject. Martinez and his wife were having their first baby, a girl, sometime at the end of September.

"It's been hard for her lately. She's big. And it's so hot."

"She still working?"

"Yeah. One more month. Then she'll take off a week or so before she pops. She takes the train in. Gets a seat in the morning 'cause it's early. But you know, coming home at rush hour, people don't even get up to offer her a seat?"

"Assholes," Lois said, echoing their last client.

"Yeah, so you know what Gina does? God, I love that woman. I laughed when she told me about it. She presses up right in against a guy who's sitting there, pretending not to see her. Puts her belly facing him at eye level. Sometimes falls against him. But mostly it's women who give her a seat," he said. "Hey Lo, you know what I found really upsetting today?"

Lois shook her head. "What?"

"That little dog. Marie?" Officer Martinez sounded sad. "That name was on our shortlist for the baby: Marie."

"Well, you don't have to tell Gina that you saw a dog today named Marie."

"That's not even it. The dog was the only good thing we saw today. God, I used to love that name. But now I'd say 'Marie' but I'd be holding my baby girl and thinking of the dog in that stinking place. No way. That name is ruined for me forever."

***

Lily was in the office at SWIC, finishing a yogurt and checking the class lists for September, when she looked out the window and saw a police car pull up; the driver, a woman of compact proportion emerged. Lily had seen Officer Lois Lane again after the hospital, going through hundreds of photographs, until she made herself sick and dizzy staring at the faces of so much deviance. Officer Lane had been gentle and competent. But also resigned that her work would never be done, that loose ends defined too much of every investigation.

"It's ok," Lily wanted to say the time she called the station and Officer Lane was apologetic because there was nothing, nothing at all new on the case. Lily went past the front desk to greet her. Did they find something? Heart racing, she began to get excited. "Hi," Lily said, standing in Mitzi's office door. "What brings you here?" It seemed odd that Lane hadn't called and asked Lily to come down to the station.

"Lily!" Officer Lane seemed puzzled. "Are you still taking classes here?"

"Actually, I'm teaching a class," Lily said. "And helping out in the office. Mitzi and I got to be friends. And like colleagues, I guess. She's taking some time off." Lily didn't reveal Mitzi's diagnosis. "Come on in." She rolled the chair over closer, so when Lane sat down, their knees practically touched. "So? Catching any bad guys?" Lily was puzzled, too. How did the police officer know that she would be at SWIC this afternoon? Why hadn't the officer called if there was new information about the attack?

Lois Lane looked around the room. "This is a wonderful place. Mitzi Solomon is really a force, isn't she? And I'm glad to see you doing so well, Lily."

"I am." Lily sat back, comfortable in Mitzi's chair. "Doing well." Lily was wearing a white tank top and tight, grey workout pants; she appeared healthy and strong. "Can I get you something to drink, Officer Lane? A Sprite? Iced tea? A sports drink?" Lily smiled, enjoying being the generous host in Mitzi's office.

"I'm good."

Lily waited, expecting an update. Could they have possibly caught him? It seemed longer ago than—how many months ago? Though Lily could still clearly (too clearly) recall his mean, narrow face. And, particularly when stressed, her hand went to where the knife blade cut across her neck.

Officer Lane went on to describe her encounter last week with the nurse in the parking lot, the arrest of a man breaking into her car. Then she described the condition of the crime scene.

"Echh." Lily cocked her head. "What did he look like?" she asked, confused.

"Who?"

"The guy who attacked the nurse. Same description as the one who attacked me? Skeevy white guy with matted hair?"

"Oh," Officer Lane stopped. "No, he wasn't." Then she added. "Oh, I'm sorry, Lily. We're talking about two different things. He was a Black guy. Older. No. I'm actually not here about your attack."

There was laughter and chatter in the hall. A class was just getting out. A knock on the door. Two young women popped their heads in before Lily could even respond. "No one's at the front desk," one said. "Can we still sign up for the next session?"

"Sure," Lily said. "Come next week. It's fine. Just leave your names on her desk."

Both the girls noticed the policewoman. The one in front put up her hand—"Sorry. Sorry to interrupt—" and quietly closed the door.

Lois turned back her attention to Lily, leaning even closer in her chair. "See, my partner and I just came from another call. Not the one in the hospital parking lot. This one was in an apartment off Lawrence. A neighbor called 911…there was an altercation in the apartment upstairs."

Lily looked puzzled.

"And what was interesting," Officer Lane continued, "was how similar the crime scenes were. Quite unusual. The mess surrounding them. Both in the parking garage at the hospital and in this woman's apartment. Looked as if these guys had suddenly heaved their guts up. It wasn't just a little…" Officer Lane paused as if waiting for an explanation, her eyes narrowed.

There was a long silence. Lily blinked a couple of times. "Oh," she said. A door opened and shut down the hall. Then silence. She took a breath and let it out slowly. The kind of deep-cleansing breath she used to relax.

"Lily? Hon? I'm on your side," Officer Lane assured her.

"My side?" Lily asked.

"I mean, no one's in trouble here." Officer Lane added: "Except for the bad guys."

"We teach self-defense here at SWIC," Lily said carefully. "And have classes where we show…certain products, you know. Deterrents. For self-protection."

"A deterrent," Office Lane said. "For self-protection."

"Yes, a useful deterrent that causes no significant damage," Lily said warily. Those were actually her father's words. And Mitzi's. Words that would be on the package if they ever advertised the product.

"Look, dear," Officer Lane began. She was not so very much older than Lily, but felt maternal toward this young, brave girl sitting in front of her, her chin set. "Lily," she said tenderly, "I don't exactly understand what's going on, but you are not in trouble."

Lily breathed out audibly, got up, and opened the bottom drawer of Mitzi's desk, taking out a key. She went over to a drawer in the file cabinet and took out a box, opening it to reveal a line of large silver pendants; each had the face of a woman so when Lily opened the box the white row stared straight ahead. "They're empty now," Lily said. Then she took a key, opened a separate drawer, and took out a glass jar with a plastic lid. The jar was filled with tiny, brown nuggets, like dried cat food. "These are mycotoxins. It's animal feed that's been contaminated," Lily explained. "From a farm in Iowa." Then she reached down to the larger drawer and took out some disinfectant, placing it on the desk next to the pendant and the glass jar: Lemon-scented all-purpose cleaner. Kills 99.9% of bacteria. Cleans and disinfects tough grime.

She lined up the three items on the desk like a science experiment: a silver pendant. A glass jar with pellets. A plastic bottle of kitchen cleaner.

Lily opened the woman's silver head to reveal two small compartments. "This substance," she said, pointing to the liquid, "before it's activated, lasts a really long time," she said. "We don't know how long. We set it up when we give out the pendant. But it's not really ready to go until this little clasp is flicked over to the side." On the side of the object was a tiny catch. "Flick, then press. You can wear this like a piece of jewelry around your neck. I mean, it's pretty enough. Though it's heavy. Many women put it on a key chain. If they're walking alone, going somewhere where they feel uncomfortable, they might hold it, ready to use. You activate it with your thumb. Mixing the liquid with the pellet. Flick. Then press. But you have to hold your breath right before the release. Otherwise, you'll get sick too."

Officer Lois Lane watched in amazement. What she was looking at was the same object that the nurse held after the attack in the hospital parking lot. The silver head of a woman. And it was the same piece of jewelry that she had seen in the apartment of Rhoda Mersh.

"I'm not going to do it now," Lily said. "Activate it. Well, you wouldn't want me to."

"No," Officer Lane said.

"From all reports, it works really well. As a useful deterrent to attack that causes no significant damage." Lily repeated the phrase as if it had been practiced. "But there's no patent on this and the substance has not been approved," she said.

"The substance?"

"The substance. It was discovered by a scientist in Iowa who does research with porcine disease." Adding, "He's a toxicologist."

Officer Lane turned the pendant over in her palm. "You're from Iowa, aren't you?"

"I am," Lily said, firmly setting her jaw. If the officer asked, Lily wasn't going to lie. They had decided that. One lie would beget another. And while her father was the one who discovered the process, for most of the summer, he was pretty much out of the loop. "Two scientists in the same lab worked on this. One is my father. The other is his research assistant. She's actually been the one in charge. And the woman who designed the piece. She's an artist. A jewelry maker. They might both be moving to Chicago. Mitzi offered to help set them up here in the studio."

Officer Lane picked up one of the objects out of the box. "A silver head of medusa. It's very pretty. Also, she looks fierce."

"By all accounts, using it is quite safe. All you have to do is hold your breath. The substance is effective for antiperistalsis for less than thirty seconds. And anyone warding off an attack is able to hold her breath for that long."

"And you say it's easy enough?" Lois asked. "To work?"

"Apparently it is. From all reports."

"You've tried it?" Officer Lane asked. "Yourself?"

Lily shook her head. "I haven't needed to." Lily thought then—not of her attack—but of the guy in the street, standing by his truck. So would you like to sit on my face? Perhaps he didn't deserve her severe reaction. Or maybe he did. Still, lucky for him, screaming was all she did that day.

"And you show others how to use it?"

"It's not complicated. We have practice devices. The women here go through training. They use it lots of times before they get one that's filled with the real thing. But then some women gave it to friends. They can come in and get it filled again and again. We started out by taking names of the women who have them. Like, at the beginning they were all people who had signed up for a class. We knew the ready pendants were out there and we knew who had them. The spore and the cleaner were not mixed until activated. And they last in their separate compartments, apparently for months. Since I've been working here, I'm trying to keep better records of where they are, how many have been used."

"So, getting back to what you said. The substance is not yet approved. Approved by whom?"

Lily couldn't help noticing that Officer Lane used correct grammar. Who and Whom. He and I. I feel bad, not badly. Her mother had been a stickler. "Well, the FDA for one," Lily said. "The Federal Drug Administration."

Officer Lane shrugged. "I don't work for the FDA."

"Some products can be marketed without being approved," Lily said. "It's about whether or not the benefits to users will outweigh the risk. But still, there's clinical testing that needs to be done. And the university—that's where my father works—has some pretty clear guidelines about animal research That's why he's not really involved any longer. I don't want him to get into any trouble."

"I don't work for the university either," Officer Lane said.

"I know," Lily said.

"But here, I assume, the benefits outweigh the risks?"

"They sure do." Lily smiled broadly.

"Well, Jeez…" Lois Lane relaxed in her chair. She looked out the window and saw two young women leaving the studio, each in black leggings, with backpacks, and ponytails bobbing as they talked.

Lily leaned in closer to her interrogator. "You know, women have been using this all summer in Chicago. Successfully from what we've heard. Probably hundreds of times. Of course, it hasn't always been used to prevent a rape. Sometimes. But there are all sorts of reasons. But I don't know any stories where women have used it in circumstances that were unwarranted."

Officer Lane was thoughtful. "What if the attacker grabbed the keychain just as it was activated and turned it back on her? You know, like Mace? That happens more often than you think."

"Well, it would make you pretty sick, I guess. But only for a few minutes. Then it would be over." Lily added a further talking point recently discussed in her classes at SWIC. "But you know what? No man wants to sexually assault—maybe even rob—a woman who is throwing up. Projectile vomiting is a turn-off."

"I would say so." Officer Lane was a professional. And usually, professional behavior indicated that she maintained a certain distance from victims. She asked for information. She offered solace. But she tried not to register her own feelings, at least openly, with the people she met every day. If she empathized with all the assault victims she saw, she would be crying all the time. If she were personally repulsed by the likes of Rhoda Mersh and her lifestyle, well, those feelings should not ever be displayed in the interview. But Lily Lerner—how could anyone not like and admire this kid? "You're doing great," Officer Lane said before she took leave. Pausing at the door, she stood next to Lily and gave her a quick hug.

Outside, Officer Lane took a deep breath. The air was muggy and close. She had turned down Lily's offer of a pendant for her own use, saying she was protected enough with both a taser and a gun. Although she would have liked to try that substance on a perp. Lois smiled, just thinking about it. Who would know? Causing someone to throw up? Not exactly police brutality. But as a rule, she was not allowed to take anything. No gifts. Nothing that might be considered a bribe.

Officer Lois Lane was a good and righteous cop. And also a woman who had seen too much over her tenure. Enough. Enough. Certainly, she had worked with angry men during her time on the force. Men who became police officers were drawn from a mix. Both ends of the spectrum. The self-important ones, the bullies, who liked the uniform, the authority, who relished the idea of wearing a gun.

But also the good guys. And no matter what people thought, there were many good guys. Cops who wanted law and order to make the world a better, safer place. Luckily, none of the angry assholes had been one of her partners. Like Rico Martinez, a good man, looking forward to having a baby. And he never minded taking directions from a woman. Some of the guys—even the young ones—down at the precinct acted out. They thought they were funny when they were really just… well, stupid.

Soon this would come to the attention of the press. Someone would figure out what was going on this summer in Chicago. And then what would happen? In the meantime, the bad guys would be stopped in their tracks. And the jerks. Of course, no law against just being a jerk. God knows how many men would be doing time if there were laws against being a jerk. Nope, Lois would be keeping quiet about this. "Jeez," she said again, getting into her car, baked hot during the August afternoon. Damn. She didn't know what would happen. But she could not help smiling at this turn of events.

Chapter 23

September: Labor Day (Joyce Corning)

She was feeling mixed about her upcoming retirement in only a few more months. She promised Larry that he could book a cruise to Alaska for June, agreeing that they should go before the glaciers melted into the ocean. Joyce promised her granddaughter Nora that if she stayed dry three nights in a row, Grandma would take her to Target and buy any toy she wanted. It occurred to Joyce that she had spent a lot of her life accommodating the needs of others and making promises to keep them happy. In all, this was not a bad thing.

She was feeling more at ease, too, about leaving Dr. Lerner who seemed in better spirits lately. The aura of sodden gloom has definitely lifted. Joyce knew him well enough to know that his general disposition was one of sober calm. And while others might confuse this with disapproval, she understood him. In some ways, Dr. Lerner was a man a lot like her Larry, just with more education. Larry was a person who was quiet in a group. Not a showoff ever, even when some guy was holding forth about something that Larry knew a lot about. Like fishing. Or how to lay a foundation. Or Civil War battles. Both Larry and Dr. Lerner were respectful of women. It occurred to Joyce that she was lucky to have spent most of her adult life with these two good and trustworthy men.

It rained off and on during the weekend, but Monday of the Labor Day weekend was lovely. After a period of drought through August, the creek behind the house was swollen, and the rock pool Larry made, had enough water for the kids to enjoy themselves. Joyce sat on the glider to keep an eye on little Nora. Larry came up the path and sat beside her, a beer in his hand. He offered her the can. "Finish it," he said. She took a sip and handed it back. "Finish it," she said. They did this frequently with a drink or with dessert in a restaurant. Back and forth, sharing, until what remained was the tiniest taste.

"Are we waiting on the pie?" Larry asked. "I could go for a slice."

Joyce brought her hand to her waist. A few pounds every year since her late fifties. Those pounds sure added up. "Honey, we just finished eating. I am still so full." It annoyed her that when Larry wanted to take off a few pounds, he did. Just like that. "I thought I'd let the kids play for a while," she said. "Then I'll go cut the pies."

"What kind?"

"There's two blueberry. Caroline brought over a pie that she made when she was over at Mason's yesterday. She won't tell me what it is, though. Said it's a surprise."

"Caroline makes good pies," Larry said. "Almost as good as you. I hope that doesn't turn his head. Anyway, what kind of name is Mason Delgado? Eye-talian?" Larry always pronounced the last name with a long 'I' but Joyce did not correct him.

"I guess." Caroline had met Mason online. He worked at the Department of Transportation and was also divorced, with a couple of kids he saw every other weekend. Mason seemed nice enough, but Joyce was withholding judgment.

Though Royce had never been nice enough, even from the get-go. And yet Caroline didn't see that he would never make a suitable life partner. Grudgingly, Joyce admitted that Royce might be a good enough father. He was on time for all Nora's visits, and Joyce saw that her granddaughter was always happy to see him.

Joyce and Larry rocked on the glider back and forth in companionable silence. "Caroline looks good," Larry said after a few minutes. Caroline had been going to Weight Watchers with friends from work. She had put blonde highlights in her hair. Today Joyce thought Caroline looked really cute in white capri pants and a black and white top she bought at Kohls. Joyce wished Caroline didn't have that heart tattoo on her calf that she had done when she was engaged to Royce. Could have been worse, Joyce supposed. She could have a big tattoo on her arm or one peeking out of her cleavage.

Joyce looked up at the bluest, clearest sky. "It's a 9/11 day," she said. Larry nodded. Joyce always said this when it was this heartbreakingly beautiful in early September. It always brought her back. On that historic morning, Joyce was not listening to the radio on her drive to work, but a CD, Dolly Parton, with a voice as sweet as cotton candy. Joyce didn't know what was happening in New York, a place she had never been. But oh, it was the most perfect Iowa morning. Not too many days like this were left, she was thinking on the drive to work.

Dr. Lerner hadn't come in yet when she arrived at her office. Anaya, of course, wasn't there. Joyce didn't even know her then. How old could Anaya have been in 2001? Joyce thought of Anaya as a little girl. Oh, she must have been a handful. Her poor parents.

She remembered Dr. Lerner that morning, still wearing his bike helmet, coming in the door, looking more serious than usual, and asking her to turn on the news. The radio reception was fuzzy in the office so she and Dr. Lerner and one of the Asian post-docs went across to a lecture room where there were already people craning their necks at a television—there were two televisions mounted on each side of the classroom, but everyone stayed together as a group, looking at the same one. They stood, watching as planes crashed into buildings; then the announcement that a plane had crashed into the Pentagon as well; speaking from Florida, President Bush declared the events in New York City an "apparent terrorist attack on our country;" on CNN John McCain said the attack was an act of war.

Students came in for class scheduled in the lecture hall, and they too watched as the buildings buckled and fell. There was a respectful hush. Oh god. Hands flew to open mouths. Could this be happening? But what was happening? Eventually, people started leaving the classroom, going to meet with friends, and going back to their dorms. Dr. Lerner asked Joyce if she wanted to go home, and she realized how much she wanted to. Be home.

There weren't that many cars on the road. Joyce did not turn on the radio, afraid to listen alone. She drove the fifteen miles home as Dolly Parton sang her heart out.

That September afternoon, she and Larry had sat on this very same glider, holding hands, looking at the woods and the creek and the sky, just the way they were doing now.

It was so quiet then, too. Peaceful. They could have been all alone in the world. Of course, that September there were no grandchildren playing in the water. Strange, she thought, how the grandchildren appeared, real people out of nothing. Little people who so totally filled up their lives.

The day, THAT day was the same, beautiful and so still, that the events hardly seemed real. Crashing planes into buildings. It was incomprehensible. Who could do such a thing? They both asked. There were Japanese kamikaze pilots; Larry's father was stationed in the Philippines in World War II and had mentioned them sometimes. Larry's father hated the Japs; that's what he always called them. Years ago, Joyce was shopping at Fareway and there was an Asian man in front of her in line. Caroline looked fearfully at the man and then whispered: "Mommy, is he a Jap?"

But we were at war with Japan. A declared war. In 2001 we weren't at war with anyone who would bomb our country. Or maybe we were. Larry had been puzzled but also angry. "Bastards," he said, his jaw clenched. "Son-of-a-bitch bastards." Joyce didn't say a thing, though Larry hardly ever cursed, and she was unsettled by how angry he was.

***

Nora squealed in the creek as one of the boys showed her a worm and pretended to put it in her hair. An older cousin came to her defense, splashing him away.

"Now you look out for her," Larry yelled down. "No teasing. She's a little one."

"Yes, Grandpa," the splashing boy said, sweet as could be.

Joyce had filled out all the papers and set the date with Dr. Lerner for her retirement. She was ready. Joyce would interview and help find her own replacement, although Dr. Lerner said that Joyce could never be replaced. He was off with a new project and that was good for him, Joyce thought. Something important, she knew, reading about those pig organs. Something that would help save lives. Lily would stay in Chicago with her new job, running that women's gym. Well, there was a life-saving quality in that kind of work as well, Joyce supposed. And Anaya. Joyce saw her in a different light now, a force for good.

Joyce looked at the remains of the garden beyond the mowed part of the yard. "There's so much kale," Joyce said. Soon there would be more squash and then pumpkins galore. "I still have boxes in the garage to bring downtown to Food at First."

"I can do it tomorrow," Larry said. "And I'll put some bags in the car for you to take to work."

But why did they ever grow so much kale? Anaya made kale chips which were tasty but left little green flakes all over the office. The tomatoes, by the east side of the house, had had a good year. Last week Joyce made tomato sauce and soup and even fried green tomatoes which she knew weren't very good for Larry with his high cholesterol, but oh were they delicious when soaked in buttermilk with a crispy breading and that burst–in–your–mouth of sour-sweet tomato. Larry wanted to get rid of the raspberry bushes which got so very buggy, but she convinced him to let them be one more year. There would be frozen raspberries this year for winter as well. Good over vanilla ice cream.

Slowly, Joyce got herself up from the glider and her knees hurt when she took the first steps on the uneven grass. Her old friend, Arthur-itess, always came calling when she sat too long. "Watch the kids," she told Larry. "I'll go set out the pies." Ambling across to the back porch, she paused, turning again to watch the kids. She had grown up in a house only a few miles from here. Larry had lived with his family on a farm in a neighboring town. Although they went to different high schools, Joyce had met him at a basketball game and boldly invited him to her senior prom. All her friends predicted that they would one day marry.

Now, walking to the deck Larry had built, Joyce turned and looked down again to the garden, to the creek, to her husband on the glider, the children playing in the water, past them to the trees of pine and poplar lining the horizon. This is mine, she thought. This is all mine.

Chapter 24

September: Labor Day (Anaya and Vera)

They took turns paddling. Labor Day weekend, and the air already smelled like autumn; the light had changed. Maybe that was because they were north, camping near Decorah, canoeing along a stream that connected to the Upper Iowa River. "This is so peaceful," Vera said. She was in touch with nature, with the seasons, with her spiritual side. Bashert. Meant to be. Vera learned that word from Mitzi Solomon.

Anaya nodded, letting her hand drift, and looking at the bugs in the water, trying to determine whether she was correctly identifying an aquatic Heteroptera in the water alongside the boat. Aquatic bugs of this sort were predators who obtained oxygen primarily from the air, not the water, and were not useful indicators of water quality compared to groups like mayflies. Anaya was concerned about water quality in the state. Too little environmental control was mandated in Iowa; farmers did not like being told what to do by the government; corporate agriculture liked it even less.

In the late afternoon, they pulled their canoe up to one of the small islands that dotted the shore. Anaya carried the cooler and Vera spread a blanket under a tree on soft ground redolent of pine. Anaya opened two cold beers and busied herself with setting up the plates: cold, basil-grilled tuna with radicchio, a sweet and sour eggplant caponata, and crusty French bread. Vera thirstily downed half her beer. "When we begin, I won't be drinking any longer."

"Begin?"

"The baby. I think as soon as we start trying to get pregnant is when I should stop drinking. Even if it doesn't take the first time." Vera broke off the end of the bread, chewing slowly.

"A beer every now and then. That wouldn't hurt. In the old days, doctors advised women to have a glass of wine to relax," Anaya said. "Besides, you don't drink that much." Anaya had a larger capacity. Three or four beers and she could still drive, although Vera never permitted that. "You sure we should start this year, hon?"

Vera nodded "Yes. It's harder to get pregnant after thirty."

"You have a couple of years..."

Vera interrupted her: "We don't know how long it will take."

"All that paddling builds an appetite," Anaya said, filling her plate. "I'm starving,"

"No, you're just hungry," Vera said. "In India, the children are starving."

"Not any longer. Now they're all working in call stations."

Recently, Howard received a large grant from an anonymous donor in Chicago; this was to work on his new transplant project. More money would surely come from the established scientific channels when his work was successful—which it was sure to be. Anaya, a true scientist at heart, felt as excited as he was, reimagining opportunity rather than obligation. If transplantation of pig organs could be made safe and successful there was potential to help thousands of people waiting to receive an organ.

She and Vera had made the decision to go to Chicago. There was a continuing source of contaminated spores and a ready supply of the standard cleaning solution. As a scientific challenge, that part was over. Now the production of this unorthodox defense product became a business venture. Vera's creative life would be funded by a grant also from an anonymous benefactor in Chicago. How much money did Mitzi Solomon actually have? Anaya wondered. Her generosity seemed boundless, checks kept coming for more supplies, for hiring help, and a substantial salary for Vera's direction and expertise. Vera had enough time to pursue her own artistic interests, and the pendants could eventually be patented. Mitzi had introduced them to a patent attorney. They would make money. Vera could do her art. Success and freedom would be theirs. Wasn't this the American dream?

Vera wanted to start their baby-making adventure. A baby. Which, in Anaya's mind was a boy: little Diego Pran-Perez. Anaya herself would make no biological contribution, but she would be a damned good role model. Vera poured over internet sites of sperm donors, men who were athletic, college-educated, and medically sound.

There were loons on the lake, calling softly. And jumping frogs at the water's edge. "Are you going to tell your mom?" Anaya asked. "About trying to have a baby?"

Bringing food to her mouth, Vera paused. "I won't tell her about trying. I don't think she'd understand. But I'll tell her when I get pregnant." The relationship with her mother made Vera sad. Her father had left long ago but there were aunties and cousins galore in Mexico. Two undocumented younger brothers lived in California and worked as landscapers. "My mama loves babies," Vera said wistfully. "When I have a baby, she would visit her first grandchild. I hope."

A canoe floated past, going slowly, containing a man with two young boys, both in life jackets that took up most of their torsos. Vera waved. The man raised his paddle in a polite salute, but one of the boys began to wave back wildly. "Hi, ladies! Hi ladies!" he called. Vera noticed that the boy, a towhead, had Down Syndrome. He started to blow kisses. Anaya stood up and blew some back as the canoe passed out of sight. Anaya said, "That kid is sure adorable!"

Vera looked at Anaya. "Do you think that is a sign?" she asked softly.

"A sign of what?"

"A sign that we shouldn't do this. That we shouldn't try to have a baby."

"Why?" Anaya asked. "It's what you always wanted. You're going to be a great mom."

Vera started to cry. "You know. Because sometimes I just worry. Is this right? To have a baby like this?"

"Like what?" Anaya asked.

"Like with the seed of someone I don't know. Not us. Not because of us," she added. "But a baby with a stranger. What if there is something wrong?"

"If there is something wrong, we will handle it. We will be the best parents, the best advocates ever to make it as right as can be," Anaya said with some conviction. "The world is different now. And people are more accepting of difference."

"Not my people," Vera said sadly.

"They will," Anaya said, ever optimistic. "You're young and healthy. The guys who volunteer to be sperm donors, they're young and healthy, too. Lots of smart medical students." Anaya tapped her head.

"I would like a child with my artistic ability," Vera said, sitting up straighter on the blanket.

Two birds circled the water, then dove, one coming up with a fish. "Oh, I have a surprise, hon," Anaya said, after they finished their meal and packed away the paper plates and tableware in garbage bags to bring home. "Want something sweet?" She opened the cooler, took out a plastic container, and carefully opened the lid. "I hope this didn't get smooshed."

Vera, who loved desserts, looked over in anticipation.

"Ta-dah!" Anaya presented two carefully sliced pieces. "Tres Leches."

Vera's hand went to her chest. "Oh, mi Alma."

"It looks a little runny," Anaya said, always her own toughest food critic. Tres leches cake, Vera's favorite. "I'll make it after you're pregnant whenever you want," Anaya said, inspecting the icing. "Tres leches. Three milk. Which is good for a nursing mother. But I want you to know what a pain in the ass it is to make right."

Afterward, they lay together on the blanket and looked at the sky. One solitary fluffy cloud floated above as if painted by the hand of a child. "I wish you went to church with me," Vera said. Vera herself was reverent, although she attended church on an irregular basis.

"Why?" Anaya asked.

"It is a comfort," Vera said.

Anaya leaned over on the blanket, a smeary dab of cake frosting on her upper lip. "You are my comfort, mi alma," she said.

Chapter 25

September: Labor Day (Howard and Betsy)

After they returned home from Prague, Betsy cleaned out the basement, painted the front porch, signed up to deliver Meals on Wheels, and accepted a part-time job at the public library starting at the end of September.

Howard went back to work, excited by the unusual research opportunity, relieved to be free from the intensity of his last project. He had been invited to participate in a conference about genetically modified animals. Pigs in particular. Scientists were discovering how pig organs could be suitable for human use. Unfortunately, retroviruses, embedded in porcine DNA caused rejection by the human immune system, thereby thwarting interspecies transplant. Now, scientists were discovering ways to stop these retroviruses by genetic modification. The Mayo Clinic had developed a colony of pigs bred to be germ-free, whose organs would be safe enough for even an immunosuppressed person. There was a realistic potential to save thousands of lives; a person in need of a transplant would not have to wait so long to receive an organ. Exciting. And the five million dollars recently donated to Dr. Howard Lerner from an unnamed philanthropist in Chicago would make it possible for him to participate and maintain his own lab in Iowa.

After his family's harrowing year, he began to think more about how science was less an academic exercise in the search for discovery and more a way to directly help people in their everyday lives. Discovering the strain and turning it into something so useful and valuable had taught him this. This was the kind of science he would commit himself to from here on out.

***

Betsy was making dinner. Just burgers and corn on the grill. Just the two of them. Other times there were Labor Day picnics at the Vet school or neighborhood barbecues, but tonight there was just the two of them, sharing gin-and-tonics on the patio. Betty had brought out a plate of fried green tomatoes, crackers, and a white, hard cheese that Howard liked but could never remember the name of. The fried tomatoes were crispy on the outside, sour and bursting after a bite, just like Joyce said. "These are delicious!" Howard said, reaching for another.

"Joyce gave me the recipe when she brought them to a potluck last year. We're up to our knees in tomatoes." Ripe. Over-ripe. Green. Everyone they knew in Iowa grew tomatoes. "Yesterday I slow-roasted two trays in the oven."

"When I was growing up, I never knew what real tomatoes tasted like," Howard said.

"Well, your mother always puts them in the refrigerator."

"My mother puts everything in the refrigerator. If butter was left out on the table, she thought we would all get botulism."

"Is the grill ready?" Betsy asked. "I'm pretty hungry. I think I forgot to have lunch." Howard wondered how anyone could forget to have a meal. He still thought about food as the chubby boy he used to be, thinking about what to eat for breakfast as he took a morning shower.

They were eating late, and the light was changing. Bees hovered among the coneflowers. And butterflies. Betsy had planted Milkweed along the side of the house. "Who ever imagined that we'd be planting Milkweed?" Betsy said. "Those were pesky intruders to be pulled when I was growing up. Eradicated." Now the milkweeds were welcomed helpers to attract butterflies. "My grandma made me pull milkweed every summer out in the country. She hated Milkweed. And I hated pulling them."

"Manchego," Howard said.

"What?"

"Manchego. That's the name of this cheese. Where'd you get it?" "Fareway," Betsy said. "It's not anything exotic. You always say how much you like it. Then you can never remember the name."

"I know. I'm forgetting nouns."

"I don't think you pay attention is all," Betsy said. "Besides, no one really needs to have a memory any longer. Just Google anything you forget."

"Sometimes I forget what it is I am trying to remember," Howard said.

By the time the burgers were ready, the bugs were out in full force, so they brought everything in, pulled out the tray-tables in the TV room and Howard turned on the news. Politics as usual. Wars. Weather. Shootings. "I can't watch this while we eat, Howie," Betsy said. "It's too awful."

He switched to an old Seinfeld, one of the many he had automatically recorded; he laughed in the same places he had laughed when they watched it years ago. It was the one where

Jerry forgets a girl's name. A name that rhymes with a part of the female anatomy. "I forgot what the name actually is," Howard said. "Not Mulva? Shit, I can't remember names. It's too early for me to have all the nouns going out of my head. It's the beginning of the end, my friend."

When the show ended, Betsy said, "Tell me something positive. That things are getting better."

Howard began the litany: "Our girls can be whatever they want to be. Anaya and Vera are a married couple and planning to have a family. My lab is going to make organ transplants for whoever needs them." He took a bite of his burger and leaned over the tray, so the juice didn't run down his shirt. "You don't have to pull Milkweed any longer. It's tough now, but hey, a black man once was president of this country. For eight years! Could your grandmother even imagine that?"

"My grandmother wouldn't have voted for him," Betsy said. "She was a good person, but still. I don't think she would have done it." Betsy and her family did not talk politics.

"My grandma would have," Howard said. "Although I'm not sure my grandma was even a good person. She would always hush us up when she was watching the news. I think she found kids an annoyance. She wasn't very grandmotherly. But I knew her politics. If she were alive when Obama was running for president, she would have said: 'I'm going to vote for that smart shvartze!'" Howard thought for a moment, "Actually, I think it was my mother who said that."

Betsy shook her head. "But now look at where we are now. It's unbelievable really…"

Howard interrupted, "Oh, Delores!" he said as the episode of Seinfeld came to an end. "That's the name. I couldn't remember. The one that rhymes with a female part of the anatomy."

"Tell me again how it's going to be, George," Betsy said wistfully. This was another of their routines. Of Mice and Men was one of Betsy's favorites, a book she made both Lily and Megan read when they were in junior high, although Megan complained that she would rather just watch the movie.

Howard was aware that they were trading places. It was now his responsibility to cheer up his wife. "The world will be getting better. And for us, too," Howard assured her. "This is how it's going to be: I will have perfected the interspecies transplant and then probably I will get the Nobel Prize for medicine. You will have to help me with my acceptance speech, to make sure that I sound humble enough."

Betsy smiled. "Not you, my darling. Anaya is the one who might need help with expressing some humility."

Howard continued, "Megan will pass all of her courses and even go on to graduate school. She will find her true calling."

"And what would that be?"

"I'm not sure. But Bets, have some faith. She'll find her way. Megan's a great kid."

"Go on."

"And Vera will get pregnant. She and Anaya will have a beautiful, healthy baby with big, brown eyes and we will be named godparents. And we'll visit them all in Chicago when we visit Lily."

"Oh, Howie, I like that," Betsy said. "Practice for when we're grandparents."

"Please. Not so fast," Howard said, "How about this winter, you and I will go to someplace warm and exotic over break. Maybe Boca Raton to visit my mother?"

"Howard, Boca Raton is not exotic. Maybe my parents would come, too. Boca Raton would be exotic for them."

Howard went on. "And Lily, who actually has found her true calling, will also meet a wonderful caring and kind man…"

"That would be nice. I don't want to be snobby, but I don't think she ever had a boyfriend who was her intellectual equal."

"Ok. Someone who has a PhD in macroeconomics. And a trust fund. But she won't need it because Lily will follow in Mitzi's footsteps and make SWIC even more successful than it is now…"

Betsy interrupted him. "Mitzi…What about Mitzi?"

"Mitzi," Howard said, shaking his head. He was quiet, sensing that their game was over.

"She's really sick now, isn't she?"

"Yes." He sighed, pointed the remote, turned off the television, and faced her. "Lily might be with her now. She texted me that she was going over to the apartment again. Mitzi's family was coming. And she wanted Lily there too."

"Oh, Howie, that makes me so sad." Betsy had never met Mitzi, yet she was as real as anyone could be, so important was she in Lily's life. Lily, always a good mimic, skilled at describing people to her parents, friends from school, her college teachers, did a great impersonation of her mentor: "Sweetie, girl. Listen to me. Who the hell knows how this is gonna turn out? But I got an idea…" Indeed, Betsy felt she knew who Mitzi was. She knew. "This will be hard for Lily," Betsy said now. "Mitzi will be the first person Lily ever lost."

Howard remembered when he was a little boy, how his mother used that euphemism when explaining his father's death. "I lost my husband," she would say when describing her young widowhood. "My children lost their father." And still, Howard then had a glimmer of hope. He thought for years that the expression was a 'glitter' of hope, and in his mind that glitter sparkled when he believed that his father might return to the family, that his father was merely lost, driving his Pepsi truck that day in the Bronx and then taking a wrong turn. Young Howard still had a glitter of hope that his father was lost and someday would find the way home.

"We would go to the funeral, wouldn't we?" Betsy asked.

"I don't know. Lily said there wouldn't be one. And she would know." Lily had spent nearly every afternoon with Mitzi going over the transfer plans for SWIC and was privy to her mentor's wishes.

"Really? How would that happen? She's like such a famous person in Chicago? Her family wouldn't go along with that, would they? For her kids and grandchildren?" Betsy couldn't understand.

But Howard could. "Mitzi does what she wants," he said.

Later in bed, he tossed and turned, imagining his own demise. Maybe, like Mitzi, in his own house, in his own bed. What time did he have left? How many years? To work as long as possible. Transplants of pig organs for immunosuppressed persons were becoming a reality. Hearts. Livers. Kidneys. A stew of organs. He wasn't totally kidding about the Nobel Prize. Some prize. Not that he cared much, but why not? He imagined first Anaya and Vera's baby, then the babies of his girls, his grandchildren going to school; it would be interesting to have boys. He figured how much he and Betsy would have in his TIAA/CREF retirement plan, by taking out a modest 4%. Figuring in social security if he didn't take it until he was seventy. He started doing the math in his head. And then finally: sleep.

Chapter 26

September: Labor Day (Laura Murphy)

Schools were still out in Chicago, but Labor Day was hardly a vacation for Laura Murphy who drove over to the elementary school where she taught to set up the classroom. While she mourned summer's end, there was always a flutter of excitement starting the school year. Miss Murphy was known for making a beautiful environment for the children in her first-grade class, with nooks and crannies where they could work and play comfortably; places where children whose home lives were sometimes filled with noise and disruption might find a peaceful space.

Morning, but it was already hot; she parked close to the front door, leaving the car's hazard lights blinking and went around to the open trunk. A police officer, athletic and fit, jogged down the steps and offered to help carrying some of the boxes. He introduced himself: "Officer Mac," he said, extended a hand. "I'll be the new community resource officer at the school this year. Welcome back. Nice to meet you."

"What happened to Officer Smiles?" Laura asked. She thought about Officer Smiles as she drove up, feeling embarrassed after the long summer when she recalled his confusion about her stalker, George Murphy, remembered the elderly officer's puzzled face when she told him she was afraid. He didn't understand her fear. And why would he, seeing George Murphy, that unremarkable man?

"Oh, he retired," said Officer Mac, taking the heaviest box out of the trunk and heading up the stairs, two at a time.

"He was a nice man," she said, following him with a box of her own. "The children really liked him." Still, she was relieved he was not there.

"I'm hoping they'll like me, too." Officer Mac looked to be about Laura's age and handsome in a wholesome way. He had a broad nose and twinkly, blue eyes. Irish, Laura Murphy thought.

"Oh, I didn't mean anything by that; I'm sure they will like you very much," Laura said. "Just that he was kind of a grandpa figure, you know. He always had candy in his pockets."

"Yeah, they told us we weren't supposed to do that. Give the kids candy. I mean that was ok. He wasn't fired or anything. He retired. You think carrying some candy is a good thing?" Officer Mac seemed earnest and sincere, wanting to do a good job.

"Well, he also played basketball with some of the children in the after-school program," Laura said. "He wasn't very good. I don't think he even had to pretend to let the children win."

"Well, that would be harder for me," Officer Mac said. "I'm competitive. But thanks, I want all the tips I can get."

Officer Mac brought out a cart and helped her pile the boxes onto it. "Good luck," he called as she steered the cart down the hall. "You, too," she called back over her shoulder, smiling, as she went toward her room on the first floor. She thought: yes, there was a wedding band on his left hand. She was sure of that. She was attracted, yes, but oh well. She was still pleased that she was going to start her every day being greeted by cute Officer Mac.

She loved the smell of school: wood and polished floors, paste and chalk. Later it would have the sweet smell of the children—which was still pleasant in first grade. Upstairs, in the upper elementary rooms, there was a rank odor of athletic shoes and hormones, T-shirts that needed to be washed after even one wearing.

There were other teachers in the building; Laura was about to close her door, knowing she would not get much work done if she spent too much time chatting, when one of the kindergarten teachers came by. He had a polysyllabic Italian name, but everyone just called him Mr. B. Even the other teachers called him Mr. B. (or simply 'B'): "And so it begins…" he said. "Arrival of the hordes. Hug? How was your summer?" B was comfortable and eminently huggable. "I missed you, girl."

"Oh, B," Laura said. She stepped back before she put her arms around him. "You look good. You've lost some weight?"

"Always," he said. "Anxiety before school begins. I'll gain it back in a flash." B married his college sweetheart, a man of similar generous proportion who was an art collector for some of Chicago's top galleries. They had spent much of the summer traveling through Europe. "You, too? You've lost weight," B said, sizing her up.

"Stress," she said.

"Well, I will fatten you up, girl. There's a new bakery across the street. Cream doughnuts to die for. Napoleons."

Laura moved in for her hug. B smelled like lemons and spice. "Missed you, too. B. It's been a crazy summer."

"Too fast," he said. "Summer went by way too fast. We'll have to catch up." Pulling back, he looked her full in the face.

"What finally happened with that creepy guy? Your stalker?"

"I'll tell you all about it, later," Laura said firmly. "I have to do my room this morning." She smiled, adding, "And B, it's a good story."

"A late lunch? Will you be here? My treat," B said, clapping his hands in anticipation. Nothing B liked better than gossip. Last year the macho, mean gym teacher was caught in flagrante delicto with the father of one of the students. It wasn't B who caught them after school in one of the showers, but he provided enough detail to make it seem as if he were there.

Of course, B wanted to hear all about Laura's stalker. The elaborate ruse to meet him and her disguise. The support of her girl posse at SWIC. She decided she would tell him about the new art of defense from SWIC. Everyone would know soon enough. "It's a date," she said, "Meet me back here at one."

B looked out the door to see if anyone was in the hall, then whispered, "I looked at your class list in the mailroom. To see who you have this year."

"You snoop," Laura said. "I didn't even see the whole list. The final version wasn't up yet online.

"Jayden," B went on. "He's a nightmare. Still pooping in his pants. The Dunn twins. They're not splitting them up this year so they'll both be in your class. But that's good. They were always crying for each other when anything went wrong. Crying almost every day the whole first month of school. Little babies!"

"B, they were kindergartners!" Laura said laughing.

"They were still assholes." Then he leaned in, "And I saw you have Fiona MacKenna." he said, his voice taking on a somber tone.

"Oh, she's a sweetie," Laura said. There were two kindergarten classes. More than fifty children. Laura knew most of them.

"Poor thing," B added.

"Why poor thing?" Laura recalled a cute, little red-headed girl with corkscrew curls. Laura imagined Fiona as the little red-headed girl Charlie Brown was in love with in the Peanuts comics.

"Oh, you didn't know?" B said, his eyes big. "Fiona's mom was killed in a car accident, B said. "Last year, right after spring break. "Someone ran a light on Clark."

"Oh god," Laura's hand covered her mouth. The air in her classroom with its bright bubbles of color seemed close and still. "Oh god," she said again. "Why didn't I know that?" Even though Fiona wasn't in Laura's class then, she felt guilty. "That poor family."

"Then she wasn't back at school for the last few weeks. I think that's when you had changed your phone and were living with your friend," B said gently. "Remember—to avoid the crazy stalker?"

"Fiona? Oh, poor, poor baby," Laura said. Her own father had been killed in a construction accident when she was a senior in high school, and she still thought of him almost every day. Now she crumpled to the chair by her desk and began to cry.

"Oh girl, I am so sorry," B said. "I shouldn't have just blurted it out like that. Are you ok?"

"I'm all right," Laura said, "You didn't know, B. I'm glad you told me." The tissues she had brought in were on top of the supplies on her desk. She took one and blew her nose.

"We started a fund for Fiona and her dad," B said, approaching for another hug and then starting toward the door. "Want it closed? I won't bother you. I'll be right down the hall if you need me."

Laura nodded. "Please."

Before he left, B said, "Officer Mac? The new community resource officer? That's Fiona's dad. He requested the post here for this year, so he could be near her. Just to make sure she was ok. He used to be downtown."

"He's here today." Laura said. "I just met him when I came in." B nodded. "He seems very nice," Laura added. "Like he'd be good with the kids."

B shut the door quietly and she sat, immobile at her desk, listening to his footsteps down the hall. Books in one of the boxes spilled over: posters, a calendar: TODAY IS SEPTEMBER. There was a big clock with hands made out of movable plastic, though most children wouldn't even learn how to tell time that way because everything was digital. Also, few of them in first grade learned how to tie their sneakers. Laura looked at the real clock on the wall. It wasn't even ten o'clock in the morning.

She put some of the I Can Read books on the shelf by the window, all organized by color-coded levels. She set out her animal corner with pictures of cozy koalas and baby chimps. The picture of an elephant mama helping her baby out of a river made her heart hurt. She was glad Fionna would be in her class. And also (she wouldn't tell anyone this—certainly not B) she did feel a flutter of excitement thinking of Fionna's father, that sweet Officer Mac.

Chapter 27

September: Labor Day (Mitzi and Lily)

At the SWIC in the Westside Loop the day before, ten women sat in a circle as Lily Lerner introduced various self-protection options; she discussed the pros and cons of each device, passing it around so that everyone could understand how each might be used. "Be careful, with this one," Lily warned, holding up the pink, cat key ring with ears of deadly sharp spikes. There were piercing whistles on pretty necklace chains. Mace, of course. And mini-tasers. A flashlight of blinding intensity was added to the display, a recent invention by a Dutch company that also made windows. There were apps for phones to signal location at the same time it emitted a siren call. Lily demonstrated, instructing everyone to prepare for the nerve-shattering sound.

"And this is also a newer addition," Lily said. In the palm of her hand was a large silver pendant, which she said contained a substance that was sure to incapacitate a perpetrator. Lily didn't tell her audience exactly what was inside. Nor how simply the substance could be made. The two ingredients were in separate compartments. Pressing the catch on the flat side of the object created the mix. Everyone understood what it did. Lily told them in graphic detail. "I'm passing this around for practice. Don't worry. This one is not filled with the actual deterrent." The women laughed.

After Howard and Anaya had brought the first shipment to Chicago, Vera Perez began to engrave a number on the back of each pendant. Lily recorded that one-hundred and ninety-seven pendants had been given out during the summer in Chicago, though possibly not all continued to remain in the city. Almost four hundred refills were recorded; a few individual pieces were refilled a number of times. What was going to happen was anyone's guess. The future was unknown. But so many women in the country were affected by the moral chaos of the time that perhaps this was just another footnote to change.

***

Lily arrived in the afternoon of the holiday and found the housekeeper in Mitzi's kitchen, saying something in Polish under her breath as she plunged deep into the bottom shelf of the refrigerator, reorganizing. "So much food. Everyone bring so much food. Why am I here? I don't have to do no cooking. Throwing out food. Terrible..." Wanda tsked in disapproval.

Since Mitzi had been bedridden, Wanda came every day. She had been with Mitzi for years, cleaning and shopping and preparing meals for seder and Yom Kippur break-the-fast. Wanda probably knew more about Jewish rituals than most of Mitzi's family. Now well into her sixties, Wanda was sturdy with wide hips, a generous chest that collected stains, and an indefatigable work ethic.

"Wanda, why don't you take some food home with you? It shouldn't go to waste," Lily said, comfortable giving this suggestion.

"Yes, shouldn't go to waste," Wanda repeated, taking a shopping bag and filling it with mysterious packages wrapped in foil. "This pan I bring back tomorrow," she said, inspecting a casserole. "This, I am sorry, but must be thrown out because of expired. What is this?" She opened a container and took a sniff, then plopped the offense into a plastic bag. "I take to the garbage on my way out."

"I can do it," Lily said.

"You keep Mrs. Mitzi company. She likes that better," Wanda said. "You want soup? Before I go, I can heat up good vegetable soup. Very delicious."

"I don't think so," Lily said. "I was just going to make some tea."

"How is she?" Wanda asked. "I did not go in this morning before everyone was here. She was still sleeping."

"The same," Lily said. "Maybe a little weaker. She doesn't seem to be having as much pain as yesterday. The pills help."

"She needs to eat more," Wanda said, "The cat still in there? She has also not been eating." Wanda did not like the cat and looked with distaste at Meow's bowl.

"You know, you can't make Mitzi do anything she doesn't want to do," Lily said. For the last few days, Mitzi was hardly eating; now she needed help walking to the bathroom. But she was still clear-headed. And sometimes even funny. What kind of tea do you want, Lily asked. Mitzi shrugged and said she didn't care. "How about arsenic and old lace? Hold the lace."

"I pray for her," Wanda said, "Every day. I light a candle, too, in church."

"I'm sure she would like that," Lily said.

Wanda looked at Lily and narrowed her brow. "Mrs. Mitzi. She doesn't care about prayers."

"I know," Lily said, "But I'm sure she would be pleased that you're doing it anyway."

Wanda untied her apron and hung it on the back of the pantry door. "I see you tomorrow?" she said.

Lily nodded. "I'll be here again in the afternoon. That gives Mr. Berg a chance to get out."

"I be here too," Wanda said, "She has lists, things for me to do. Tomorrow, she wants me to take all the winter clothes from the hall closet. Not clothes for me. For my church. They give clothes to poor people. Nice clothes. I can find some people in my church like her. Not too many."

"Not too many like her?" Lily asked.

"You know. Small. Little, like her. Maybe a child could wear the clothes. Some very good winter coats. Mrs. Mitzi says she doesn't need no more winter coats."

Lily was not family, but she didn't feel like an intruder. Mitzi wanted her there, in her home, sometimes sitting next to the bed, bringing in her mail. Mitzi's old friends still wrote real letters and sent cards. There were visitors, but most did not stay long. Wanda bustled about and always had food prepared. Lily wanted to be there, and the family, including Mitzi's husband, seemed grateful for her presence.

After Wanda left, balancing all her bundles, Lily waited for the water to boil and took down two mugs for tea. Outside the foliage on the penthouse balcony was green and overgrown, needing a trim. Colorful zinnia and purple asters edged the outer brick before the evergreens. Over the tops of the trees, Lily could see Lake Michigan, which this afternoon was calm blue all the way to the horizon. Lily thought maybe she could walk Mitzi outside for a bit. It was September, but still very much summer.

Lily reported that the SWIC studio was running smoothly. She was there each morning and had hired an office assistant to take over in the afternoon when she left to be with Mitzi. Lily was the only one to give out the silver pendant which involved a special interview, and sometimes she shared the story of her own attack in Union Station just to show that she understood, that she was one of them, a sister. The pieces she gave out were not returned and didn't have to be. Who knew how many of them were eventually used? It certainly wasn't as if all the women in Chicago were armed and ready.

Anaya was coming soon, and all the information was ready for them to meet with the patent lawyer. Vera's studio was set up on the second floor of the SWIC building.

Mitzi was grateful for Lily's soothing presence every afternoon. Perhaps there would be jealousy usurping the role if Mitzi had daughters. Her sons, nice as they were, came in and out, mournful and awkward. In Mitzi's voluminous bedroom, they sat on the couch, looking at their phones which annoyed Mitzi greatly, although she did not tell them. "How you doing, Mom?" they asked. "I'm going out," they would say from the doorway. "Do you need anything, Mom?" Mitzi smiled benevolently. Closer now to death, she seemed still herself but softened. "No sweetheart, you go home now. You need to rest. You look tired."

Both of her sons had brought their own boys over a couple of times in the recent weeks, but the children were noisy and bored. Today, Labor Day, they stayed too long. Mitzi was relieved when they decided to go out for an early dinner and asked Ben to come along, even though there was enough food in the refrigerator to feed them all a dozen meals. Ben had been padding through the house in his slippers, quietly walking along the furniture, sighing audibly. That morning Mitzi heard him crying as he talked to someone on the phone. She urged, "Ben, go, go with the kids," assuring him, "Please. I'm ok. Lily is here with me. We have some business to talk over." Her voice was not strong. "Please," she added. Meow sat curled up next to her on Ben's side of the bed. "There's a new Chinese place on the corner, next to the dry cleaners. The boys will like it. They have crispy noodles." Ben and the boys did as they were told. They came into the bedroom to kiss her goodbye. "Go. Have a good time," she said. When they were out of earshot she added, "Don't rush back."

The constant company exhausted her. Yesterday, her sister Grace and one daughter-in-law came by; old friends, close friends; others she didn't necessarily count as friends. Sometimes she felt hostage in her own bedroom, unable to even go to the bathroom without someone waiting to see her. Mitzi asked Lily to keep the visitors at bay. Ben was not strong enough to do that. And he probably needed the company himself.

"I'll get us some more tea," Lily had said, heading for the kitchen. "Herbal? Any preference? Ginger and lemon? Bengal Spice?" Mitzi didn't care. Surprise her. Life was full of surprises.

***

And so, in the last month, Ben had seen to it that everything was taken care of. Even in his grief—and it was apparent that his grief was deep and real—he had seen to it. Going to work, and giving financial advice was what he knew. Mitzi heard him say often enough to a client, "How much money is enough?" The answer always was, "Enough money means you don't have to think about money."

Done. Done. Done. All four of her grandsons had college accounts that would take them through graduate school and beyond if they so chose. Who knew how things would be in this country when the boys were grown and making their way in the world? It was both difficult and interesting times, and Mitzi was sorry not going to be able to stick around and see.

May you live in interesting times. These were interesting times. Terrible times in many ways. What was going to happen to families who could not provide college accounts for their children? That was most people. And climate change. Oy. What world were they leaving to the grandchildren? Why couldn't everyone understand that we were all in this together?

Benjamin, under Mitzi's directions, had the three other SWIC studios sold as franchises with reasonable costs and liberal regulations to enterprising young women who were thrilled to take over this successful business. The SWIC name would be kept for three years, the leases assumed. Each studio would be permitted to design its own classes, whatever would work for the clientele: Yoga, spin classes, Zumba. Weightlifting. Mitzi yielded that women could make themselves strong in different ways, and she did not have to leave her mark only in the area of self-defense.

Ah, but SWIC in the West Loop was different. Unique. That was given to her protégée, Lily Lerner. Given. The studio alone would produce a profit, but in addition, Mitzi owned the building, and the rental units above the studio—a dental clinic and two apartments on the third floor—were all transferred over to Lily Lerner with a tidy benefit to pay the taxes that were due at the end of September. Lily had not told her parents the exact numbers. She did not even know them herself for sure. There was a studio rent-free for Vera Perez and an office upstairs for Anaya who would be coming at the end of the month. Those women were smart and righteous enough to help make this studio a success. What Mitzi knew was that teaching women how to protect themselves was what Lily wanted to do with her life. That legacy at least would be passed on.

Lily kept better records than Mitzi had over the summer. There was still a drawer full of silver pendants in velvet boxes when Mitzi was too sick to come into work. Mitzi had started writing things down but soon gave up. How many pieces were out there? She had not kept track.

Women used the gift. Scared, some of them. Then thrilled. It worked! Oh, how well it worked! Women came in for a refill and sometimes passed their pendant on to a friend. Or wanted another for a sister, for someone they worked with. How many pieces was Vera Perez still making? The drawer was always full. The boxes kept getting delivered from a Main Street address in Iowa. And now they would be able to produce more here in Chicago.

Mitzi heard the stories that pendants had shown up in other states, in Indiana, and a few in New York. Well, how could such a valuable resource possibly be contained? There was one unfortunate story she heard. It was only rumor and even then, not so awful. It happened during a summer school session at Whitney Young—the very high school that was Michelle Obama's alma mater. Some high school boys heard girls talking in the cafeteria, passing something around the lunch table. One of the girls was explaining how it worked, and what would happen. There was a ruckus, and a teacher came over to investigate and…it didn't matter. Even on a good day, a high school cafeteria lunchroom was sure to be a disgusting place.

Life was full of surprises and perhaps death would be as well. Mitzi wasn't so much afraid as astonished. How could life have gone by so quickly? She wasn't ready, not by any means, but what the hell—this decision was not in her power. Everybody had to die sometime. She was no one special. She would have wanted more time. But she did not want to end up losing her physical prowess and be one of those frail old ladies, slow and unsure in her step. Getting the dwindles, her mother used to say. Not her. Not Mitzi. Was this a rationalization? Perhaps she was just too proud to admit incapacity. Having spent her whole working life with younger women whom she encouraged to find their strength, she didn't now want to appear the weak sister.

She had presumed that Ben would have died before she did. He was four years older, with high blood pressure, and lived a sedentary life. Well, except for golf. She would have survived better alone than he. She could manage; she always had. She worried about Ben, but his kids would be attentive. He liked spending time with the grandchildren. More than she did, to be perfectly honest.

And Ben's practice, such as it was. Retired from his job with the firm but he was still sharp, very good indeed at financial consultation. And he would be the one to give financial advice to Lily and Anaya for as long as they needed.

Meow purred contentedly next to her. "Just us, old girl," Mitzi said. Maybe a vet could come to the house and put Meow to sleep when Mitzi died. They could have their ashes mixed together. She knew this suggestion would appall her family, but it seemed like a reasonable plan. Meow was on her last legs—all four of them—and without Mitzi, the cat would be bereft with no one to attend to her feline needs. Mitzi certainly couldn't trust Wanda to continue to prepare the cat's special diet. Yes, she would tell Lily her idea. Ashes co-mingled. That was the word the cremation society used. Mitzi had already given instructions that she was not to be buried. For all practical purposes, a cemetery plot seemed a waste of good real estate. After the unveiling, she had never visited the graves of her own parents who were buried with matching headstones somewhere in the Jewish section of Westlawn.

Lineages were complicated, with remarriages and adult stepchildren on both sides and some of Ben's extended family she didn't even want to sit at the same table with at a bar mitzvah. Ben had a prepaid plot next to his first wife. He was distraught, loving the two women as he did, when he asked Mitzi this some years ago: where would he be buried? He didn't know what to do. He cried, confessing this. Mitzi told him she didn't care what happened to her body after she died and that was the truth. Dead was dead, she said, "Ben, darling, it's not me anymore," she told him. "Not the real me-me." She told him that she was grateful to be next to him in bed each night. That had been enough.

The fact was that recently she had been thinking about her second husband, dreaming about him, often in these last few weeks. Her Ira. Gone so quickly there was no chance to say goodbye. Her dreams of him were of his departure. On a train pulling out of a station. Of walking down the street and getting into a strange car. "No, wait," she would call in the dream and he would look out of a window and shrug. What could he do? He was young in the dream. Still so handsome. But she always woke angry at him for leaving.

Ambien produced a peaceful night's sleep, welcomed and deep. But once in a while, early in the morning, almost half awake, she had dreams. This morning, she dreamed she and her Ira were on a cruise, leaning over the rail looking out on a moonlit ocean. They had been on a cruise for her fortieth birthday to the Greek Isles of Rhodes and Santorini, where the white-washed stone looked scrubbed, the sky so blue and brilliant that it seemed like a fake movie setting. Could anything be that bright and beautiful?

In her dream, it was early evening and she and Ira were on a ship, looking over the darkening sea. Ira raised one of his legs over the railing and told her he was going to step off. "Come with me," he urged, taking her hand. She shook her head, crying, telling him that she wasn't ready. They hadn't even eaten dinner yet. "Yes, the food is good on this ship," he said, kissing her goodbye before he leaped into the ocean.

This dying. She hoped it didn't take too long before she became even more decrepit and disgusting than she was now. Before she started peeing the bed and talking gibberish. She liked when the hospice nurse came and massaged her feet. A coma would be nice to quietly slip into. She wondered if she would still be able to hear everyone around her. She had read that people in comas were still able to hear what was going on around them and hoped no one would say something stupid like she looked so peaceful lying there. Or worse, that she finally was going to a better place. It would be difficult to hear something ridiculous like that and not be able to respond and say what kind of bullshit is that?

Mitzi had a few favorite quotes attached to a bulletin board in the study, one from Rabbi Abraham Heschel that she had memorized:

> *Our goal should be to live life in radical amazement, to get up in the morning and look at the world in a way that takes nothing for granted. Everything is phenomenal. Everything is incredible. To be spiritual is to be amazed.*

Mitzi did not think of herself as a particularly spiritual person, but perhaps she was. "Everything is phenomenal," she said, reaching for her cat. Meow had the softest, fluffiest fur. Mitzi had been told that a long-haired cat would shed all over the place, but she had never minded seeing puffs of Meow's hair, floating along the wood floor of the living room like tiny tumbleweeds. "Everything is incredible," Mitzi said. "Amazing," she added before nodding off into sleep.

www.ingramcontent.com/pod-product-compliance
Lightning Source LLC
Chambersburg PA
CBHW070635100726
47907CB00007B/1998